RECOVERY COMPLETE.
PROCEEDING TO ELIMINATE

"Inverted
Spirit
Barrier!"

→Lia Lagoon

"There's no rush. Feel free to take a bite of me whenever you like."

My Status as an Assassin Obviously Exceeds the Hero's

NOVEL

2

WRITTEN BY
**Matsuri
Akai**

ILLUSTRATED BY
Tozai

Airship

Seven Seas Entertainment

CONTENTS

ANSATSUSHA DE ARU ORE NO SUTETASU GA YUUSHA
YORI MO AKIRAKA NI TSUYOI NODAGA VOL. 2
© 2018 Matsuri Akai
Illustrated by Tozai
First published in Japan in 2018 by OVERLAP Inc., Ltd., Tokyo.
English translation rights arranged with OVERLAP Inc., Ltd., Tokyo.

Seven Seas press and purchase enquiries can be sent to
Marketing Manager Lianne Sentar at press@gomanga.com.
Information regarding the distribution and purchase of
digital editions is available from Digital Manager CK Russell
at digital@gomanga.com.

Follow Seven Seas Entertainment online at
sevenseasentertainment.com.

TRANSLATION: Colby W.
ADAPTATION: Leigh Teetzel
COVER DESIGN: Hanase Qi
INTERIOR LAYOUT & DESIGN: Clay Gardner
COPY EDITOR: E.M. Candon
PROOFREADER: Meg van Huygen
LIGHT NOVEL EDITOR: T. Anne
PREPRESS TECHNICIAN: Rhiannon Rasmussen-Silverstein
PRODUCTION MANAGER: Lissa Pattillo
MANAGING EDITOR: Julie Davis
ASSOCIATE PUBLISHER: Adam Arnold
PUBLISHER: Jason DeAngelis

ISBN: 978-1-64827-659-0
Printed in Canada
First Printing: November 2021
10 9 8 7 6 5 4 3 2 1

CHAPTER 1

A New Adventure Begins

POV: ODA AKIRA

"*MASTER! MASTER!*"

I awoke in the top of a tree to the sound of Night calling out to me. I opened my eyes to discover he'd shrunk down to the size of a house cat and was standing on my stomach, peering into my eyes with concern. It felt like it had been quite a while since I'd last laid eyes on him.

Some time had passed since my duel with Kilika, which was the last time I'd seen him. He'd apparently had no interest in watching the bout and headed off to catch up on his beauty sleep in a nearby tree. I'd complained about his unwillingness to support his master, to which he'd simply grinned wryly and replied that there was no chance of me losing to "one such as her." I appreciated the sentiment, but I wasn't really sure where his confidence in me was coming from or whether I should be flattered by it.

I leapt down from the tree and stretched my arms up high and then behind my back. Night hopped down after me with feline grace. Sleeping on tree branches was by no means comfortable, but it beat sleeping on the cold, hard ground of the labyrinth by a mile. Thankfully, I didn't do much tossing and turning in my sleep, so I didn't have to worry about falling off. I also wasn't particularly worried about insects, especially since there were no mosquitoes in this world to annoy the hell out of me throughout the night.

"Morning, Night," I said.

"Good morning, Master. You seem to have slept well, which is excellent. I was wondering if perhaps you'd like to accompany me on my morning stroll? The others won't be awake for some time yet."

"Wow. It's not every day I get invited on your walks. In fact, I think this might be a first!"

I knew he had been in the habit of pacing around his old boss arena for a while after waking up, and that he called the act his "morning stroll." But I'd never been invited along before. I could tell from the look in his eyes he had more in mind than just a carefree stroll. If it was something he felt compelled to wake me up over, I assumed it had to be important.

Throughout our little walk, Night continued to alter his size via Shapeshifter to suit the varying width of our path. In a flash of light, he'd shrink down to the size of a kitten, then a second later, he'd be the size of a panther or a large dog.

"That's a handy little Extra Skill you've got there," I whispered, side-eyeing him.

"It does have its drawbacks, but yes, I'd say the good generally outweighs the bad."

A long silence followed this brief exchange. My footsteps were the only sound. After quite some time, Night finally raised the question I assumed he'd been waiting to ask.

"So what do you intend to do now, Master?"

"Are you asking me as a servant of the Demon Lord or as my familiar?"

Night seemed a bit taken aback by the retort at first, but then he let out a weary chuckle; our pace had slowed from a stroll to a saunter by this point.

"Why, as your familiar, of course. The only remaining connection I have to the Demon Lord is through my five senses. I have no intention of betraying him, but I also have no intention of serving him ever again. Though I suppose one could argue that refusing to serve him would constitute a betrayal..."

"You sure about this? I mean, I have to assume you were living the high life among the demons, given your lofty position."

Granted, being confined to the lowest level of a labyrinth for eternity seemed like quite the demotion to me, but given Night's fastidious nature, I couldn't imagine his placement had been a punishment for a blunder of some sort. He had probably been entrusted with the task because he was the Demon Lord's most faithful servant. And I could only assume his ability to shapeshift and communicate meant he was treated more like an equal than any other monster. I'd met so many beings with Extra Skills that it was sometimes hard to remember only the true elite could even dream of acquiring them.

"You told me once that if it ever came down to it, I was free to take His Majesty's side, but the truth is, I don't see myself leaving

you... But back to the topic at hand: if you truly don't have a next destination in mind, there's somewhere I'd like us to go."

"Wow. You don't generally make requests like this. All right, where do you wanna go?" I asked, going along with the change of subject while being secretly touched by the notion that he would pick me over his old master.

"To the wildlands of Brute, where the great beasts roam free."

"The beastfolk continent, eh? And what exactly do you wanna do there?"

"There are many skilled blacksmiths among the beastfolk. And I think it's about time you had that blade of yours looked at."

I followed Night's gaze over my shoulder to the hilt of my black katana. The blade had been a gift from Commander Saran and had saved me from death countless times, but it was now on the verge of death itself. I supposed that was to be expected after seeing so much use against monsters more susceptible to magic. It wasn't that I hadn't been trying to take proper care of the blade— I'd simply pushed it to the point that it now looked quite brittle, as though a skilled martial artist could karate-chop it in half.

"Yeah, it probably would be a good idea to get some work done on it," I admitted.

"See? Your partner's a rather observant little kitty, isn't he?" said Night, puffing his chest out in a display that made me snicker. It was likely this wasn't the only errand he had in mind for our journey to the beastfolk domain, but I decided to wait to broach the subject.

"Then I guess it's settled. We'll head out later today," I proclaimed.

"Today?!" Night sputtered in disbelief.

I couldn't blame him for being surprised—it *was* quite the bombshell, but my mind was made up, and I had a good feeling about leaving right away. "To be honest with you, I was hoping to get the hell out of the Sacred Forest ASAP, but this business with Kilika really delayed our plans. It's unfortunate we got held up here for so long, but we can finally move on."

"I see. Guess I'll go get ready, then," said a voice that was decidedly not Night's. No, this was a woman's voice, and I whirled around to see a beautiful girl listening in on our conversation, her silver hair fluttering in the breeze.

Eavesdropper.

There was a mischievous glint in her bright-red eyes, pleased with herself as she was for having successfully sneaked up on me.

I groaned. "Why, hello there, Amelia."

"You weren't planning to leave me behind, I hope? Because I'll follow you to the ends of the world, Akira." She smiled. She hadn't done a lot of smiling since we'd arrived in the elven domain, so it was nice to see.

"Of course I wouldn't leave you behind, silly. I don't care what your daddy, the king, has to say—you and I are a team," I assured her, but Night gave me a dirty look. "Er, you and I *and Night*, I mean," I amended quickly. They both gave me a satisfactory nod. "But there's no telling if or when we'll make it back, so you should probably tell the king and your sister before we go."

"There's no 'if.' We *will* make it back, so there's nothing for them to worry about. I don't need to tell them a thing," Amelia asserted coolly.

"Fair enough." I smiled. Perhaps I was the only one who was feeling a little apprehensive. *She's right; we'll be fine,* I reassured myself internally. *We'll be just fine.*

"Princess Amelia! Would you like a drink of water?"

"Princess Amelia! How are you feeling?"

"Princess Amelia! Maybe we should..."

"Princess Amelia...!"

"Princess...?"

"Gaaaaah! Would you all just SHUT UP, already?! Leave us alone!"

I shooed away the swarm of elven attendants crowding Amelia, all the while wondering what I'd done to end up in this situation.

"You're leaving *today*?!"

"This is...awfully sudden, to put it lightly."

The king and Kilika were both quite taken aback by my announcement of our departure. Amelia's father immediately shot up from his throne, knocking it to the ground with a loud thunk. But the king paid no mind to his fancy chair, instead walking over to grab me by the collar. I didn't flinch, but I could feel an immense ire emanating from the girl standing beside me. *No, it's okay, Amelia... You don't have to give your father the death glare, it's fine...*

However, the king did not falter under Amelia's gaze as he shook me violently by the shoulders, though this felt like hardly more than a gentle jostling to me. The king was by no means a weakling, but the difference between our stats was substantial.

"That is much too soon!" he yelled. "Perhaps a child like you wouldn't understand, but there are procedures for things like this! Steps that must be taken! You can't just waltz over to another continent on a whim!"

"Yes, I'm aware," I quickly retorted.

The king simply shook his head. I'd thought I had a pretty good handle on things, to be honest, but now I was feeling just a little bit bad for the guy—mainly because I knew the real reason he was so reticent to let Amelia go so soon.

"Fine, have it your way," the king relented. "Though I guess this means we won't be having that homecoming party I planned for her after all..."

I knew that he and Kilika had been planning a grand party to celebrate Amelia's return to the forest, which was part of the reason I insisted on leaving posthaste. The other part was out of spite for her father, who clearly didn't want his daughter to leave despite our agreement.

"Hey, look at it this way: maybe this would be the perfect chance for Kilika to experience what it's like to be Amelia," I suggested.

"Wh-what it's like to *be* her? Surely you're not suggesting that I disguise myself as my sister and attend the party in her stead?" Kilika balked.

"That's exactly what I'm suggesting, actually." I frowned, disappointed that she didn't seem fond of the idea.

Kilika and Amelia's relationship had come a long way, and they seemed to be trying to set their differences aside, but I was still worried that some fragment of Kilika's deep-seated jealousy would resurface from time to time. Not that I doubted Kilika's good intentions—the two sisters had been practically inseparable ever since our little duel—but elves like them lived extremely long lives, so it was crucial to ensure the sisters reached a point of true mutual understanding.

"Now there's an interesting idea," mused the king. "You may not realize it yet, Kilika, but being a princess comes with its fair share of difficulties. Perhaps by learning to stand tall above your people without the help of Mesmerize, you'll be able to better understand and gain a deeper respect for your sister."

"A-are you truly entertaining this idea, Father?!" Kilika cried.

"Oh, what I do really isn't all that hard," Amelia said, patting Kilika on the head. "You'll do just fine. I promise."

"Sister..." Kilika whimpered, then nodded enthusiastically.

No one could resist the one-two punch of Amelia's smile-and-head-pat combo. At least, I certainly hadn't found a way to say no to it, let alone to her puppy-dog eyes. Both were top-tier attacks that utterly ignored her opponent's stats and did a huge number on their mental fortitude. They couldn't be blocked or countered either. Perhaps Amelia was the true MVP of this world.

"Very well, then. I'll disguise myself as my sister and attend the party in her stead!"

"Good. Make me proud, okay?" Amelia smiled sweetly.

"Okay!" Kilika beamed.

Sweet. That was one problem taken care of, at least. I looked over at Amelia—she didn't seem quite as stoked about the idea as Kilika now was, but it did seem like she was happy for her sister.

"And where are you three headed? Off to the Demon Lord's castle?" asked the king.

"Nah, I need to get some work done on my sword, so we're gonna head over to Brute first," I answered. At this, the king scrunched his face up a bit. *Right, I forgot the elves and the beast-folk aren't big fans of each other. Well, I guess the elves aren't big fans of any race other than themselves, so perhaps it'd be more accurate to call it a one-sided beef. Still, I can definitely see why the elves, who pride themselves so much on elegance and tradition, wouldn't see eye to eye with the rugged, burly beastfolk.*

"I see. In that case, allow me to at least see you safely to port."

"Thanks, but we'll be fine."

"Now, now. There's no need to be modest."

"No, really. Your coming along seems like a recipe for disaster, so I think we'll pass."

"Not a very agreeable one, are you?"

I don't really care if you think I'm agreeable, Pops. The thought of you accompanying us all the way to the port seems fishy to me, even if there is an entire ocean between us and them. There's no telling what sort of helicopter-parent BS you might be planning.

"There aren't many ships from here to Brute, and you

certainly won't be able to get on one without a royal writ of passage. Though if you truly wish to keep moving illegally between continents without doing any of the necessary paperwork, I suppose that's none of *my* concern. Just leave my daughter out of it."

"Tch."

"Speaking of which, how *did* you three manage to illegally trespass into elven territory in the first place?"

Crap. I was kinda hoping he'd forgotten about that. I clicked my tongue in frustration. *Really don't want to get into the whole "came here via a magic teleportation circle" thing right now, let alone the fact that I'm not from this world to begin with.* I forced a smile and made a desperate attempt to evade the question. "Fine, fine. We'll do it your way, I *guess*," I relented.

"Not if you're going to condescend to me like that, you won't," said the king.

"Sorry, can't help it," I said. *Jerkwad. I wasn't even trying to be rude that time.*

I folded my arms, and the king sighed, apparently realizing that trying to rectify my behavior was a lost cause.

"Well, take some time to gather up your belongings. I'll meet you down in the plaza later, and you can head out from there."

"We'll be ready and waiting."

I didn't have much luggage to speak of, other than my weapons and the clothes on my back. After counting up my throwing knives and helping Amelia sort through which of her belongings she wanted to bring, we headed down to the plaza as requested.

"All right, men! Forward march!"

"Hey, King Dingaling! You mind telling me what the *hell* is going on here?!"

When we arrived at the plaza, we were greeted by what must have been nearly a hundred elven archers. They were all standing so perfectly still that I honestly thought they might just be empty suits of armor at first.

"Father, don't you think this is a bit much?" asked Kilika, despite being in full armor herself—which was fitting, given that she was the greatest swordmaster in the entire elven domain. Having her along for the trek probably wouldn't slow us down, but the other ninety-nine archers were definitely overkill. And to my utter dismay, it seemed the king was hell-bent on accompanying us as well.

"There are many dangers out on the open road, and there's strength in numbers," proclaimed the king, trying to carry himself as though he didn't look utterly ridiculous in his soldier's uniform. Also, had he never heard of keeping a low profile? Sometimes it wasn't ideal to be traveling with an entire battalion of soldiers, believe it or not. Most times, in fact. "Oh, come now. Surely a little protection wouldn't hurt?" The king smiled sheepishly.

"A little? You call this a *little*?" I spat back.

I could have punched his stupid face—and probably would have, if Amelia hadn't stopped me. In the end, Kilika managed to talk him down to only sending a handful of the soldiers along with us, and she (thankfully) convinced him to stay home and take off that ridiculous suit of armor.

Flash forward to the present, as we continued to make our way through the forest with a posse of soldiers in tow. Though only about a quarter of the original number, it was still twenty new and unwanted traveling companions. And if that weren't bad enough, they were all men.

I hate this. Even after shooing them away for the umpteenth time, I could still see them shooting occasional glances over at Amelia. *These bastards just don't know when to lay off.*

"Won't be long now till we reach port," said a smiling elven youth who dared to approach me despite my obvious frustration.

Granted, "youth" was relative. Compared to Amelia and the others, he might have been young, but he was probably several decades older than me at least. And just like all the other elven men, he was blessed with extremely good looks.

Get bent, pretty-boy.

He misinterpreted my baleful gaze somehow, as he quickly gasped and proceeded to introduce himself in a flustered panic. "Th-the name's William, milord!"

"Why does that sound so familiar?" I asked, cocking my head.

"Erm, it's a bit embarrassing, actually...but my parents were both big fans of Lord Liam, so..."

"Oh, I see. They included his name in yours as a tribute or whatever." Apparently naming your offspring after someone you respected was a thing in Morrigan too.

"Correct. I have a lot of respect for Lord Liam, so I'm perfectly happy with the name. Even if it *is* a little embarrassing."

"I still don't see what's so great about that prick," I whispered to myself, thinking back on his stupidly confident face during our duel.

"Did you say something, milord?"

"Nope, sorry."

To be fair, I had to give Liam credit for his actions since he'd been freed from Kilika's spell. He was working tirelessly to stabilize the elven nation, and he had formally canceled his engagements with both Amelia and Kilika in order to focus on his work, even issuing an official apology to that effect. Hell, he'd even gone as far as to prostrate himself before me with such emotional intensity one might have been forgiven for wondering if he was secretly Japanese.

"Lord Akira, you have my deepest, sincerest apologies! I should have stopped Princess Kilika and saved Princess Amelia, but my own inadequacies forced you to do those jobs for me! And I even had the gall to try to kill you when first we met! Forgive me for my transgressions!"

"Hey, whoa, whoa, whoa! You don't have to get on your hands and knees, buddy! And where'd you learn to apologize like a Japanese person, anyhow?! Though you're doing a stellar job of it, I've gotta admit! C'mon, lift your head up!"

"I've heard this is how the people of the human country of Yamato apologize or plead with their superiors. And since your homeland apparently bears a striking cultural resemblance to Yamato, I wanted to apologize in the manner you'd most appreciate!"

"All right, all right! That's enough! Just get up off the ground, already!"

I did end up caving to the emotional display and forgiving him.

Perhaps not realizing my mind was elsewhere, William had continued to wax nostalgic about his love for Liam. "He really is the perfect role model, though, wouldn't you say? It's said elven society would collapse if not for our king, but I honestly think you could say the same about Lord Liam. I'm told he works deep into the night, day after day, trying to rebuild our economy, though I honestly don't have a clue what his job actually entails, since I'm still just a student myself. But he doesn't pride himself too much on his status as a civil servant, and he still participates in hunts just like any other capable elf. His archery skills are second only to Amelia's, and his prey has never escaped him. That's our Lord Liam for you—he's the best of both worlds, blessed with both brains *and* brawn!"

"Yeah, very cool, kid. Anyway..."

After expertly ignoring William's long and fanboyish tirade, I noticed a commotion had broken out somewhere up ahead of us in the caravan, bringing our steady forward march to a standstill. William had said we were getting close to our destination, but I didn't think we'd arrived. Shortly thereafter, the boy confirmed my suspicions.

"Oh, no! We've got hostiles!" he said in a panic.

"Hostiles? You mean bandits or something?" I asked.

The soldiers formed a circle around Amelia and drew their respective weapons. Given that we were still in close quarters and there were elves all around me, I couldn't exactly draw the Yato-no-Kami and join them yet. Plus, it seemed like our assailants had us far outnumbered.

"No, these aren't just your average bandits! They've been kidnapping women and children around these parts! And none of them ever return!"

"Elf traffickers, eh? I imagine they're selling their victims to rich and powerful foreign buyers willing to pay a little extra for a slave with an 'exotic' face?"

"So you've heard of them before. Yes, they steal away our elven brothers and sisters, then sell them off to human and beastfolk buyers at a high price!"

William was now clenching his fists so tightly that blood was trickling down his palm. He watched as the kidnappers slowly closed in on us with a deep and fiery hatred in his eyes; the innocent Liam fanboy from a minute ago was nowhere to be found. I had a hunch that perhaps someone very close to William had been kidnapped, and it seemed like several of the other elves bore similar vendettas.

Elves seemed to be unified by tribe mentality. They wouldn't hesitate to lay down their lives for their fellow countrymen, regardless of whether or not they were related by blood, and they would stop at nothing to exact revenge. To make an enemy of such a society—let alone brazenly kidnap dozens upon dozens of their brethren—these traffickers probably had the backing of a powerful group, maybe even a government.

But as our circle grew tighter and tighter, I decided now

probably wasn't the time to be thinking about such things. For now, I had to figure out how to get us out of this sticky situation—I could worry about the true culprits later. Unfortunately, I was the only frontline fighter here. I found myself wishing we'd brought Kilika along with us after all, though perhaps more than anything, I wished they had warned us that there were kidnappers lurking around these parts!

"Now then, my little elves—give up Her Highness, and we'll let you live. Resist and die," said one among the kidnappers.

"Her Highness?"

"Don't play dumb, boy. Princess Amelia! Hand her over right now!"

These guys clearly weren't messing around—they certainly had balls to demand we hand over Amelia, I'd give them that. So offended was I by this notion that I accidentally shattered the throwing knife I was squeezing tightly in my hand. *Should I just off these goons? No, I probably shouldn't kill them, but I could at least restrain them with Shadow Magic, right? Maybe take off an arm or two while I'm at it.*

"L-Lord Akira?"

"What is it, William?"

"Y-you just broke your own weapon..."

"Yes, but I've got more where that came from. Don't worry about it."

"Lord Akira, your tone—why has it changed?"

"I'm offended by the nerve of this man."

"O-oh. Well, if you say so."

The elves standing in my immediate vicinity, William included, all took a few steps back, but the raging waves of malice flowing from my very pores were soon calmed by a lone woman's voice.

"I believe in you, Akira. Don't let me go, okay?"

"Of course not, babe. I'd never hand the woman I love to a bunch of thugs."

One touch from Amelia's fingers on the arm I'd used to shatter the knife was enough to calm me right down, and she smiled upon seeing I'd returned to normal. Then she took a deep breath and began shouting out orders to the soldiers, most of whom were still shaking in their boots.

"Look alive, men! The enemy has us outnumbered! But as long as we have Akira on our side, they'll never defeat us! Let's show these villains what we elves do to those who dare to lay a finger on our countrymen!"

All of the soldiers let out a roaring cheer. Then Amelia, having completely reversed troop morale, began preparing to cast her signature Gravity Magic. It seemed she intended to fight alongside me.

"Well, I'm gonna go take these punks out like the assassin I am. You be careful, Amelia."

"You too."

With that, I activated Conceal Presence. I figured I would take out the leader first, then deal with his cronies, so I slipped out from the circle of elves and headed in the direction the first man's voice had come from. Thanks to my high-level Assassination skill,

I was able to dash as fast as I wanted to without making a sound. I knew the others would be all right—there was no way any of these thugs could hold a candle to Amelia. Realizing that perhaps one of our assailants could still see me if they had Mystic Eyes like Commander Saran's, I stuck to the shadows behind the trees as I approached. However, it seemed like none of them had any idea that I'd slipped away right under their noses.

"Heh heh heh... Whaddya say, Boss? Think they'll hand over the girl?" I heard one unsavory voice ask.

This was enough to get me fuming all over again. *Like I'd ever hand over my precious Amelia to a bunch of goons like you.*

"Well, she may be their so-called 'crown jewel,' but don't let that deceive you. These people consider a slight against any of them a slight against all of them, so I don't think they'll be too eager to negotiate after we've taken so many of their brethren," came a calmer voice, apparently belonging to the leader of the group.

With a throwing knife in one hand, I moved closer. Using Detect Presence, I was able to determine that there were about fifty of them in total. Three of the presences seemed far too weak to be kidnappers—hostages, perhaps.

"Well, should we let 'em have it, then?" asked the first voice.

"I suppose so. Wouldn't want to keep Lord Gram waiting on his princess for *too* terribly long, now would we?" said the boss.

Gram. Now there was a name I hadn't heard before. If he was the one doling out orders to these thugs, then it would be prudent to make a note of it. Regardless, it seemed they were preparing to go on the offensive, so it was about time I got to work. Waiting for the sun to be hidden by a passing cloud, I took advantage of the meager veil of shadow and made my move.

"Gugh?!"

"Blarrrgh!"

"Hey, what the—grgghk!"

I incapacitated nearly a dozen of them in an instant, then sped off toward my next target. The kidnappers were caught completely off guard, and I continued to knock them out one by one before they could even pull out their weapons.

"Hey! What the hell's going on?!"

"We're under attack, Boss!"

"What?! You're kidding me!"

Apparently the boss hadn't even considered the possibility we'd dare to fight back while they had other hostages in tow. They should have pulled back right then and there, but their leader seemed to have other ideas.

"Grr! I dunno what these pointy-eared freaks are thinking, but I don't care! Kill anyone you don't recognize!"

The lowlifes let out a war cry, disguising their fear and confusion, then charged straight into the middle of the circle.

"Only ten of 'em left, eh? Guess I'll let Amelia and William handle them while I go take care of the boss and the hostages," I said decisively. It seemed the perpetrators were indeed human, which meant Amelia could easily handle them even without the help of her archers. I ordered Night to keep a close eye on Amelia via Telepathy.

"But of course, Master," he responded confidently. He seemed

rather excited to have the chance to trounce some humans again; he hadn't completely let go of his boss-monster roots just yet.

"Hey, goddammit! What's gotten into you idiots? Wake the hell up!" cried the leader to his fallen comrades. He was holding a knife to the throat of a female elven hostage, who looked awfully gaunt and malnourished. His unconscious companions remained still.

I noticed another elven girl, this one a fair young maiden, trembling nearby. There was one other hostage lying on the ground next to her, and though I couldn't quite make out their face, they seemed to be an elven woman as well. Perhaps she'd fainted. All three of them were bound and gagged, unable to escape despite the pandemonium.

Saving the hostages was my top priority, so I used Conceal Presence again and moved toward the boss, though I probably could have sneaked up on him without it, preoccupied as he was with rousing his comrades. First, I picked up the unconscious woman, laid her down in the shadow of a nearby tree, and cut her bindings with a throwing knife. Then I headed back for the young girl. I didn't want her to scream and alert the boss, so I karate-chopped her neck to knock her out before dragging her behind another tree. Amelia would probably have some choice words for me had she witnessed that, but I figured she was too busy to notice, and the risk of the girl assuming I was one of the kidnappers was too great to ignore. However, it was the final hostage who would be the trickiest of all. How was I supposed to wrest her from the boss's stranglehold?

"Hey, buddy," I whispered in his ear from behind. "Unless you want this knife shoved into your neck, I suggest you let the lady go."

"Bwaaaaaaagh?!"

The boss, utterly oblivious to my presence until I spoke, nearly jumped out of his skin in terror and released his grip on the woman.

Thanks for being so predictable, sucker.

I pulled the girl away while I had the chance, and she seemed just as surprised by my sudden appearance as he was. Using my throwing knife, I cut the ropes around her and pointed over to the tree where I'd left the young girl. She immediately knew what I was getting at, and though she still seemed a bit wary of me, she headed to the tree. The other hostage was lying at the base of the tree next to it, so I could only hope she would watch over the other two. I kept my eyes locked on the boss, who was so furious that his entire face was bright red and veins bulged out of his forehead.

He could probably stand to work on his blood pressure.

"You rat bastard! Those hostages are the property of Lord Gram!" he screamed.

"Sorry, who's this Gram guy, exactly? Can't say I've heard of him," I responded.

"I don't have to tell you anything!"

Damn. Guess he's not quite stupid enough to sell out his client. But I was at least able to learn that these three women were apparently on loan from this Gram guy for use as bargaining chips in Amelia's kidnapping. The thugs' boss wasn't so happy about losing his leverage.

"Now then. I've got a few questions I'd like you to answer. I don't mind leaving your buddies out here to sleep on the dirt, but I'm afraid I'll have to bring you in."

"Do you even realize who you're talking to, you little prick?! I'm the leader of the Sharks! We're a blue-rank crime syndicate! Maybe you've heard of us?!"

He seemed awfully proud, but unfortunately, I'd never heard of ranked crime syndicates, let alone the Sharks, so I was far from impressed. The thought of there being a governing body that ranked crime syndicates did amuse me, though, and I found it rather quaint that the "Sharks" would be given the color blue. It just seemed fitting, even if I didn't know whether blue was a high rank.

"Sorry, can't say that I have. No offense," I said. Realizing there was no point in trying to get any more information out of him, I slammed my fist into his stomach, and despite attempted resistance, he fell to the ground with a lethargic groan. "Great. Time to go see if Amelia's done with the stragglers yet."

After tying the boss up tight with some vines growing nearby, I slung him over my shoulder. He deserved no dignity after trying to kidnap Amelia. I looked up and saw that the young girl I'd knocked out had regained consciousness. I helped her stand. One of the other hostages, presumably her mother, embraced her, and they sobbed together.

All's well that ends well, I guess. I sighed to myself, looking away to give them some privacy during their touching reunion.

But while I didn't know it then, I'd eventually come to realize this kidnapping was only the beginning of something much, much bigger.

"Welcome back, Akira. No injuries, I take it?" Amelia asked.

"Of course not. Who do you think I am? Anyway, uh... What the hell happened here?"

As I walked around the pile of kidnapper bodies, back toward the center of our brigade, Amelia jogged over to meet me. Then came Night, whose fur was looking awfully shiny. The elven soldiers cleared a path for him, and I squinted suspiciously at the cat. What had he done *this* time?

"I know what you must be thinking, Master, but I've done nothing wrong."

"You *sure* about that?"

"Wow! You won't even believe your own partner?! Tell him, Lady Amelia! Though I'll admit, I'm glad my face alone can still strike fear into the hearts of people."

Night's countenance, though feline, was also that of a fearsome monster, so it did give me cause for concern, but as Amelia confirmed he hadn't done anything wrong, I walked up and pressed my cheek up against his giant toe beans, each now the size of my face after Night's shapeshifting. *Yes, this is heaven. I'll have to ask Amelia to squish them with me later.*

"Night's not lying, Akira. These criminals all just fainted the minute they saw his face," Amelia assured me, and I believed her.

It wasn't the best look for a so-called prestigious crime syndicate, and I hoped they wouldn't get demoted to a different color for this. We decided to let the elven soldiers take care of the kidnappers. As we were discussing our next move, William walked tentatively up to us, clearly terrified of Night.

"Um, Lord Akira? I was hoping to ask you something, if that's all right," he said, turning his gaze toward Amelia. Presumably, he wanted to make sure she approved, as the highest-ranking official present. I found it amusing that he was so concerned with this particular formality while simultaneously interrupting our conversation. Amelia nodded, and he finally turned toward me. "Um, so is Lord Night your familiar?" William asked.

"I dunno. *Is* he?" I responded, looking up at Night.

"Of course I am! Or did you think the matching emblems on my forehead and your wrists were just a coincidence?!" he roared.

"Well, there you have it," I said, ignoring Night's tantrum and looking back at William.

"Um, then would you mind if I took a look at your wrists?" he asked.

I kept them hidden under my long black sleeves most of the time, no matter how hot it was, since I didn't want to be seen walking around with the markings and get mistaken for an edgelord with matching wrist tattoos, but I rolled up my sleeves and let William take a gander. The black emblems had darkened since Night and I made our pact.

"Th-thank you. I have to admit, I never thought I'd meet a monsterlord in my entire life, even with an elven lifespan."

"Sorry, a 'monsterlord'?"

It sounded a little too close to edgelord, even for me. Usually, cringeworthy titles like "monsterlord" were reserved for the protagonist alone, but I had no idea where our intrepid hero even was. He was skilled enough to not be lying dead in a ditch somewhere, and I assumed he'd made it out of the castle by now, but that only made it harder to guess where he might have gone.

"It's an elven term," Amelia explained. "Though I think it's been adopted by the other races over time."

"Yes, it was originally a derogatory term used to refer to demons specifically, but over time it was expanded to include humans, elves, and beastfolk who've made pacts with monster familiars," said Night.

"Monsters can almost never establish a bond with non-demon races, which is why there have been virtually no studies on the topic. With your cooperation, we could make huge breakthroughs in the field of monsterlord research!" William swooned, gazing up at Night. This visibly disturbed the poor feline, and he quickly shrank back down to house cat size to take refuge on my shoulders. William stepped closer to me, undeterred. "Fascinating! So Lord Night has the ability to adjust his size at will! How unique!"

"Look, William. You're a nice kid, and I get that we're a fringe case, but please don't scare my poor kitten," I said.

"Oh! Of course, sir! My deepest apologies! I suppose I let myself get carried away, since I'm not sure I'll ever get the chance to see you again. Forgive me!" he said, turning away from Night in shame.

"Well, you have to admire his passion, at least," said Amelia.

"Passion? The guy needs to learn some self-control," I replied. *"I don't like him. I don't like him one bit."*

As we offered our respective thoughts on William, I noticed the leader of the kidnappers had begun to stir. He was still slung over one of my shoulders (where Night usually sat), while Night perched on the opposite one (and seemed none too pleased that his usual spot was taken).

Well then. I suppose it's about time for a little interrogation. Hopefully we won't have to rough him up too much—it'll be nice if he just tells us what he knows without putting up much of a fight. I threw the man roughly to the ground, which woke him right up. He glared up at me with hatred in his eyes. *Wow, I bet this guy wakes up ready and alert for work each day. As someone who's never been much of a morning person, I'm honestly kinda jealous.*

"Okay, you're gonna tell us everything you know. Why don't you start by explaining who the hell this 'Gram' guy is?" I suggested, pressing a throwing knife against his throat. The man's eyes quivered with fear. I had no intention of killing the guy, of course. These were just intimidation tactics, plain and simple, but he didn't need to know that. Although my recent cruel streak *did* make me wonder if perhaps I was becoming more demon than human.

"I—I don't gotta tell you nothin', kid!" the boss squealed with tears in his eyes. I could tell from the way his body quaked that he was on the verge of passing out again. Maybe he really would sooner die than give up his intel.

I let out a sigh. "Fine, whatever. Unlike you, I'm no villain, and I honestly don't care who the hell this Gram loser is. I was mostly just asking out of curiosity. But if you elves still can't solve this problem on your own, feel free to call me for help," I said to the soldiers. I retracted my knife, and the boss's jaw dropped, along with the jaws of everyone else in attendance. *Why are you all giving me that look?* I didn't think I'd said anything particularly strange or controversial.

"Akira, are you saying you don't wanna stick around to help solve the kidnappings?"

"I am. Sorry, Amelia."

I wasn't some fairy tale protagonist who felt compelled to put a stop to any wrongdoing he happened to encounter. As long as my friends and loved ones weren't suffering, I couldn't have cared less what happened to random strangers. Besides, at least the elves were one unified nation and people. Every country had its fair share of crime, and if a few kidnappings were truly the biggest problem they had to deal with, I thought they should consider themselves lucky. At least they got to live out their peaceful lives far away from the fires of war.

"Well, okay," said Amelia. "I'm sticking with you no matter what, so I'll defer to your judgment."

"Wh-what?! No!"

"You can't leave us, Princess Amelia!"

William and the other elves cried out in dismay. *C'mon, guys. Quit treating us like heroes, will ya? You can't expect other people to solve all your problems.*

"Sorry, but them's the breaks. Oh, and by the way, I rescued three hostages and left them over there. They'll probably come join up with you soon enough," I said, pointing a finger in the direction I'd come from. Sure enough, the three hostages walked out from between the trees a moment later, and the little girl ran up and wrapped her arms around me.

"Thanks so much for saving us, mister!" She smiled.

"You're very welcome, kiddo," I replied.

The other hostages expressed their deepest gratitude to me as well, and I noticed Amelia pouting jealously out of the corner of my eye. I'd have to give her some special attention later.

"Are you sure about this, Master?" Night whispered in my ear.

I simply ran my fingers through his fur in response. Suddenly, I was reminded of a peculiar symbol I'd noticed earlier—the one that had been engraved on one of the kidnappers' weapons. "Hey, Night?" I asked. "Have you ever seen a symbol like a circle with three claws on top?"

"Why, yes. That's the national crest of Uruk, the largest of all the beastfolk nations. Why do you ask?" Night responded. Then his eyes grew wide. *"Wait! Surely you don't mean—?!"*

"Yeah." I nodded. "That symbol was engraved on one of those guys' swords. I'm thinking our little 'kidnappers' might have been hired by beastfolk or disguised Uruk knights or something."

"Kn-knights of Uruk kidnapping elves? But why would they not use more nondescript weapons in that case? Surely they would be smart enough to realize such an indicator could blow their cover."

"Beats me. It was only one guy, so maybe he broke all the other weapons he brought with him and had no other choice," I posited. The man *had* been swinging his sword around rather wildly, perhaps in an attempt to hide the crest, but unfortunately for him, his flurry of slashes had been no match for my stellar kinetic vision.

"Have you told Lady Amelia and the other elves about this?"

"No, and I don't intend to. I don't have any hard evidence, and it's too serious an issue for baseless speculation. Plus, Amelia might be the ruler of the elves someday, and I don't want her to be left with a society that's even more prejudiced toward the beastfolk than they already are." I might have told the elves I wanted nothing to do with this problem, but it was starting to look like I'd have to do a little digging of my own whether I wanted to or not.

"Very well. I'll go along with whatever you decide, Master."

"Thanks, Night."

I had no working theories as to why the beastfolk country of Uruk would be abducting elven women and children, nor why they seemed so determined to kidnap Amelia, but I knew one thing for sure—they'd have to pry her from my cold, dead hands.

"So I guess the next big question is: who the hell is this Gram guy?" I wondered aloud.

"I don't believe that's the name of the current king of Uruk, if that's what you suspect, but, if I remember correctly, there was a prime minister with that name at one point..."

"Meh. Don't worry about it. Unless he tries to come after Amelia again, I'm willing to let weeping dogs cry."

"I don't believe that's quite how the idiom goes, Master."

As Amelia watched the two of them exchange a hearty chuckle from a distance, she let out a wistful sigh. "I hope one day you'll learn to let me in, Akira."

In the end, we decided to release the leader of the kidnappers out into the forest. The elves and I agreed there was little chance they'd have any more luck interrogating him than I did, and it was far more likely he was just a pawn who didn't actually know anything at all. For a leader of a group of ruffians, his sword skills weren't up to snuff, and while I didn't have any frame of reference for how infamous a blue-rank crime syndicate was, their modus operandi for kidnapping seemed sloppy at best.

After he was gone, the group of archers split in two—half returning to the Holy Tree with the hostages and half accompanying us the rest of the way to port. With the soldiers watching our backs at every turn, the three of us would be able to enjoy the rest of the journey without having to stay on guard. At one point, Amelia got tired and asked Night to turn big so she could ride on his back.

"You think letting them go was the right thing to do, Akira? If they really were part of a major crime syndicate, we could've gotten a reward for turning them in, y'know," she said, pouting, probably envisioning the fancy meals we could have enjoyed with some reward money.

"Hey, we rescued some kidnap victims, and that's good enough for me. You know what they say: a bird in the hand is worth two in the bush," I said wisely.

"People say that?" asked Amelia.

"Not that I've ever heard," said Night.

The two of them looked confused as I explained the meaning of the expression.

"Ah, I see. I must say, the people of your world certainly have a knack for crafting peculiar expressions, Master." Night and Amelia folded their arms and nodded in understanding. The two of them looked like grumpy old coots who'd finally found something they could agree upon, and I couldn't help but laugh.

"Okay, people! We're here!" said William, who'd been walking at the head of the pack. The rest of us stopped in our tracks.

It was hard to make out much with all the trees still in the way, but I did spot a large ship moored at what looked like an underutilized wharf. Amelia and Night, meanwhile, seemed utterly spellbound by the vast blue ocean spreading out in front of them.

"That, Lord Akira, is the *Searunner*—one of the only ships that travels between Brute and the Sacred Forest on a set schedule, and the one you'll be boarding today," said William, handing me a letter adorned with the seal of the elven royal family.

The king had instructed me to give it to the guildmaster of the Adventurer's Guild branch in Ur, the largest port city in the beastfolk domain. He said they would be of great help to us on our journey. *How very thoughtful of him. He probably thinks this makes us even, doesn't he? Yeah, I don't think so. Not after I just saved those hostages for you, buddy. Wish I could see the look on his face when they make it back and he realizes he's even* more *indebted to me.*

"This is as far as we can take you," said William. "Lord Akira, Lord Night… Saying this might make me appear pathetic, but I don't care. I have a request for you—not as a representative of all elves, but as a man named William." I could tell he was struggling to hold back tears as he scrunched up his face. "Though I'm ashamed to admit it, I used wind magic to listen in on your conversation earlier, and I heard that you suspect the kidnappers hail from the nation of Uruk. If it turns out they do, then I beg of you: please save my wife and daughter, and ensure they make it home safely!"

"M-mine too!"

"Please, you have to help us!"

The elves bowed to me in unison. These proud people, who generally didn't interact with other races, were lowering their heads and asking for help in an uncharacteristic and potentially torturous display. To them, we humans were inferior despite our greater numbers, yet they were giving me the ultimate show of respect. I could see the resolve written all over their faces.

"Eavesdropping isn't good, you know, and I'm sorry, but I've got my own ailing mother and sister I need to hurry back to in my homeland. Bye now."

"L-Lord Akira!"

I clenched my fist as the elves continued their whining, but I stopped myself.

"But if I happen to run into any of your loved ones along the way, I suppose I wouldn't mind setting them free," I offered in my own uncharacteristic display; I never would have been so altruistic before coming to Morrigan. It seemed I'd changed an awful lot after meeting Amelia, for better or worse.

The faces of the elves lit up.

"Oh, thank you, Lord Akira!"

"Be careful out there, Princess Amelia!"

"Please take care of yourselves!"

The elves waved and called out to us as we boarded the vessel. I immediately headed away from the railing to avoid embarrassment, leaving Amelia to deal with them herself.

"You be careful on your way back too, everyone," she said.

"Yes, ma'am!"

And so we set sail, with Night still on my shoulders, savoring the salty ocean breeze.

"What a tremendous feeling this is, Master."

"Yeah."

Personally, I didn't like the smell of salt water one bit, especially the way it clung to your clothes and skin. I'd have to give Night a good bath to wash it out of his fur.

"Akira, I wanted to talk to you about something," Amelia said, appearing behind me with a blank expression.

I had an idea of what it might be.

"What is it, Amelia?"

"Are you sure...there isn't anything I can help with?"

"Not right now, no. Your time to shine won't come for a while yet."

"I see," she murmured, hanging her head.

Any other time, I would have rustled her hair to reassure her, but not now. "Listen, Amelia, if you don't fully believe in our cause, maybe it would be better for you not to come. There's still time for you to catch the soldiers and get an escort back to the Holy Tree."

"Wha... Why would you say that...?"

Believe me, this isn't a fun conversation for me either. The crest-fallen look on Amelia's face was like needles through my beating heart. "I'm just saying, I don't give a rat's ass what happens to the elves or their society. All I care about is that those closest to me are safe and happy."

"Does that not include me?"

"No, it does. It totally does."

Hence why I would never forgive the country of Uruk for trying to take her from me. But if we went on a wild goose chase trying to get to the bottom of these kidnappings in Uruk, our journey to the Demon Lord's castle would be delayed. I was worried enough about the hero and the classmates I'd left behind at the Retice's castle as it was, and if we kept signing ourselves up to solve more and more problems...there was no telling when I'd ever make it back to Japan. The part of me that wanted desperately to go home to my family was constantly at odds with the part that wanted to help Amelia and keep her safe. Perhaps Amelia could read my mind, and perhaps she couldn't, but either way, she got up on her tiptoes and ruffled my hair.

"You're free to do things your way, Akira. And I'm gonna do things my way."

"Fair enough."

I couldn't help but let out an exhausted chuckle at how unconditionally this woman accepted me. She was far, far too trusting and naïve. But I knew she'd take offense to that notion, so I kept the thought to myself.

"Erm, Master? While I certainly don't mind being subjected to this touching conversation, perhaps there's a better place to have it than up here on the deck, in front of all the crew members," Night suggested, snapping me back to reality.

I looked around to see various crewmen going about their designated tasks, trying their very best to ignore us. The three of us were just getting in the way.

Come to think of it, I'd noticed the working class in this world seemed to comprise mostly humans, regardless of what continent we were on. All of the crew members on this ship, and even the kidnappers who'd attacked us, had been human. Perhaps it had something to do with the human population constantly growing while the elves and beastfolk stayed relatively the same, leaving humans to seek work on other continents just to get by. We'd only seen a small fraction of human society back in Retice, after all, and while it didn't seem like any of the humans I'd met resented their lot in life, there was no denying that they were treated differently than the other races of this world, for better *and* worse.

CHAPTER 2

The Land of Beasts

POV: ODA AKIRA

WHILE THE VOYAGE itself was relatively uneventful, true trouble came to greet us the moment we made landfall. Though, in fairness, I might have had a hand in instigating it.

"Hey, shrimp. Leave the elf girl with us and get lost."

"I beg your pardon?"

Right, I almost forgot that a scrub like me sticks out like a sore thumb next to a bombshell like Amelia. Before long, we were surrounded by beastmen who reeked of booze and had clearly been drinking all day. They were red in the face (or at least I thought they were—hard to tell under all that fur), with yellow Adventurer's Guild dog tags hanging proudly around their necks. Judging by their equipment, they seemed like a party full of warriors. *What rank was yellow, again? The fourth highest?* I knew it was the third lowest. Maybe that was a better frame of reference.

Using World Eyes, I determined none of them had any particularly threatening combat abilities. They were just small fry—

if this were a manga, the author probably wouldn't have even bothered to draw faces on such forgettable background characters. I wasn't sure there was much of a market for big, burly dudes with cat ears and curly tails, and they were kind of creepy. *Either get plastic surgery done on that face or get rid of those ears and that tail—one or the other.*

The beastmen, having no idea that I was currently roasting them in my mind, took my speechlessness as a sign of fear and let out a collective hearty chortle.

I heaved a quiet sigh. "Welp, there's another trope I can check off the list, I guess. Yay for me."

"Want me to squash 'em for you, Akira?"

"Nah, I'll take care of it."

I'd somehow completely forgotten about my original concern that having a pretty girl for a party member would draw unwanted attention, but this was also the first time she and I were walking together through a society where humans weren't considered a novelty.

"Whaddya still hangin' around for, shrimp? Leave the girl and go. I ain't interested in dudes," barked the leader of the pack, now visibly irritated. "I know I'm a fine hunk o' man, but I don't swing that way, freak."

I'd been trying to keep my temper in check, but this pushed me over the edge.

"Who said anything about what way I swing, douchebag?" I snarled.

The corners of my mouth stretched into an evil grin. I could hear Night protesting on my shoulders, begging me to stop, but I wasn't having any of it. I was too preoccupied with deciding how exactly I was going to punish this asswipe. Calling me gay was one thing, but if he thought I'd let him get away with ogling Amelia like he was, he was dead wrong.

"You wanna go? Fine by me. Which of you kitty cats wants to die first?" I asked, beckoning them with curled fingers. I left my katana in its sheath—I didn't want to actually kill them, just rough them up a little bit.

"'Scuse me? You think a little hairless brat like you can take on all of us at once?"

"*You're* the only one who's gonna die here, kid. Why don't you run back to mommy?"

"Yeah, aren't you late for your daily breastfeeding?"

"Go on, beat it, shrimp. Better start running if you know what's good for ya."

The rest of the beastmen joined in with the taunting, and this pushed Amelia over the edge as well. Night simply shook his head disappointedly at the both of us from his perch on my shoulder.

"And what about you, huh?" Amelia said. A crowd of onlookers had gathered around us to see what all the commotion was about. "You're adventurers, aren't you? I see those dog tags. I don't think the Guild would take kindly to its representatives picking fights in the middle of the street."

Suddenly, the beastmen's faces went bright red, but not out of rage. They weren't even paying attention to the words Amelia was saying—they were simply entranced by her beautiful, soothing voice.

"Holy crap, did you guys hear that?"

"Yeah, man. Chick's got the voice of an angel."

"Now we *definitely* can't let her walk away with a loser like him."

"How much do you guys think she'd sell for?"

Now I liked to think I had been controlling myself quite well up to that point—the old me certainly wouldn't have let this go on as long as it had—but every man's patience had its limits, and these bastards had just crossed mine.

I reached out my hands. Amelia, realizing what I was about to do, reached out her own to try to stop me.

But it was too late.

"Shadow Magic, activate."

I had no intention of using such a deadly skill to its fullest extent here in the middle of town. While plenty of the ordinary onlookers were gawking at Amelia like she was a fine piece of meat, they at least had the decency to not actually make a pass at her like these jerks had. And now that we'd drawn so much attention to ourselves, I didn't think we'd be able to keep a low profile anymore, which meant my only option was to send each and every one of these drooling horndogs packing.

"Don't do it, Master."

"Gwaaaaaagh!"

"Ugh! What the hell *is* this?!"

"Crap, crap, crap! It won't come off!"

I'd sent tiny little shadows hurtling into each of the men's eyes, rendering them temporarily blind. It was by no means a display of what I was truly capable of, but I thought it would do a decent job of conveying to the crowd that I was a force to be reckoned with and deter at least a few presumptuous brutes from trying to mess with us later.

"Well now. That's a fancy trick if I've ever seen one," came a voice from the peanut gallery. The sea of onlookers parted, and a tall man sauntered slowly up to us through the murmurs of the crowd. He had the ears and tail of a leopard, was garbed in dark clothes, and carried himself like a wise and eloquent individual. His face, however, was like a mask—expressionless, unfazed.

The beastmen who'd been taunting us panicked at the sight of him.

"Th-that voice…!"

"O-oh, crap!"

"W-we're in deep trouble now!"

"What the hell is *he* doing here?!"

Judging by their reactions, as well as the murmurs from the crowd, the man was either highly respected, highly feared, or both—which was impressive, given his apparent youth. The way everyone seemed to crap their collective pants the moment he arrived on the scene was a little cliché for my tastes, and I wished they would all just shut the hell up.

"Now then. I suppose some introductions are in order, hm?" said the man. "I am Lingga, and I am the administrator of the local Adventurer's Guild branch here in the port city of Ur. It's a pleasure to meet you, human child."

"I'm Oda Akira. Nice to meet you too, bud. If you're the local guildmaster, then I guess you've saved me a trip. I've got a letter for you here from the king of the elves."

"Oh? A letter of introduction from His Majesty himself? You must be here on important business indeed; that man deeply abhors all manner of written correspondence."

The crowd seemed incensed at the idea that anyone would refer to this apparently important man as "bud," but Lingga didn't look bothered, so I carried on like normal. I handed him the letter from the elven king, and he broke the seal to start reading it.

"I see, I see... Fascinating stuff, to be sure. Even if the penmanship could use a little work."

"Careful what you say in front of his daughter, pal," I said, shooting Amelia a glance. She didn't seem offended in the least and was still trying to size the guy up for herself.

"His daughter, you say? Then you must be Princess Amelia," Lingga said, before raising a hand to hide his mouth and lowering his voice to a whisper. "You're awfully brave to come here at this time of year, when lovely young ladies like yourself are in grave danger."

"Wait. What's so different about this time of year?" I asked, genuinely confounded.

"You don't even know, yet you came here anyway? Oh, never mind. This is hardly the time or place. Let's head on over to the Guild, shall we?" Lingga turned sharply on his heels and looked with disdain at the beastmen who had accosted us. Then he turned to another young man standing nearby. "Ah, there you are, Yamato. Excellent timing. Would you be a dear and process expulsion paperwork for these ruffians, confiscate their dog tags and other effects, and see that they're banished from the city? Thank you."

"As you wish, sir," said the young man.

As Lingga began to walk back the way he'd come, the crowd parted once more, fear in their eyes as they looked upon him. I wondered what he'd done to deserve such a reputation. Perhaps more surprising was the fact that they seemed equally as scared, or maybe even more so, when they saw Night sitting on my shoulder.

"That was quite the cunning little plan you cooked up, I must admit," Lingga said to me as we made our way to the Guild down some less-trafficked side streets.

"I'm just glad they fell for it." I grinned. "Don't think anyone in this town's gonna try messing with Amelia again anytime soon."

"Huh? Akira, what's he talking about?" asked Amelia as she and Night cocked their heads in confusion.

I wasn't sure if they were trusting or naive, but they were awfully bad at seeing through traps and schemes. I was about to explain when I realized we were still in public, so I figured I'd fill them in once we were somewhere private. You never knew who might be listening, after all, and I still didn't know what kind of technology this world had in terms of transferring information quickly. It was equally likely someone had eyes and ears inside the Guild, but I decided to bank on the office of the feared guild-master being a safer place to have sensitive conversations than the middle of the street.

"And here we are. Welcome to the Adventurer's Guild," said Lingga, placing his hand on the door to what looked like a shady dive bar.

When we set foot inside, however, I couldn't help but gasp.

Unlike its rough exterior, inside, the building was startlingly clean. The service counter looked like it had been a bar at one point, so I posited the Guild had renovated an old pub. Flyers with various work requests were posted all over the walls, each separated by a rank color based on the expected difficulty of completing each job. It was almost exactly as I'd imagined it.

It seemed the establishment still functioned as a bar as well, as I noticed a few groups of adventurers chatting and drinking at tables set up around the room. The moment Lingga entered the building with us, the whole place went silent. The drunken adventurers seemed to immediately sober up upon seeing him and Night, and all the color drained from their faces. Other than the sudden change in atmosphere, it looked like a fairly cozy establishment.

"G-Guildmaster! What business brings you here today?" asked a flustered guild employee who looked a bit like a puppy.

"Hello, Myle. These people are with me. Be a dear and bring some drinks up to my office, would you?" said Lingga, and the boy dashed back behind the counter.

Using my exceptional listening abilities, I picked up his conversation with the other bartenders.

"Ugh, that Lingga, I tell ya... You never tell what's really going on in that head of his."

"Hey, at least he seems to be in a good mood today. Be grateful for that."

"No kidding. Though I wish he wouldn't drop in on us out of nowhere like this with unexpected guests and force us to drop everything we're doing."

"Yeah, and it's not like he just brought in one guest either. A human, an elf, and a monster familiar walk into our bar... Sounds like the start of a crummy joke, doesn't it?"

"I didn't think familiars were even a real thing. Which one is its master? The boy?"

"Gotta admit the elf girl's quite the looker... I'd let her walk all over me any day."

"Oh, shut the hell up. Myle, go deliver these, would you?"

"Whoops... Sorry, will do."

So they're afraid of Lingga because they can't tell what he's thinking...? That's dumb. The average person can't tell what any other person is thinking.

"Have a seat wherever you like," said Lingga once we were all in his office. "Though I suppose there aren't really a lot of options left with all this paperwork I've got piled up."

The guildmaster's office was in the hallway behind the bar, first door on the right. The only furniture to speak of was some packed bookshelves, a sofa, a desk, and a couple of chairs. It was certainly not the sort of room that could be used for leisure as well as work, and everything except the sofa and one chair was piled high with documents. Based on that and the conversation I'd overheard between the bartenders, it was plain to see that Lingga didn't stop by here very often; he probably did most of his work from home or out in the field. Or maybe he just came in through a secret entrance? But why would he need to do such a thing?

"Now then. I believe you were about to say something?" said Lingga after he'd sat behind the desk and Amelia and I had found our own places to sit.

"R-right." I remembered Amelia's question from earlier and began explaining my rationale for the actions I'd taken against the ruffians. "So you guys know I have an insane amount of control over my magic, right? Like, I could shoot my shadows through the eye of a needle from a meter away."

The two of them nodded, both fully aware of how difficult it was to achieve that level of control over one's magic. I'd condensed my Shadow Magic into tiny beads, shot them into the miscreants' eyeballs, then commanded the shadows remotely to expand and cover their eye sockets, rendering the ruffians temporarily blind. I was sure Night at least would fully comprehend just how difficult this was, since he knew from experience that it was impossible to properly shapeshift without a clear picture of your goal in your mind. I used my magic in a similar way.

"So basically, I wanted to make my skill clear to everyone watching without being overly showy about it. Amelia, why do you think I did that?" I asked, trying my best to sound like a college professor.

"Uhhh... Because anyone with a modicum of skill can make a big fireworks show out of magic, and it's the little things that show you're truly a master of your craft?"

"Correct," I said, patting her on the head as a reward.

"Yay! Tee hee," she giggled, her cheeks turning pink.

"Now it's your turn, Night," I said. "Why would I ever want to make my abilities known in such a public manner?"

"I assume because it would deter all but the most foolish of challengers from trying to disturb us again?"

"Right you are," I said, rustling his fur with both hands. "Now, what potential drawbacks might there be to this plan?"

"Well, now the extent of your abilities is out in the open. If there was a witness in that crowd who saw the level of control you have over your magic and still wasn't impressed, that individual would likely feel even more emboldened to pick a fight with us."

I lifted Night up off the sofa and buried my face in his fur. *Yes, that's exactly right, my friend.* While there was certainly the possibility of a few more overconfident challengers wanting to press their luck after today, especially among a race that had a reputation for being a little hotheaded, I still believed I'd taken the best possible course of action.

"Plus, by giving Lingga the elf king's letter in front of all those people, we also made sure everyone knows Amelia's lineage," I added.

"And you expect that the average citizen will be less likely to interfere with her, knowing she's royalty?" Lingga chimed in.

"I do. Sorry for not asking permission first, Amelia."

"No, it's fine," she said with a little smile, shaking her head. "You can use me however you want. I don't mind one bit."

"Amelia..."

"Shall we give them some privacy, Guildmaster?" asked Night sarcastically, clearly a little bit peeved by our PDA.

"And miss the best part? I think not!" Lingga joked.

"What about Lingga?" Amelia asked me, ignoring those two. "Were you counting on him being there from the start too?"

"Not from the start, no. That was purely coincidence. When my eyes tipped me off to the guildmaster's attendance, I decided to rope him into my little spectacle," I said, tapping the corner of one eye, so Amelia would know what I meant.

Lingaa pouted like a child. "Could you please explain that again in a way that all of us can understand?" he asked grumpily, and I gave him an intentionally vague explanation as to what World Eyes did. He might have been the guildmaster, but I wasn't comfortable revealing *everything* to him just yet, even if it wasn't confidential information. Maybe after he'd earned my trust.

"Fine, have it your way," Lingga relented. "But there are still two things which I'd like to be crystal clear on. Oda Akira, were you summoned here from another world via the recent hero summoning ritual?"

Apparently rumors of the hero summoning ritual's success had spread even to this continent. Given the way the common folk had greeted my classmates and I like we were in a parade on our first trip to the labyrinth, I supposed it wasn't too surprising that word had gotten out. I exchanged glances with Night, wondering if it was really a good idea to admit this.

"I see. On to my next question, then." Lingga nodded, apparently satisfied with what he'd learned from one glance. I really needed to work on my poker face. "Now, this familiar of yours— 'Night,' as you call him—he wouldn't also happen to be the

Demon Lord's infamous right-hand monster, would he? The one known as Black Cat?"

Wow. I'd known that Night had been a fairly important servant of the Demon Lord, but his right-hand monster? Why the hell had the Demon Lord let us steal such an important assistant? Maybe he truly hadn't foreseen the possibility of Night betraying him.

"I was once called that, yes," Night responded. *"But now I answer only to Master. Rest assured, I have no intention of going on another rampage through your country as I once did back in my younger and more mischievous years."*

Whoa, whoa, whoa. Violent rampage? What?! I was going to need an explanation for such an atomic truth bomb, and fast. Seeing the bewilderment on my and Amelia's faces, Lingga thankfully obliged.

"It's true. When that familiar of yours was still the Demon Lord's right-hand monster, he went on a rampage through this country. The entire continent, in fact. Thanks to the tireless efforts of the hero at the time, we were able to stop him before he had a chance to destroy more than the capital city and a single wing of the royal palace, but the casualties were still immense. We are a resilient people, of course, and we did manage to recover, but to this day you'll find that most beastfolk fear black cats far more than even the fiercest of beasts."

I shot Night a look, and he immediately became very interested in the ceiling and started whistling innocently. He had concealed this information on purpose. Now I understood why the people in the city had looked at us the way that they had; perhaps the hoodlums who'd tried to mess with us had been too drunk to notice Night. It wasn't me the commoners were afraid of—it was the little brat riding on my shoulders.

"I was on orders from His Majesty, okay? And we were at war at the time. I really don't think what I did was wrong given the circumstances, and I don't intend to apologize for it," Night said, puffing out his chest.

"Yes, I assumed not. Just wanted to verify your identity, that's all," said Lingga.

Amelia was clearly having a hard time believing our cute and cuddly cat companion was really a mass murderer, as her jaw hung open for quite a while following this revelation.

Guess you really can't judge a book by its cover. This is the same cat who tried to attack us with dragon breath the first time we met him, remember? I can totally see him being some harbinger of destruction.

"Er, Master? I picked up most of that via Telepathy, you know..." Night said despondently, disappointed to have me think of him in this light. He certainly didn't look like a convincing right-hand monster when he sulked like that.

"So what they say about a master and familiar being able to communicate via Telepathy *is* true. We've been looking for definitive proof of that for a while now," Lingga said.

Oh, you have, have you? Suddenly suspicious, I looked around the room and noticed what looked like a camera on the ceiling. It wasn't quite as conspicuously evil-looking as the ones back in the castle of Retice, which perhaps explained why I'd overlooked it at first.

"Got security cameras in your own office, huh? I take it you're awfully careful," I said. Though perhaps it was an understandable security measure, even for a simple branch manager.

"Yes, well. We often have to temporarily store priceless artifacts and treasures here. Can't be too careful."

"Treasure, eh? You sure you should be mentioning that to strangers like us?" After all, we could have been simple burglars who'd only come to scope the place out for our next heist.

"I'm sure it's fine," Lingga said, shaking his head. "If you were planning on breaking and entering, you wouldn't have brought a familiar along. That would be too conspicuous, and all the more so given that we're already cautious around black cats."

He had a point. If we were truly burglars, then we weren't making much of an effort to keep a low profile. Especially with a knockout like Amelia tagging along with us. Though on the topic of keeping a low profile...

"Hey, so what does that Extra Skill of yours do?" I asked him. "The Inconspicuous one, I mean. Does it let you waltz right past people without them noticing you?"

"Using those special eyes of yours again, I see..." Lingga sighed. "Yes, that's what it does, but I'll remind you that I am nothing more than a simple civil servant at this point. I was never cut out to be an assassin, to be honest with you—I've got aichmophobia, a fear of pointed objects. Can't even look at a butter knife without feeling faint."

Apparently he couldn't use forks either, and he had to have chopsticks imported from the country of Yamato just to eat. I looked again at Lingga's stat page. It did still list his class as an assassin, like me. That shouldn't have been surprising, since it was one of the more basic classes out there, though very few of us ever went on to do any actual assassinating. Still, I did feel a tiny sense of kinship with him.

He told us about how he'd been using his Inconspicuous skill to sneak into his office each day and take care of his paperwork without causing a stir every time he walked through the bar downstairs, which explained why the bartenders thought of him as some mysterious enigma. I was sure any assassin worth their salt would consider such a powerful Extra Skill wasted on someone like him; even I felt that way for a brief moment. But he'd chosen his path in life, and it was none of my business. If he really did have a fear of sharp objects, then it wasn't his fault he'd been born into the worst class possible for his condition.

"Now, I think this little tangent's gone on long enough," Lingga said, and the mood in the room became tense. "Let's get down to brass tacks, shall we?"

It seemed he was finally ready to talk business, though not before taking a big sip of one of the drinks Myle had brought up for us a moment ago. It was some sort of non-citrus fruit juice— smelled a bit like grape, but I couldn't say what it tasted like, as I'd opted not to drink mine. Amelia seemed to be enjoying hers quite a bit, though.

Noticing I hadn't touched my drink, Lingga narrowed his eyes at me. "So what brings you three to our fair continent?"

Maintaining eye contact with him, I walked up to his desk and slammed the Yato-no-Kami down in front of him, sheath and all. He looked up at me, as if asking permission to take a closer look. I nodded, and he drew it about halfway out of its sheath.

"I see. So it's a blacksmith you're after," he said, inspecting the well-worn blade before setting it gently back down. "Quite fine craftsmanship, I must say. How did you ever do such a number on it?"

A well-crafted sword was far sturdier and sharper than a poorly crafted one, and katanas were no exception. Lingga was asking how I'd ever let a blade like this, which was clearly a masterpiece even to the untrained eye, fall into such a state of disrepair.

"I need to get to Level 100 ASAP. I was trying to do that by grinding monsters down in the Great Labyrinth of Kantinen, but I guess I went a little overboard," I responded.

Lingga froze in place for a moment, just like Night had when I'd first told him the same information. "I'm sorry, did I hear that correctly? It sounded like you were implying you tried to take on the labyrinth of the human continent with only this sword."

"Yes, that's correct."

"Wow. You're far dumber than you look," Lingga said, so matter-of-factly that I honestly had no comeback.

Night, up on my shoulders, nodded as if to say "See, I told you so," and I shot him a spiteful look.

"Please tell me you didn't delve deep into that particular laby-rinth without even knowing it's designed to be a *magic* training ground." Lingga sighed. "Or did you run in with a death wish and somehow miraculously make it out alive?"

"Look, I didn't know about the magic thing until Night told me, okay? And I dunno if I'd call it a miracle. Sure, luck was on our side a lot of the time, but mostly it was just my own strength and Amelia's help that got us through," I said petulantly.

Lingga sighed yet again. "I assume you're after the Special Skill that people supposedly get upon reaching Level 100, but to put your life on the line over an old wives' tale is brazen at best and suicidal at worst."

I grinned. Yup—it was rumored that anyone who managed to reach Level 100 would be rewarded with a so-called "Special Skill," a type of unique ability far, far stronger than even an Extra Skill. Commander Saran had told me the rumors about these fabled skills during one of our late-night conversations, though I now knew they were more than a mere wives' tale. I'd sworn to do whatever it took to reach Level 100; it had been my final promise to him.

"Special Skills *do* exist. I know they do," I said defiantly.

A brief silence fell over the room as Lingga peered deep into my eyes, sizing me up.

"Judging by your expression, it looks like you truly believe that. Or perhaps you somehow know for a fact? But that can't be; there are no heroes who've reached Level 100 in this world. Certainly not any living ones, at least."

"Not now, perhaps, but they did exist, and I can assure you people really do receive a Special Skill upon reaching Level 100. I've seen it with my own eyes."

Though where and when I saw this, I wouldn't say. Not yet, anyway.

"Hmph. Believe what you will, I suppose." Lingga shrugged. "If you need any assistance while you're here, you know where to find us. The Guild and I are happy to be of help."

"Akira, is it true what you said in there?" Amelia asked as we made our way through the crowd after leaving the Adventurer's Guild.

With Night riding on my shoulders, the beastfolk pedestrians were quick to make way for us, and with the news of Amelia being high elf royalty having made its way around town, there wasn't a single person who dared to mess with us. It was exactly the outcome I had been aiming for, and I patted myself on the back for a job well done. I still wanted to get off the main drag and into an alley or something to get away from all these prying eyes. Amelia's question was vague, but I was pretty sure I knew what she was referring to.

"*Yes, I was about to ask the same thing. I've never even heard of there being some sort of bonus for reaching Level 100, Master,*" said Night, clinging to my head as he struggled to maintain his balance on my shoulders, his soft tummy fur tickling my ears.

"Yeah, well, you're a monster, so I'm not too surprised. I'm sure Amelia's heard the rumors at least a few times before, right?" I asked, turning to her for validation.

"In old fairy tales and stuff, yeah." She nodded hesitantly. "It's always presented as something only the best of the best can ever hope to achieve, kinda like how most people can never reach Max Level in a given skill. It's just not possible for the average person to reach Level 100. Even getting to Level 99 is a massive struggle."

Yes, that's how the stories go. But it's more than just a fairy tale.

"The first person to ever discover the Level 100 bonus was the Hero of Legend. He was on the verge of death, and all his allies had already been wiped out by the Demon Lord. But when all hope seemed lost, he slew the last of the Demon Lord's minions, and suddenly he awakened to a brand-new ability, which he then used to slay the Demon Lord and get a happy ending...or so I was told. You see it all the time in hero-versus-villain stories, honestly—just when the good guys are about to lose, the hero unlocks some special ability that increases his power tenfold."

According to the legend, the sheer force of the attack had obliterated the upper half of the demons' continent too. I could totally believe that, since I'd almost taken out an entire gigantic forest with my Shadow Magic, and that was only an Extra Skill. It wasn't a quaint little forest like the ones we had in Japan either—this was one of those gigantic forests like they had overseas, the size of a small country. Still, it probably wasn't comparable to half of an entire continent.

"And you think monsters don't get these Special Skills?" asked Night, sounding more than a little disappointed. As I patted him on the head reassuringly, Amelia tilted her head in confusion.

"Wait. So if there aren't even *stories* about them where Night comes from, could that mean neither monsters *nor* demons get Level 100 bonuses?" she asked.

"Sure seems that way, yeah. Though I guess there *is* another possibility," I mused.

"And what might that be?" asked Night.

"It could be that the demons are concealing the existence of Special Skills on purpose," I said, stopping dead in my tracks at the entrance to a secluded alleyway. I turned around and saw Lingga staring at us with shrewd eyes from among the crowd of pedestrians. He didn't seem to be using his Inconspicuous ability at the moment—perhaps there were some limitations on how and when he could use the skill, or perhaps he was just bold enough to believe he could avoid my detection even without it.

"Is something the matter, Master?"

"Nah. Must've just been a stray cat," I said, pretending I hadn't noticed Lingga tailing us. One thing was for certain: something very fishy was going on here.

"All right, Miss Amelia—one deluxe room for you and your party. Will you be needing breakfast in the morning?"

"Oh, no, thank you. We'll just grab a bite to eat in town, I'm sure."

"Very well, then. I'll have someone show you to your room shortly. One moment, please."

We were standing at the reception desk of a local inn, all breathing a collective sigh of relief upon seeing it did indeed appear to be a reputable establishment.

An hour or two earlier, Amelia had mentioned she was feeling a bit peckish, so we settled on a random restaurant nearby to have our first meal in Brute. The beastfolk proprietor who greeted us looked like a calico cat, and the interior of his establishment resembled a posh English-style café. They served some beastfolk favorites (like catnip, for example) in addition to more traditional fare. There were a few human adventurers seated at a corner table, but it seemed the lunch rush hadn't quite hit yet. As Amelia stuffed her face ordering plate after plate of food—hey, who was the guy here?—I got to talking with the owner and asked him if he knew of any good inns in the area he could recommend.

Apparently, he'd already heard the rumors about us and knew of Amelia's noble status, so he let us in on a bit of insider information. He told us that you should never judge a beastfolk establishment by its exterior, as many of the nicest-looking buildings were notorious for having terrible service and being run-down on the inside, but there were plenty of nicer places hidden in plain sight, like the Adventurer's Guild. The owner suggested an inn not too far from his establishment known simply as The Coop.

It turned out to be a combination establishment with a nice bar on the bottom floor. The innkeeper was a kind avian beastman with slumped shoulders who didn't flinch at the sight of Night and treated Amelia with a suitable level of respect.

"Hi there! I'm Haru, and I'll be showing you to your room," said the spry female attendant who dashed out to greet us. She was a cute human girl with prominent upper canines and deep black hair. If her eyes had been black instead of green, I might have been fooled into thinking she was a Japanese person just like me. Even her name sounded Japanese. Maybe she'd come here from the Japan-inspired country of Yamato.

"Hey! That's the elven princess you're talking to, girl!" the innkeeper yelped, reprimanding Haru for greeting us so casually. The innkeeper bowed his head to beg our forgiveness, but Amelia stopped him.

"Please, there's no need for special treatment," she assured them. "We're traveling here in secret at the moment, and we haven't even gone to pay our respects to the king of the beastfolk yet."

"But, milady..." he sputtered incredulously.

A lightbulb seemed to go off in Amelia's head. "If you want to be of help, then why don't you tell us some of your favorite restaurants in the area?"

"Why, of course! I'll write up a list of a few choice establishments and have it brought straight to your room."

Amelia nodded at the innkeeper, then indicated for Haru to lead the way.

The poor girl had done a complete about-face, her peppy demeanor dissolving into something appropriately serious. "If you'd just follow me right this way, madam," Haru said, guiding us through the dining area before stopping in front of a room clearly reserved for only the most esteemed guests. "Here is your room, Madam Amelia. In case of emergency, you'll find an exit right over there. If you need anything—anything at all—just ring that bell there, and we'll be right over to serve you."

One look inside, and I could tell it was probably the nicest room in the building by far. Maybe not quite as luxurious as the rooms in Retice Castle, but fancy nonetheless. There were two large beds situated in the center of the room. *God, how long has it been since I slept in a real bed?*

"Oh, and the walls are completely soundproof, so feel free to be as loud as you like tonight, byeee!" Haru added quickly before leaving us alone in the room.

So much for her fake formality act.

"Don't worry, Master. I can take a hint," Night whispered in my ear. *"I'll be sure to go out on the town alone tonight so you two can have some privacy. I won't even use Telepathy to listen in, I promise!"*

"C'mon, Night. You don't really think I'm that type of guy, do you?"

"I don't, but you know what they say: when a fine piece of tail presents itself on a silver platter, it's only good manners to at least take a bite."

"I beg your pardon? Where the hell did you learn to talk like that?"

"It's something His Majesty always used to say."

"Oh, great. I haven't even met the guy yet, and I can already tell he's a prick."

Night seemed a bit too pleased with himself for having scandalized me. *Man, I'm too old for this crap.* I grabbed him by the cheeks and started wrestling with him on the floor.

"What are you two whispering about over here?" Amelia asked, suddenly appearing out of nowhere.

"Nothing!" we said in unison.

Amelia squinted at us, unconvinced, but ultimately gave up and went back to unpacking her luggage. Night and I let out sighs of relief. We made an unspoken agreement then and there to keep such topics to Telepathy, then I went over to unpack my own luggage beside Amelia (not that I had much to speak of).

"I wouldn't mind Akira taking a bite of me," Amelia mumbled grumpily, but I pretended not to hear it.

"How do you like it, Amelia? Is it good?"

"Mmfhm!"

"Good, good. I'm glad."

I couldn't help but crack a smile at the sight of Amelia stuffing her face and talking with her mouth full. Back in my world, I'd often heard people say there was no sight more beautiful than watching the one you love eat their fill. I'd always thought the saying was a little weird, but once I met Amelia, I finally understood.

Of course, I was making a total pig of myself too. I didn't even know what kind of meat I was eating—the texture was a bit like chicken—but I couldn't have cared less. It was far better than anything I'd eaten down in the labyrinth, and the special sauce it came with was to die for. Night was munching on some purple leafy vegetables beside me, and while they certainly didn't look appetizing to me, he seemed to be enjoying them well enough. After filling our bellies, we decided to walk off a few calories as we made our way back to the inn.

When we returned to our room, I crashed on the bed and finally began to feel the weariness of our long journey starting to abate. This was the first time I'd truly taken a load off since I was summoned to this world—hell, maybe even in years. I did a quick inspection of the room to make sure no mana-based surveillance devices had been installed while we were away, but I didn't find anything. Perhaps I'd become a little too paranoid after the many betrayals and close encounters with death I'd had since arriving in this world. It did seem like the sort of world in which you had to generally be on your guard at all times, but even so...

"Man, I can't stop thinking about that guildmaster's Extra Skill," I muttered to myself. "Sure wouldn't want to have someone like that turn out to be our enemy."

Hell, he could have been listening in on us right then and none of us would know. It felt almost like cheating for someone to have an ability that made everyone around them utterly oblivious to their presence.

I say as someone at Max Level in Conceal Presence...

Apparently Night had somewhere he wanted to go alone, so he left us immediately after dinner; maybe he had an old acquaintance somewhere in the city.

The beds in our room were fit for a king—so soft and comfy it was hard to do much thinking without accidentally drifting off to sleep, especially after all those nights sleeping on the cold, hard ground in the labyrinth. I could see Amelia was starting to nod off in her bed too. Not that there was any reason we *shouldn't* have fallen asleep—we'd both already changed into our pajamas and were fully ready for bed.

I was suddenly reminded of the thumbs-up Night had given me as he went off on his own after dinner. Did he really believe I had any intention of making a move on Amelia tonight?

Granted, I didn't think there was a man alive who wouldn't kill to sleep with a girl like her, but she was way too far out of my league, and I didn't have any sexual experience to speak of. I'd never had time for dating back in my world—I'd been too focused on working all night, every night, trying to make ends meet for my family to have any social life to speak of. Besides, even if I'd had a girlfriend, it wasn't like we would've ever had the chance to do anything, since my sickly mother never left the house. *Though I guess the bigger problem would have been finding any self-respecting girl who would ever date, let alone sleep with, me.*

So transfixed was I on this train of thought that I didn't even notice when Amelia got up off her bed and came over to lie down next to me. She certainly felt at ease around me, that was for sure.

"What's wrong, Akira? Something on your mind?" she asked, rubbing the sleep out of her eyes.

"Y-yeah, sort of. Just thinking about that guildmaster again," I said, trying to play it cool even though my heart was skipping beats left and right.

"What was that skill of his, again? Noncontiguous?" she asked, nuzzling up to me like a cat. When I petted her on the head, I almost expected her to start purring.

"Inconspicuous. And yeah, that's the one that worries me."

"So, hey, not to change the subject, but...don't I look pretty enticing right now?"

My thoughts ground to a halt. *Sorry, what?*

"What are you trying to say?" I asked, propping myself up on my elbows so I could look down at Amelia, who was now pouting.

"I mean, I'm right here, y'know. But you don't seem interested in doing anything with me at all. Maybe I'm just not sexy enough..." she said dejectedly, and I went slack-jawed in disbelief. I couldn't believe the words coming out of Amelia's mouth.

I placed my hand softly on her cheek and let out a sigh. "Not sexy enough? Please. You're way *too* sexy. It's honestly hard to control myself around you sometimes," I admitted at last. At this, her eyes widened ever so slightly. *Man, what the hell am I doing?* I could feel the heat gathering in my cheeks, and I didn't think I was coming down with a fever. I turned my back to Amelia, unable to maintain eye contact any longer.

"Tee hee. Well, okay. If you say so," she giggled, wrapping her arms around me from behind. I could feel two soft mounds pressing up against my back as she whispered seductively in my ear. "There's no rush. Feel free to take a bite of me whenever you like."

"Hnnngh...!"

Damn it. She had me right in the palm of her hand, and she knew it, but I couldn't give in to her feminine wiles just yet. I twisted around and planted a kiss on her cheek.

"Better watch out, 'cause as soon as we take care of business with the Demon Lord, I'm gonna rail you like there's no tomorrow," I whispered back. "So get ready."

"Will do!" she nodded enthusiastically, her cheeks flushed bright red.

Damn, that wasn't the reaction I was expecting. I was hoping to make her knees quake a little.

"Okay, we'd better hit the sack. Tomorrow, we'll start looking for a blacksmith who can repair the Yato-no-Kami," I said, turning to face Amelia again.

I discovered she was already drifting off to sleep, though she still clung to me like her life depended on it. *I guess she did seem pretty sleepy earlier.* The two of us sank deep into the pillowy mattress, wrapped up in each other's arms. In my drowsy and uninhibited state, I placed yet another gentle kiss on her peaceful, angelic face.

"G'night, Amelia."

POV: NIGHT

"MASTER? I'm baaack..." Upon returning from my little errand a few hours later, I noticed a large bulge under the covers in Master's bed, while Amelia's bed lay vacant. Lights out had long since passed, and the room was pitch-black, but thankfully I could still see just fine with my feline eyes. I slowly made my way over to the bed, peeled back the covers, and let out a silent chuckle.

"Well, would you look at that... Good for you, Lady Amelia."

There Master and Lady Amelia were locked firmly in each

other's embrace. I could tell from the way their clothes weren't rumpled or askew that they hadn't actually done anything, but seeing the satisfied smile on Amelia's face warmed my heart nonetheless. I knew she'd been feeling anxious about Master and his feelings lately. I gently tucked them back under the covers, then made myself comfortable on the empty bed. It felt like a waste to enjoy only a small portion of such a fine bed, however, so I made myself large enough to fill it.

"*Good night, Master. Good night, Lady Amelia. We have a busy day ahead of us tomorrow,*" I whispered, my thoughts drifting back to the man I'd just gone to visit as I closed my eyes.

POV: ODA AKIRA

WHEN I AWOKE the next morning, I found myself lying next to a beautiful girl. After a few moments' confusion, I wrapped my head around the situation. *Right, Amelia and I fell asleep in each other's arms last night.*

Lying in a soft and sumptuous bed against the skin of a veritable goddess... Had I died and gone to heaven? Or was this a hell designed to keep me from ever accomplishing my assigned tasks? As I mulled this conundrum over in my head, I heard a creak from the bed next to ours. I lifted myself up to look over Amelia's shoulder to discover an embiggened Night waking up. I watched as his cheeks wrinkled with a massive yawn—he wasn't much of a morning person. But then he got up and circled around behind me, bit my pajamas, and dragged me out of bed.

"Whoa, hey! Night?! What's the big idea?!" I hissed, releasing Amelia from my arms so as not to wake her up. As soon as Night got me on the ground, he set about pulling my pajamas off without a word. I shook my head violently but begrudgingly got myself changed at his insistence. Then he went and woke up Amelia and made her get dressed as well.

"What's gotten into you, Night?" I asked, averting my eyes from Amelia as she changed clothes.

The cat let out another big yawn, then finally began to explain. *"Last night, I went and visited an acquaintance of mine. A blacksmith. He'll be dropping by shortly,"* Night said, then sauntered lethargically back to his bed.

Amelia and I looked at each other, utterly perplexed.

"How do you know he'll be here so soon?" Amelia asked, but just then, there was a rather loud knock on the door.

"Come in," I replied, hiding a throwing knife behind my back just to be safe.

Haru opened the door and entered the room, followed by a feline beastman with deep black fur. I knew I wasn't one to talk, but he didn't look very friendly—there was something in his eyes that made him intimidating and unapproachable. I didn't know what typical blacksmith attire consisted of, but he was wearing a sleeveless version of what I'd seen many of the male beastfolk wearing.

"This is Crow the blacksmith," said Haru. "He claims to be an acquaintance of your familiar, so I gave him a quick pat-down and let him in."

The beastman named Crow glanced over at Night lounging on the bed before sizing me and Amelia up from head to toe. I sensed no negative intent or distrust behind his gaze, weirdly enough.

"C-cool. Thanks, Haru," I said, and she bowed and left the room.

After waiting a while to make sure she was truly gone, Crow finally spoke. "Well, I can already tell you've got some skill, but in terms of mentality, you're still just a kid. And don't even get me started on the elf chick. Hard to believe the two of you somehow managed to bumble your way into taming the Nightmare of Adorea."

Jeez, this guy's a real charmer. He had an awful lot of gall to start spouting cutting remarks before we'd even introduced ourselves. Though more than anything, I was just curious about that last thing he'd said. *Nightmare of Adorea? Isn't Adorea the capital of the whole beastfolk continent?*

"*Master, I know he's not the friendliest man, but I daresay he is the finest blacksmith in all the world. His skills are second to none, even if his personality drives away the vast majority of his clients,*" Night murmured to me from his sprawled-out position on the bed.

"Why, thank you for the introduction," Crow said. "Coming from the Nightmare of Adorea, I take that as quite the compliment. In fact, I think I feel a blush coming on."

While he certainly didn't blush, he did seem genuinely flattered by Night's evaluation of him, as he raised his tail ever so slightly.

I see how it is. This guy's got a rough exterior, but he's probably a total softie on the inside. "Nice to meet you, Crow. I'm Oda Akira, and this is my high elf companion, Amelia."

Crow gave us a little nod and extended his hand. When I reached out to shake it, he pulled it back and raised his voice in frustration.

"No, you idiot. Show me the weapon you want me to fix."

I nodded and pulled out the Yato-no-Kami. When Crow laid eyes on the blade, his eyes widened for a brief instant. I barely noticed this—just handed him the sword, sheath and all.

"Humph. Well, it's certainly seen better days. I assume you took it dungeon-diving down in the Great Labyrinth of Kantinen? You should've brought it to me sooner."

"Whoa," Amelia murmured, clearly amazed he could tell that much from a cursory glance.

"Can you fix it?" I asked.

Crow smiled and shook his head in amusement. "Just who do you think I am? I can repair a blade like this, no problem. The hard part's gonna be gathering the materials I need to do the job." Crow ran his eyes down the length of the blade, gave it a good flick, then held it up to the sunlight to examine it closer.

"He only does the repair work himself," Night explained. *"It's up to us to provide the materials he needs as well as recompense for his labor. We can probably scrounge up enough cash just hunting monsters, but getting the materials could be a bit tricky."*

I nodded, then turned back to Crow, who was still scanning the blade up and down.

He popped the hilt and handguard off the sword and returned them to me. "I won't be needing those. But the blade itself stays with me. That monster of yours has the list of materials I'll need," he said, then left the room without another word.

A moment later, Amelia chased after him.

POV: AMELIA ROSEQUARTZ

"WAIT A MINUTE!" I cried, grabbing Crow by the arm after chasing him down outside the inn.

He stopped walking and let out a heavy sigh. "What do you want, little elf princess?"

He looked down at me, and my breath caught in my throat. His piercing gaze cut right through me. These were not the eyes of a simple blacksmith—these were the eyes of a man who'd narrowly escaped death's grasp time and time again, just like Akira.

"I have a feeling I know who you are," I said, and Crow tilted his head curiously. Averting my gaze, I looked down at the Yato-no-Kami he clutched in his hand, its deep black blade forming a stark contrast with the white cloth in which it was wrapped. "You were one of the previous hero's party members, weren't you?" I asked, trepidation seeping into my voice.

The previous generation's heroes had failed in their quest to defeat the Demon Lord, and it was said that only the hero and his lone beastfolk companion had made it out with their lives. The other humans and elves in his party had been slain just when it seemed like they had the Demon Lord on the ropes.

I was about to say more when Crow squinted down at me with contempt and I froze in place.

"Yeah? And what of it?" he snarled.

I couldn't give up now. I mustered all my remaining courage and forced myself to look him straight in the eye.

"I want you to teach me how to fight."

POV: ODA AKIRA

As soon as Amelia dashed out of the room, Night hopped down from the bed.

"Are you sure you don't want to go after her, Master?"

I tucked the bladeless hilt and handguard of the Yato-no-Kami into my shirt. That way, I knew I wouldn't lose or misplace them, barring an encounter with a pickpocket—not that they were of any value to a thief without the sword itself.

"I'm sure Amelia has her reasons. She can take care of herself," I replied at last, counting up my remaining throwing knives and checking their sharpness before hiding them in various folds and pockets of my clothes. Night shrank himself down and leapt up onto my shoulders, dropping a single sheet of paper into the palm of my hand. It was the list of materials we needed to gather in order to get my sword repaired.

"We all have our own tasks we need to focus on right now," I continued. "I'm gonna focus on gathering up the money and the materials... Maybe *you* should go after Amelia."

"But, Master! Isn't this the perfect opportunity for the two of us

to go on a little adventure together?! A master and familiar, setting off on a journey to deepen their bond?!"

Night had evidently been looking forward to tagging along with me more than I realized, and he sounded utterly crestfallen. I grabbed him by the scruff of the neck and held him in front of my face. I'd learned recently that grabbing him in such a way when he was house cat size rendered him completely powerless. The fierce dragon inside him was nowhere to be found.

"Listen, bub. You and I are connected by our bond no matter where we go, but Amelia doesn't have that luxury. If all we have to do is hunt some monsters, I can just pop down into the Great Labyrinth of Brute and slay a few by myself, no sweat. Lucky for us, that labyrinth just so happens to be right here in this town," I said. Night pouted, but he seemed to understand the point I was trying to make. "Now you be a good boy and go stay by Amelia's side while she does whatever it is she's trying to do... I dunno what it is about this place, but I've got a feeling something bad might happen to her if we're not careful. Be sure to tell her to be back here by nightfall, okay?"

Night stared at me with his little golden eyes for a while, then closed them in resignation. *"As you wish, Master."*

I set Night down, and the two of us left the inn. I headed off toward the Adventurer's Guild, while Night followed Amelia's scent in the opposite direction. Apparently in Brute, you needed permission from the Guild to even enter the labyrinth, and in order to get that, you had to prove you had a certain level of skill— or so the avian innkeeper had claimed. It made sense, though, and

I had to wonder why there weren't similar restrictions back in Kantinen.

Without Amelia and Night tagging along, I didn't stand out from the crowd very much at all, and I was able to move through the city without drawing any unwanted attention...but I had to admit, it felt a little lonely being all by myself again. Even if keeping a low profile was undeniably a good thing.

I couldn't remember exactly where in the city the Adventurer's Guild was, so I decided to follow a group of armored fellows who thankfully led me straight to it; perhaps I had my Luck skill to thank for that.

When I walked inside, the bar was far busier than when we'd come with Lingga the day before. Countless adventurers crowded around, drinking and arguing over job postings. The place stank of booze.

"Hi, where do I go to register as a new adventurer?" I asked at the counter, trying to be as polite as I could as I addressed Myle, the young boy who'd brought us drinks yesterday. We'd been told to go directly to Lingga if we needed anything, but I didn't trust that guy one bit, and I certainly didn't want to end up indebted to him.

"Oh, you wanna register? Sure, I can help you take care of that," said the boy.

Judging by his lack of reaction, it seemed he didn't remember my face. As an assassin, being forgettable should have been a point of pride for me, but as an individual I couldn't help but feel just a little bit miffed—especially since you'd think we would have left a bigger impression, having been brought in by the guildmaster himself. But Myle really seemed to have no memory of me. *Great. Just great.*

"Are you able to write? I can fill it out for you, if not," said Myle, holding out a pen and a piece of paper, unaware of my internal woes.

"No, I can do it. I just have to fill out my name, race, and class, right?" I asked. Myle nodded, and I quickly scribbled down the necessary information.

"Great, you're all set. You're now officially a gray-rank starter adventurer. The ranks are, in order: gray, blue, yellow, red, silver, and gold. Here are your gray dog tags; they also act as a form of identification, so try to wear them at all times and be careful not to lose them."

"Cool, thanks," I said, sliding the tags onto the chain and fastening it around my neck before tucking them in my shirt. "Any advice on how I can go about increasing my rank as quickly as possible?" I'd been told that access to the labyrinth was restricted by rank and that you needed to be at least yellow rank if you wanted to enter, which meant I needed to be two whole ranks higher than I was now.

"Hoping to do some dungeon diving, eh? Just to warn you, there's no clear-cut strategy that works best in our labyrinth like there is for the human and elven ones. There're all sorts of different enemies, some weak to physical attacks, some weak to magic."

So it was a good place to do some all-around training, but it was far more suited for well-balanced classes than specialized ones.

"Oh, don't worry. I'm pretty sure I can handle it," I boasted.

Myle sized me up for a minute, then let out a heavy sigh. "Can't tell you how many newbie adventurers have told me that and then lost their lives... In any case, we need to start by giving you a primer on guild rules and etiquette. We can talk more about the fun stuff after that."

This sucks. I just wanna go into the damn labyrinth already, I thought, even as I nodded reluctantly.

POV: AMELIA ROSEQUARTZ

THE THREE OF US walked in silence down the street, the fallen red leaves spread out under our feet like a fancy carpet. Though one of the three of us wasn't actually walking and was hitching a ride on my shoulders.

"So how long are you planning to stalk me, anyway?" Crow finally asked.

"Until you agree to teach me," I replied, and he snorted.

"Then I suggest you give up. I don't have any room in my life for an apprentice, nor do I have any intention of teaching others my secrets. Besides, they're not the kinds of skills a pretty little princess like you could ever hope to grasp."

I wouldn't be discouraged so easily. As the people who knew me liked to say, I was a lot more stubborn than I looked. "I know it'll be hard," I said, "and I'm prepared for that, but I'm gonna have to put in the effort if I ever hope to measure up to Akira."

Crow shook his head and marched off at a faster gait. Naturally, I picked up my own pace to match.

After a while, he got frustrated and turned to address Night. "Hey, furball. How do I get this chick to leave me alone?" he asked.

Night snorted out a chuckle. *"I suggest you give up on that idea. Lady Amelia might just be the most bullheaded person I've ever met."*

Finally, Crow stopped in his tracks. "You know, I did take on apprentices, once upon a time, until every single one of them left because my training was so brutal it destroyed them mentally."

I tilted my head as if to say: *And you think that'll happen to me?* "I'm not just some weakling. Even if I might be weaker than a chosen race representative like you, I'm still a silver-rank adventurer," I said in a disaffected murmur, looking down at the ground.

Crow turned his head and glared at me. "Of course you're weaker than me. Only the strongest of the strong make it in this world. It's survival of the fittest, and you could never survive the sorts of things I've lived through. You need to learn that there are some things you just aren't cut out for, Princess."

The wind picked up, sending a flurry of red leaves fluttering along with my silver hair. Night was spellbound by the sight. I knew he was following me because Akira had told him to, and that he had no intention of trying to help me plead my case.

"Maybe so, but you don't have to be the strongest to survive if you've got allies that can save you from the brink of death. Akira's done that for me, and now it's my turn to return the favor. I want to be strong enough to fight shoulder to shoulder with him—so that we can work together to make sure we both survive. So please," I said, clenching my fists, "I need you to teach me your secrets. No, teach me the secrets passed down by the Hero of Legend."

POV: ODA AKIRA

"AND, WELL, I suppose that about covers it!" Myle said, looking up from his book as he finished his long-winded lecture about guild rules and etiquette. It was pretty much the most basic, banal stuff you could possibly imagine—guild members should apologize when they recognize they've done something wrong, guild members should never dine and dash, yadda yadda yadda.

There *was* one little detail that interested me, though.

"So there's a guild-sanctioned dueling system, eh?" I asked.

Myle gave me an awkward smile. "Yes, that's right. We've actually had so many duels in recent years that they've become a form of public entertainment. The common folk can't get enough of them, and I hear many will bet away their life savings on specific contenders."

I could understand the appeal, especially given that beastfolk were, on average, far more competitive and bloodthirsty than the other races. There were no such duels held by the human and elven branches of the Adventurer's Guild. It sounded like the Guild only sanctioned them here so people wouldn't hold their own private duels with unregulated bets.

"Why, just the other day, we had an incident where a party of yellow-rank adventurers got into an unsanctioned tussle with a group of unregistered humans out on the main drag. Even though they got their butts kicked, when the guildmaster found out about it, he stripped them of their ranks and banished them from the city, still blinded by whatever black magic the human boy had cursed them with."

Huh, that sounds familiar. Must've been some random assassin trying to make a statement by showing off what he could do.

"Come to think of it, I'm pretty sure the guildmaster brought those humans here right after the fact, and one of them was an assassin just like you..." Myle looked me over again, then suddenly froze up.

"What's wrong? You don't look so good," I teased. His jaw dropped, and he lifted a trembling finger to point at me. "Hey, it's not polite to point, you know."

As Myle stood there, frozen in place, a few other employees came out from the back room. They looked me over then cocked their heads as though they couldn't quite place where they'd seen me before.

"Wait, aren't you..." one of them began. I recognized this one, but before I could remember where from, a lightbulb went off over his head. "Right, you're the assassin who showed those yellow ranks what for out on the main drag."

At the same time, I snapped my fingers, suddenly remembering where I'd seen *him* before as well. "Right, you're the Guild employee Lingga asked to file their expulsion paperwork!"

There was a brief pause, as we both gave each other a puzzled look while Myle struggled to hold back a snicker at our comedic timing.

"Well, in any event," the man said, clearing his throat and extending his right hand. "The name's Yamato. A pleasure to make your acquaintance."

"I'm Oda Akira," I said as I reached out to shake it. "Nice to meet you too."

He reminded me of Kyousuke a little bit.

Back at our room at The Coop, a very peculiar scene was taking place. I stood above Amelia and Night, who were both prostrating themselves before me. Night, being a cat, just looked like he was stretching, so he didn't appear particularly guilty next to Amelia, who was trembling either out of fear or extreme discomfort from having to hold this position for so long.

"Now, do either of you have anything to say for yourselves?" I asked, with just the slightest hint of a villainous smile. When she trembled this time, I knew for sure it was out of fear.

"M-Master, please. Look at Amelia's legs—she's clearly at her limit."

I shot Night an icy glare as he attempted to reason with me, and he shut right up. There would be no mercy for the silver-rank adventurer and the Demon Lord's ex-right-hand monster. "What do you mean, Night? Limits only exist to be broken, didn't you know?" I asked, referencing a line I'd read in some manga once (albeit in a totally different context).

"P-please, Akira... I—I can't take any more..." Amelia pleaded with tears in her eyes as she gazed up at me, and my heart finally caved.

"Well, it seems you've realized the error of your ways, so I suppose you can stand up now—*if* you promise it won't ever happen again."

"I promise!" Amelia said with a twinkle in her eyes, relieved to have finally been freed from the hellish torture.

But what she didn't know was that the true hell was only just beginning.

Flash back to two hours prior. After spending the entire afternoon trying and failing to convince Crow to teach her the secret techniques he'd learned as a member of the previous generation of heroes, Amelia had completely lost track of time. Unwilling to give in, she marched over to Crow's house and started pestering him yet again. His house was attached to a grand smithy, as befit a blacksmith of his caliber. The house itself was a simple, single-story wooden abode with no real furnishings aside from a bed, a desk, and a kitchen. Given the raging flames required by his line of work and the smithy being next door, the house was built from a type of wood that didn't catch fire easily—something not even Night's observant eyes picked up on.

"We really should head back soon, Lady Amelia... Master's going to start getting worried," warned the cat.

Amelia simply stood there motionless, her head hung, at Crow's side.

"You can bow to me all you want, Princess. I'm not teaching you a damn thing," Crow said from his seated position. He elegantly sipped his tea, not even looking up at her when he took a break to eat one of the fine-looking pastries he had arranged on a plate.

"You have to! Please!" Amelia begged, lowering her head even further.

"You really won't even consider it, eh?" said Night, shooting Crow an annoyed look.

"Sorry, but my training could very well kill her, and I refuse to have royal blood on my hands," Crow said, twisting to face Night. "Besides, didn't you say you two needed to be home by suppertime anyway? Better run along now."

Crow's dismissive response made Amelia twitch, though she pursed her lips tightly to try to contain her frustration. Night, too, was getting awfully pissed off, as evidenced by the veins bulging out of his forehead.

"Come on, Lady Amelia. Let's just go home, shall we? You know how Master can be when we break curfew—he turns into a veritable demon. Though I suppose we're already too late to avoid his wrath..."

At last, Amelia raised her head, her face deathly pale from the lack of blood flow. "I'll be back again tomorrow," she said as they were on their way out the door, at which Crow grimaced and waved his arms wildly in protest.

"Will it really take us that long to make it back to the inn, Night?" Amelia asked as they sprinted.

But her feline companion wouldn't even slow down enough to catch his breath and give her an answer, which told her all she needed to know. The two of them were greeted by a very frazzled innkeeper as they crashed through the doors of the inn, haggard and out of breath. They gave a quick apology before dashing off to the room where the horrible demon was waiting to dole out their punishment.

"Okay, Amelia. You can stand up now."

As anyone who had ever had their legs fall asleep after sitting in an awkward position (read: everyone in the entire world) could tell you, the pain of trying to walk on numb legs was not to be underestimated. To avoid the pain, Amelia remained on the floor, trembling on all fours like a newborn fawn. One did not simply "stand up" after prostrating oneself for so long.

"Lady Amelia..." said Night in sympathy.

I'd thought it might be a fun punishment to try, since I assumed she'd never experienced the pain of having to prostrate yourself for so long, given her royal upbringing, but it seemed it had been even more effective than I could have hoped. I decided this would be the standard punishment for her being late going forward.

"Next time, when I tell you to be home in time for supper, you do it. Are we clear?" I asked with a sadistic smile, and the two of them nodded several times.

Once Amelia's legs had a chance to recover, we had ourselves a late dinner. We could have had room service bring us something, but food wasn't included in our nightly rate, and Amelia preferred the local street food anyway, so we'd been eating out for every meal. There were so many options to choose from that there was no risk of ever getting sick of things, which Night seemed to appreciate, and I could tell Amelia had made it her secret goal to try food from each and every street vendor in town. After we settled on what to eat, we told one another about our days over dinner.

"So, yeah. It sounds like I'm gonna have to earn the Guild's trust and prove my skills are the real deal if I wanna reach yellow rank any time soon. What was it like when you were working your way up the ranks, Amelia?" I asked the princess, who had to gulp down the absolute shovelful of food she'd crammed into her hamster-like cheeks before she could answer.

"Hard to say," she finally responded. "The Guild branches in the elven domain are pretty sleepy in comparison to the ones here. There aren't really many quests to speak of, so most people just use 'em as places to sell off raw materials and mana stones they collect from the monsters they slay. Though honestly, yellow rank was so long ago for me that I don't even remember it... All I remember is going in one day and being surprised when they promoted me to silver rank."

Given how long elven lifespans generally were, I could totally understand how she'd forgotten something that had happened so long ago. Hell, she'd probably been at silver rank for hundreds of years.

"Well, it sounds like I'm gonna need to collect a lot of monster pelts and raw materials to get bumped up to yellow rank, so you two are probably gonna be on your own for a while yet," I said, at which point Amelia shot Night a wary look.

Now I trusted the two of them completely, which was why I hadn't asked what made them so late for dinner. However, I could tell from the way Amelia was signaling to him with her eyes that there was something she didn't want Night to tell me. He nodded to show he had received the message loud and clear.

POV: NIGHT

"BACK AGAIN, EH?" said Crow, with a cold glare and an irritated tone we'd already grown accustomed to.

Lady Amelia walked up to him and bowed her head, picking up right where she'd left off yesterday. I was hoping her efforts to degrade herself might finally get through to him, but I was immediately let down by the first thing he said.

"Sorry, but I've got some smithing work I need to do, so I'll be in the workshop all day. If you've got nothing better to do than just stare at the ground, why don't you make me some lunch and bring it over there? Got plenty of ingredients in the house you can work with."

So you intend to make her your personal maid now, is that it?

Crow noticed my scathing look and grinned sadistically. "Well, I figured if she's just gonna be getting in the way regardless, I might as well put her to work. I think it's a pretty swell idea, if I do say so myself," he said before grabbing a pile of metal hunks and monster parts and heading off to his workshop.

I let out a deep, deep sigh. *"What now, Lady Amelia?"* I asked, looking up at her only to find she was already holding purple leafy vegetables in one hand and a knife in the other. My eyes went wide. *"W-wait a minute. What do you think you're doing?"*

"Isn't it obvious? I'm chopping up some vegetables while I try to figure out what I'm gonna make," she replied, shrugging as though I were a fool for asking something so obvious and nearly dropping the knife in the process.

I snatched it out of her hands for fear she might accidentally break something and incur Crow's wrath—or injure herself, at which point I'd probably be the one to incur Master's wrath for not being a better supervisor.

"Shouldn't you at least rinse those first, Lady Amelia? Look, they've still got dirt on them. And we need to peel them too," I said, realizing that letting Amelia cook was probably a bad idea. Then I considered the possibility of *letting* her cook something that would turn out so vile, it might even poison the disrespectful oaf. I quickly shook the idea from my mind, remembering we needed Crow alive to fix Master's sword.

"So, hey, how do you and Crow know each other, anyway?" Lady Amelia asked as I balanced myself atop her head to monitor her washing the vegetables. She tried to look up at me as she did this, which almost made me tumble to the floor, but I clung to her hair.

"Well, it's a bit of a long story, and probably not all that interesting to you, but I can tell you if you like," I said. After Amelia finished washing the vegetables and I made an executive decision on what we were going to cook, I began to tell her the tale in

between cooking instructions. *"It must have been, oh, about a hundred years ago now, perhaps? I went on a rampage through the beastfolk domain at His Majesty's behest—I may have gotten a little carried away with it. There was no need to turn it into such a massacre that I gained the nickname 'The Nightmare of Adorea,' at the very least. After a while, I started to truly regret my actions."*

And so I went to pay my respects at the victims' memorial, disguised as a simple house cat. I wasn't sure what I was planning to do once I got there—I just knew I felt horrible for what I had done and all the lives I had needlessly taken. It was there that I first met Crow.

When I arrived at the hill where the monument stood, there was another person already paying their respects: a black feline beastman, kneeling before the monument with empty eyes, muttering someone's name over and over. Suddenly, to my surprise, he addressed me directly.

"Hey. I know you're there. You're the Nightmare of Adorea, aren't you?"

Frantic, I hid behind a nearby tree, thinking he was a relative of one of the many people I had killed. I peeked out from behind the tree to find him staring straight at me.

"Long time no see, kitty cat. You gave us a hell of a time back at the Demon Lord's castle. Don't think you can use your magic to hide from me."

It was then that I finally recognized him as one of the hero's party members, who'd made it all the way to the Demon Lord's throne before being done in by his own cockiness and barely escaping with his life.

"Don't worry," he muttered. "I've got no bone to pick with you. I know you're not the one who killed my little sister."

His eyes were red and damp with tears as he turned back to the monument. Sensing he truly didn't bear me any ill will, I walked over to sit beside him.

"What do you mean? Your sister died that day, but not because of me?" I asked.

"She was murdered by her own kin—by a member of the beastfolk royal family, no less," he explained in a monotone. I had no words, so I waited for him to continue. "In the midst of all the pandemonium that day, they were scrambling to get as many citizens as they could into ships and carriages to flee the capital. My sister just barely made it onto the last ship leaving the harbor." Crow clenched his fists, digging his sharp claws into his palms deep enough to draw blood. "But then this asshole from the royal family recognized her as my sister and said 'Why don't you just let your oh-so-heroic brother save you?' before pushing her off the ship just as it set sail, leaving her with nowhere to go."

His voice was spiteful as he spat the words from between his gritted teeth. The look in his eyes was not one I had seen back at the Demon Lord's castle, but one of deep despair and desire for revenge.

"I was in Ur at the time, so I was in no position to come to her rescue. She ended up being crushed under the rubble of a collapsing building, but I don't blame you for that. She'd still be alive today if it hadn't been for that bastard—that pathetic excuse for a man who still dares to claim he's a champion of the people."

One by one, the teardrops fell, forming trails along his cheeks. I looked up at the monument, motionless. At the end of the day, that building wouldn't have fallen on her if it hadn't been for my wanton rampage. My lack of self-control had still been the cause of her death, and the death of many others.

"But I'll avenge her yet," Crow muttered under his breath. "It might take some time, but I'll make him pay. I swear it."

"I see. Good luck."

I'd suffered grievous wounds at the hands of Crow and the hero back at His Majesty's castle. I probably could have taken Crow by myself right then and there, had I wanted to. But his lust for revenge was clearly far, far deeper than mine, and I could sense that nothing good would come of trying to fight him. So I offered him my condolences, then sat there looking up at the memorial for a while.

The next time I looked over, Crow was gone.

"What happened after that?" Lady Amelia asked as she fried the chopped vegetables. Master usually handled most of the cooking, so I'd never realized Amelia had some natural talent. If she kept learning at this rate, she'd be a fine chef before we knew it.

"I never saw him again. In fact, I completely forgot about him until we arrived here in town and I sensed his mana."

The day we first came into port, I felt a blast of harmless wind magic come shooting my way, so small most would have assumed it a simple breeze. I felt it at the exact moment Master activated his Shadow Magic. Crow timed his gust so it would be concealed by the overwhelming force of Master's mana, ensuring his message reached only me. Master was too focused on controlling his mana to notice, so Lingga was the only other person there who might have picked up Crow's mana.

"Come to think of it," said Amelia, "my father did tell me once that one of the previous hero's party knew how to use and control his magic almost as well as a demon. He was probably talking about Crow, wasn't he?"

I nodded. In order to be chosen to join the hero's party as a race representative, one needed to not only be exceptionally talented in either physical combat or magic, but also boast extraordinary skills no other member of said race could hold a candle to. In Crow's case, it had been his incredible mana control that helped him edge out the competition.

"When you and Master went back to the inn after dinner that first day, I went off on my own to meet with him."

"Well, if it isn't the Nightmare of Adorea."

As I had suspected, Crow was waiting for me on the same hill where we'd first met.

I scrunched my brow, annoyed by this snarky greeting. *"That's not how I generally greet a guest when they take time out of their day to answer my summons. And my name is Night now, for your information, so stop calling me that. It's been over a hundred years."*

"It's been *only* a hundred years, I think you mean," Crow said with a mocking laugh as he twisted my words. "That's barely even the blink of an eye for a monster like you, isn't it? Are you even capable of dying of natural causes? I honestly don't know."

It was true. Beastfolk generally only lived about a hundred years more than the average human, while monsters generally didn't die unless they were slain.

"Enough semantics. What did you call me here for? Why did you feel the need to send me a covert signal hidden by Master's magic?"

Crow's ears perked up. "Master, eh? I was wondering what seemed different about you. So the great and powerful Nightmare of Adorea has been reduced to nothing more than a pet for a weak little human child? Maybe the Demon Lord ordered you to do it?"

I flicked my tail angrily. This wasn't at all what I'd come to talk about; I wanted to scream at this man. This was only the second time we'd met—what could *he* possibly know about me? Where did he get off acting like he knew what was going through His Majesty's head?

"State your business," I said again.

Crow sighed. "That boy with the unbelievable amount of mana is your master, I take it? I've got some questions I wanna ask him, so why don't you bring him with you next time? Heck, I'll even fix that broken sword of his—how's that sound?"

I said nothing, just glared at Crow. Not like I occasionally glared at Master or Lady Amelia, mind you—this was a death glare that could have killed a lesser man.

But Crow simply shrugged and shook his head. "Did you really think I wouldn't notice? That sword was forged by the Hero of Legend's own hand. It has more mana embedded in it than your average human has in their entire body, and who- ever wields it will have their own mana amplified to be on par with even the most powerful of demons. His mana signature's so great, I can tell exactly what he's doing, even from here. Right now, it looks like he's about to get it on with that elf princess."

My jaw dropped in awe—not at Crow being capable of such a feat, mind you, but at Master finally making a move on Lady Amelia. Crow interpreted my amazement as being directed at the former, and he looked rather pleased with himself as a result. I decided not to burst his bubble.

"But you wouldn't have called me here just because you want to fix his sword out of the goodness of your heart, would you? What do you want?" I asked.

Crow wagged his finger at me like a misbehaving pet, which annoyed me to no end. "If I told you that, you'd just run off and tell your master, now wouldn't you? Why don't you try doing a little critical thinking? Here, I'll give you a hint: that master of yours has something no other human has."

I tilted my head, my curiosity piqued. What could Master have that no other human had? I couldn't think of anything.

"Oh, and here's a list of raw materials I'll need to fix that sword of his," Crow said, using wind magic to send a single sheet of paper flying over to me. On it was a list of parts that could only be obtained from fearsome high-level monsters. "I'll need you to bring me them within the next few days."

"Isn't this a bit much?" I asked.

"No. In fact, it's the bare minimum for a sword like that. Best of luck!" said Crow, trying not to snicker.

I looked him straight in the eye. This was the first time I'd ever heard him laugh. In that moment, I saw no lust for vengeance in his eyes, but it wasn't my place to ask if he'd managed to exact his revenge on the royal family member who'd killed his sister. Especially not when I'd had an indirect hand in her death.

"So *that's* where you ran off to. I thought something seemed off about you that night," Lady Amelia said as she plated the finished meal and hand-squeezed some fresh fruit juice into a cup.

"You noticed, eh?" I asked, pleased to know she paid such close attention to me.

"Well, it was Akira who noticed first, actually." She chuckled as she picked up the plate and cup and headed to the workshop. It was just about lunchtime, and we found Crow waiting for us inside, having taken a break from his work.

"Hey, thanks. I appreciate it. I know cooking's probably outside your usual wheelhouse," he said.

Amelia and I exchanged a wide-eyed look, unable to believe we'd just received a genuine thank-you from Crow of all people. He didn't seem to notice however, as he'd already begun digging into his food. He didn't say he liked it, but he didn't insult it either, which meant he probably found it to his liking.

"Hey, so Night was telling me about your little sister who died," Amelia said nonchalantly. "Did you end up getting revenge for her after all?"

Crow's hand froze as he was about to take another bite. I looked up at Amelia in horror, wondering what possibly could have possessed her to broach such a topic.

"Not yet. The royal bastard who killed my sister is still alive and kicking. In fact, he's the current king's nephew, if you can believe that," Crow replied with an exhausted laugh. There was a pain in his expression that I knew I couldn't possibly fathom.

CHAPTER 3

Crisis

POV: ????

*M*EANWHILE, *deep in the Great Labyrinth of Brute...*
"Shit, shit, shit, shit! W-we've gotta let the guildmaster know about this ASAP, or else the whole town's gonna be in trouble!"

In the depths of the dimly lit labyrinth, the man's frantic footsteps were drowned out by his own bestial, bloodcurdling screams. The screams were soon replaced by the sound of a young boy's high-pitched laughter.

"Heh heh heh heh... Yes, that's it. Kill them—kill them all!"

POV: NIGHT

A FTER CROW FINISHED his meal, Lady Amelia set about cleaning up. As she washed the dishes, she became lost in her thoughts. Something told me her conversation with Crow was far from over, and sure enough, Lady Amelia walked right back out to Crow the moment she was done cleaning.

"Your sister was murdered by the royal family, and what are you doing about it right now?" she asked, perhaps more intensely than she should have.

I suddenly felt queasy; there were far more tactful ways to broach touchy subjects, though I'd never known Lady Amelia to mince words. As a royal herself, she was likely used to people waiting on her hand and foot, and you could probably count on one hand the number of times she'd thought twice about how her words might make someone else feel. Luckily, it seemed her bluntness paid off this time.

"Right now? Nothing," said Crow, with a self-deprecating smirk. "At the end of the day, I'm just a weakling who couldn't even save his little sister. Besides, I realized a long time ago that she wouldn't want me to get revenge." He slammed a fist down on the table, and the heavy mace he'd just finished repairing fell to the floor. For the first time since the day we'd met, Crow was trying to open up to someone.

Lady Amelia looked at him with cold, unfeeling eyes.

It made a chill run down *my* spine. *"L-Lady Amelia?"* I whimpered, but she did not respond.

I could see the mana whirling in her deep red eyes. I'd known about her World Eyes skill, which she had in common with Master, ever since she and I had met. It let you see someone else's stats, along with countless other things—according to Master, if you channeled enough mana into the superhuman ability, you could see anything and everything in the past, present, or future.

"Well, if I were your sister, I'd want to be avenged no matter what."

Crow's eyes widened as he noticed the strange flickering in Lady Amelia's eyes and gulped down a breath. After a moment, he realized she was using a special ability. "An Extra Skill, eh? And what are those eyes of yours telling you about me?"

"Don't ask me," Amelia said, closing her eyes. "That's for you to contemplate. But I will offer one piece of advice, as one who sees all: stop using your sister as an excuse to run away from your fears. It's pathetic, and it's not fair to her *or* you."

It felt like, for the briefest of instants, I could see a face reflected in Lady Amelia's eyes—the sad face of a young feline beastwoman who wanted to comfort Crow. With her World Eyes activated, it wouldn't be all that strange to think I'd just seen a phantom of his sister for a split second. I knew Master didn't have the skill level to perform a feat like that, and it must have required an immense amount of mana to pull off even for Lady Amelia.

Crow turned away, eyes downcast. "The food was great, thanks, but I think it's time for you to go home for today."

Lady Amelia thanked him for the kind words, then left.

I chased after her, looking back at the workshop several times with concern. Finally, when we were a good distance away, I looked up at her. *Are you sure that was a good idea, Lady Amelia?*

"It's fine. Even if I somehow convinced him to teach me his secrets, they wouldn't be of any use to me when taught by a man who's given up on life, nor would they be of any use to Akira.

The man is much more compassionate than he makes himself out to be, so I think he just needs a little time to stew."

It felt strange to hear her give such a concise summary of a man she'd met only days prior, but I nodded my head and chalked it up to the power of World Eyes. For once, I felt a deep respect for a being who was not my master; though I was sure Lady Amelia would make a fine master as well.

Heh heh heh... Go, my minions. Go up to the surface and kill all those pathetic weaklings! Let the streets run red with their blood!

Just as I was chiding myself for having gone soft, my breath caught in my throat. Amelia had already noticed it. We both stared at the ground.

"What was that?"

"This is bad, Lady Amelia."

Being a monster, it was only natural that I would pick up on it as quickly as Lady Amelia had with her World Eyes. Even some of the nearby beastfolk seemed to notice it a little bit, and they either tilted their heads or looked down at the ground. We could all sense something very bad was about to happen, and that monsters most foul were about to make a move at their master's signal.

"Lady Amelia! Over there!" I cried, pointing to a cloud of black smoke spewing from the ground.

"H-hey, that's where the entrance to the labyrinth is, isn't it?"

"Has the calamity from a hundred years ago returned to destroy us once more?!"

"It can't be..."

The townsfolk began to panic as they watched the cloud billow up to blot out the sun.

"The Nightmare of Adorea," I muttered spitefully, looking up at black skies similar to those that had fallen over Adorea a century ago. Only this time, I wasn't the one in charge of the destruction—I was among the besieged.

"I want to see what's going on over there, Night!"

"On it!"

At Lady Amelia's command, I enlarged myself. The nearby beastfolk screamed, thinking the black cat who had once laid waste to Adorea had come back to destroy them, but I had no time to reassure them. With a great leap, I bounded right over their heads and sought the high ground.

POV: CROW

"S O IT'S COME BACK to haunt me at last... The nightmare that has plagued my dreams each and every night these past hundred years..."

POV: ODA AKIRA

"O KAY, I've officially reached yellow rank. Please tell me I can *finally* enter the labyrinth."

With one hand, I handed Yamato the stack of request sheets I'd been assigned by the Guild not two hours prior, fanning them out like playing cards. There were five in total, all of which were completed and stamped.

"D-damn, Akira. You weren't kidding when you said you don't mess around," said Yamato, unable to deny that I had a right to be as smug as I was.

Even Myle looked over in amazement from his station at the reception counter.

Mind you, these "official Guild requests" were nothing more than odd jobs they'd let pile up. One of them had been a long-standing request to give a crotchety old man a back massage, and it had apparently sent countless newbie adventurers running home crying for their mommies before I showed up and finished the job in ten minutes flat. In fact, the guy even made a point of telling me he'd exclusively request my services from the Guild from now on.

"How in the world did you manage to satisfy that old coot? You must have used some sort of magic," Yamato muttered incredulously.

I cocked my head and responded plainly. "Magic? No, I just made small talk with the old guy for a while, started rubbing his shoulders, and bam, he stamped my flyer... Sheesh, I can't believe you told me it'd take at least a week. Ten minutes was more than enough. I guess my job experience back in Japan gave me the skills needed to finish the job so fast."

When you're a part-timer working at a place with lots of older folks, you're going to have to learn how to give a back massage sooner or later, whether you like it or not. You also gain a knack for placating jaded old geezers. I'd had to work with some very stubborn, closed-minded old farts in my previous gigs, so this guy had been a walk in the park by comparison.

Myle looked on, mouth agape, ignoring the adventurers he was supposed to be helping as he watched Yamato change out my dog tags for yellow ones.

"And what about these other requests? Let's see, you did a house demolition gig, helped the old ladies in the neighborhood run some errands, helped a chef come up with some new fusion cuisine ideas... What was the last one again?"

As Yamato ran through the list of requests I'd been assigned, I exchanged my dog tags and fastened them back around my neck. I didn't personally think I'd accomplished very much, so it didn't really feel like I'd "ranked up."

"Oh, that's right!" Yamato exclaimed, looking over the flyers. "You helped clean out that infamous hoarder house! How in the *world* did you pull that one off?"

I could feel all the eyes in the building on us. Yamato didn't seem to care one bit, though he might have been too excited to notice the attention. I simply nodded and rubbed my chin. I wasn't exactly a neat freak, but I did try to keep things tidy, so seeing my first ever bona fide hoarder house had been a bit of a shock to my system.

"Well, for the demolition gig, the client claimed he could use a little bit of barrier magic. I had him set up a soundproof barrier, then I went in and took out all of the primary support beams, and boom. House demolished. I mean, it sounded like he didn't care how it got demolished as long as the job got done, and that seemed like the fastest way to do it, y'know?"

I could already hear Yamato concocting a retort in my head. *"But how in the hell did you break those pillars? They were about as thick as you are tall!"* I didn't really want to explain that I'd extended my Shadow Magic into the shape of a giant sword to cleave them in half, so I changed the subject before he had a chance to ask.

"As for running errands for the old women, I've got a pretty good handle on the city's layout by now from eating out with Amelia all the time, so I just drafted up a plan that let me get everything I would need at the fewest number of stores, with the lowest prices, then plotted out the shortest route between them. Easy."

I was the one who kept track of our family's finances back in Japan. If I let my sister, Yui, do it, I knew she'd buy overpriced stuff, and whenever my mother was feeling well enough to go shopping, she'd come back with the lowest-quality stuff possible. *The women in my family, I swear... It almost makes me understand why my dad left.*

Once again, I could hear Yamato's incoming response as he clutched at his face after I told him that had been the easiest job by far. *"Wait, wait, wait! Are you some sort of super genius or something?! How could you possibly memorize all of that?! And how could you carry all those groceries by yourself, for that matter?! I know how much those ladies usually buy! We generally assign those quests to entire parties of adventurers! You were assigned it by accident!"*

But I wouldn't hear it. I moved on to the next request.

"As far as the fusion cuisine ideas went, well... I do a little home cooking, so I just gave a little advice using that as a basis, and the chef was totally spellbound by my every word... Is Japanese cooking really *that* rare here? I thought I heard the country of Yamato's cuisine was pretty similar."

I could already hear his protests as he banged his head against the reception counter. *"How can an adventurer be a more accomplished cook than a professional chef?! He's the head chef at one of the city's most famous restaurants, for crying out loud!"*

I was glad I hadn't been giving him the chance to say these things out loud. If I had, his voice would have probably gone hoarse. I looked at him with something akin to pity in my gaze, but this only served to deepen his anguish. He tried to compose himself and asked me to please continue my story; the trails of blood running from his nose did nothing to help him look put together.

"Mmm, well, the last one was definitely the trickiest of the bunch," I began, shrugging. "It was a fairly standard clean-up job, all things considered, but I'd never seen a hoarder house before, so I was pretty taken aback at first. Took me almost an hour to get the place cleaned out."

It had all looked like trash to me, so I just had my Shadow Magic swallow it up; my shadows weren't picky eaters, and they probably wouldn't get a tummy ache from eating all that garbage. I didn't know what happened to the things the shadows "ate," and I didn't care to find out. All I really had to do was sort out what needed to be kept from the rest and then clean up the place afterward. The place had been so dusty, my stay-at-home-dad instincts had kicked in, and I had a blast getting everything spick-and-span.

"Wow, a whole *hour*. What an ordeal," Yamato grumbled sarcastically.

"Yup. But it was pretty fun, honestly. The client had been trying to find the key to the vault there for years and it was driving him nuts. He seemed very happy when I found it."

Like clockwork, I heard Yamato's response in his head as he shook his fists beneath the countertop where none could see. *"That was the old duke's manor, you idiot! The same one urban legends say still holds a vault filled with unfathomable riches despite having fallen into disrepair! The only reason it got so filled with trash was because the local thieves repeatedly ransacked the place over the years! They turned the whole building upside down and still came up empty! You're telling me you found it in an hour?!"*

Every adventurer in the building was now shaking with rage just like Yamato.

"Listen, uh, I've gotta go take care of some urgent business down in the labyrinth, all right? But it's been fun doing odd jobs for you guys, so feel free to send more requests my way once I get back."

I proceeded to stride gallantly out of the Guild HQ, aware of just how much the atmosphere inside had changed but pretending I was oblivious to it. Yamato and company watched in stunned silence as I waltzed out the door.

"The Patron Saint of Side Quests, eh...?"

That was what one of them called me on my way out the door, to which everyone nodded in agreement. The speed with which I had completed all the citizen requests made me something of a messiah figure in their eyes, evidently, and I would continue to be known as the Patron Saint of Side Quests by everyone in the Guild and by the townsfolk from that day forward. Little did I know, the legend of the Patron Saint of Side Quests would be heralded and passed down to future generations as they prayed for their messiah's second coming.

And so, I was able to become a yellow-rank adventurer, thanks in no small part to my experiences back home.

I might have just finished taking care of five whole requests, but I was heading directly into the labyrinth—I was getting a very bad premonition about something, and alarm bells were ringing in my head like never before. They got louder as I got closer to the labyrinth. I wanted to nip whatever was giving me the bad feeling in the bud. Thankfully, Amelia and Night were spending their days over at Crow's house, which was on the complete opposite side of town, so there was fairly low risk of them coming to harm. I wanted to get Amelia off this continent ASAP regardless, or else something told me she would end up having to use her Resurrection Magic again. Perhaps it was my Detect Danger skill trying to warn me.

"Damn."

When I arrived at the labyrinth, it was already covered in a cloud of black smoke, and I could hear the screams of monsters racing for the surface. A group of Guild members scrambled to try to seal the exit. Since beastfolk were quite like beasts, they had a sixth sense that alerted them to danger. Thus the only fools loitering around the area right now were a few oblivious human Guild members and some adventurers that had been dungeon diving in the labyrinth.

"Hey! You need to get the hell away from here, now!" yelled a high-ranking beastfolk Guild member, trying to direct a few unarmed civilians to safety.

The other Guild members, realizing the danger was closer now, fled the scene, leaving the labyrinth entrance only partially sealed. I couldn't really blame them; everyone had to look out for themselves, especially those with lesser or no combat abilities. And chances were the horde of monsters would bust through the doors, sealed or not.

"Hey! You'd better get going too, pal!" yelled a thoughtful beastfolk adventurer as he grabbed me by the arm and dragged me a few paces. "Can't you feel it?! Some serious monsters are headed this way! The type that would normally take a whole raid party to defeat!"

"Yeah, I get that. But then how are *we* supposed to stop them?!"

He and I were the only two left in the vicinity. I noticed from his dog tags that he was a red-rank adventurer—one rank higher than me—and I could sense he had someplace in mind to fall back to and regroup. I relented and started running alongside him.

"We've gotta go to the Guild and report this ASAP. They'll probably organize an emergency response team of every adventurer, ranks gold through yellow, but if we don't get there in time, we'll all be dead meat!"

"You're awfully composed. Doesn't seem like this is your first rodeo."

"Yeah, same to you."

I grinned. It was true; I'd had my fair share of near-death experiences during my long stint down in the Kantinen labyrinth—not that any of them were the sort of experiences I was especially proud of.

When we arrived at the Adventurer's Guild, there was already a large group of adventurers ranked yellow or above gathered outside the entryway. I contacted Night via Telepathy and gave him a quick rundown.

"Copy that. Try to stave them off as best you can, Master. We'll focus on evacuating civilians and minimizing casualties over on our end."

"Cool, just be careful, okay? If you die, I die too, remember."

"Pah. Just who do you think I am?"

"Right, stupid question. Let's keep each other posted. Keep an eye on Amelia for me."

Since we'd been bonded via a monster pact, our lives were now directly dependent on each other's, but something told me there wouldn't be any monsters down in the Great Labyrinth of Brute capable of endangering the life of the ex-final boss of the Great Labyrinth of Kantinen. Shortly after I cut off telepathic communications, the guildmaster, Lingga, appeared on a slightly elevated platform.

"Let's dispense with the preamble, shall we? Everyone, pair up with someone nearby. They are now your partner, and you must trust them with your life. We're going to stay in these pairs for the duration of this operation. If you ended up getting paired with someone weak, well, consider that very unlucky on your part."

Normally, I would have protested such a ridiculous order, but this was neither the time nor the place. We were in the middle of an emergency here. An ordinary-looking human like me didn't seem to belong anywhere near this emergency response team, but maybe it would be a good opportunity to rank up even further. Besides, Amelia was nearby, and I had a duty as the man in the party to protect her. Even if she *was* technically a much higher rank than me, and even if there was very little chance of her being in any real danger with Night around.

"Hey, you wanna partner up with me?" asked the red-rank adventurer I'd met at the labyrinth.

"Works for me. Thanks."

"The name's Senna, and I know I might not look like it, but I'm actually Guildmaster Lingga's younger brother."

He certainly *didn't* look like it. Lingga was a leopard-esque beastman, while Senna was more of a lupine breed.

"Nice to meet you, Senna. I'm Akira."

Well, that's the introductions squared away. Though if he really is Lingga's brother, I'll need to stay on my guard. He may be dangerous.

"Are you a frontline fighter? Or do you stick mainly to the rear?" asked Senna, wagging his bushy tail as he scanned me from head to toe.

"Frontline, usually. I'm an assassin."

"Then that works out well, 'cause I'm a fire mage, and I need someone to protect me while I cast." He grinned, and I gave him a quick nod before looking around at the other pairs. It seemed most of them had known each other before partnering up.

Once everyone was paired off, Lingga resumed his speech. "Now work with your partners, and if any of you run into any major trouble, send the other back to seek help. If any teams are especially worried about operating on your own, you're free to link up with other teams as well. We've just sent our fastest runners to warn the nearby towns and the capital, but we can't wait for them. If we're going to save our city, we need to do it ourselves. Don't let the demons defile our town!"

A roaring cheer rang out from the crowd, but I furrowed my brow. "Demons?"

How could they say for sure this was demons? I could understand why they might associate the black skies with the "Nightmare of Adorea" incident from a hundred years ago, but I hadn't heard anything about there being actual demons in that siege—only monsters. Night hadn't said a word about any demons being involved, nor had any of the townsfolk from whom I'd heard secondhand whispers, and that was something people would have mentioned from the start. Other than the fact that Night had been acting on the Demon Lord's orders, I didn't get the impression that demons had been remotely involved with it.

If these people really thought this was a repeat of the incident one hundred years ago, in which Night had led an army of lesser monsters, why would they *not* assume this was the work of another intelligent monster leading an army of minions? I couldn't imagine the guildmaster was saying the demons were involved out of pure speculation—surely he was aware that spreading those kinds of baseless accusations could be very harmful. He must have had evidence demons were involved.

"Hey, quit spacing out, would ya?" Senna chastised me, and I quickly snapped back to reality. "Now do you wanna try to link up with another group or not?"

"Nah," I said, shaking my head. "I don't know about you, but I'm not much of a team player. I generally go it alone. Increasing our numbers will only give me more things to worry about."

Senna nodded, then waved off the pair of adventurers who'd apparently come to ask us to join forces while I was lost in thought. The duo walked off, crestfallen.

"Akira. Senna. Your team is going to go provide backup for the red- and silver-ranked teams," said Lingga, just as we were about to head into battle.

"Wait, you're really gonna send a yellow rank to the front lines? Are you sure that's a good idea?" Senna asked, concerned.

It was the first time I'd had anyone doubt my abilities in this town, likely because of the little show of power I'd put on for the townspeople when we first got off the ship.

"I don't think you have to worry about this one," Lingga assured him. "But if it really comes down to it, you can always just ditch him and run back here."

"You got it, Boss."

The two brothers exchanged a mischievous grin. *Okay, I take it back. I can totally see the resemblance now.*

POV: NIGHT

WHEN MASTER got in touch with me, I was running around town with Lady Amelia on my back, trying to offer a shuttle service for older citizens who didn't have the strength to evacuate on their own. Most of them trembled in fear at the sight of me, but they were quick to hop on my back once they saw the horde drawing near.

"Quickly, Lady Amelia! We need to get out of here!" I cried, lowering my tail for her to grab on to after she helped the last citizen onto my back. But she refused to grab hold.

"There are still people who haven't been able to evacuate up ahead, and the adventurers aren't covering this area either. Someone needs to stay here and protect these people," she insisted.

I saw the monsters closing in, and I hesitated. If I left and something happened to her, I'd have no way of getting in contact with her or finding her.

"You need to go, Night!" she cried.

I regained my composure and noticed the monsters were already upon us. They were all weak, low-level monsters that surely wouldn't pose a challenge to a silver-rank adventurer like Lady Amelia.

"I'll come back for you as soon as I can," I said, then took off with the evacuees in tow. It wasn't the cleanest way to do an evacuation,

but we needed to do whatever we could to minimize casualties. I turned around as I landed back on the ground and looked back at her.

"Don't worry. It's probably gonna be me who comes running after you," she said, turning toward the horde of monsters. "Gravity!"

Her silver hair fluttered as she channeled her mana into the spell, and the silver dog tags she kept hidden in her bosom were jostled free for the first time in a good while.

POV: ODA AKIRA

"O ALL-CONSUMING BLAZE, let me wield thy raging tempest in the palm of my hand! Flaming Fist!"

The monsters closed in on Senna as he stood still to recite this incantation, then began to pull back once they realized what he was doing. He reached out his hands, from which a gigantic fist made of pure flame burst forth before sweeping across the vicinity, burning all the monsters directly ahead of us to a crisp. More monsters quickly swarmed in to take their place. We'd been fighting on the front lines for almost an hour now, and the horde showed no signs of diminishing.

It was just as Yamato had told us back at the Adventurer's Guild—the monsters that called the Great Labyrinth of Brute their home had a variety of different weaknesses, making good teamwork an absolute must. I assumed the requirement to form well-balanced parties was likely a result of the beastfolk race's unique tendencies. After all, the blood of beasts ran through their veins, and the different breeds and species they represented had a direct influence over their personalities and skills.

Beastfolk resembling predators were always quick to lose their temper and start fights, whereas beastfolk resembling peace-loving animals generally kept to themselves and tried to avoid conflict. So while there were many powerful beastfolk, their various natures meant that they didn't always get along with one another—which might have been why they left it to us to decide our own partners.

"Akira, can you hold the line by yourself for a few minutes?" Senna asked in a haggard voice.

I turned to see him carrying two injured adventurers who'd been fighting on the front lines, one over each shoulder. They seemed to be on the verge of death, barely clinging to their last thread of life. I nodded, then borrowed a dagger from one of their belts. *Good timing.*

The one I'd been lent by the Guild had just shattered to pieces after I'd sliced through an entire group of monsters, and I'd noticed the blade this particular adventurer was using didn't seem to dull or break no matter how many monsters he used it against. I was very curious to try it out for myself. I gave it a quick swing to test its weight. It was about the length of my forearm and the perfect weight for its size. A well-made blade by all accounts.

"Th-that dagger... I had it custom-made... It's Crow's handiwork... You'd better...return it when you're done..." the adventurer muttered.

Interesting. That explains why it feels so good to wield, I suppose.

I nodded and tried to remember the man's face. It seemed Night's endorsement of Crow's forging ability was well-earned indeed. As someone who couldn't even afford his repair services at the moment, I was grateful just to have the chance to borrow one.

"Sorry about this. I'll be back in a little bit," said Senna, carrying the men away from the scene of the battle.

I grinned mischievously. Now I could fight without any reservations. There were still a few dozen adventurers trying to hold the line, but none within my immediate vicinity, and there was no way the few remaining would ever guess that a lowly yellow rank was about to take out all of these monsters in one fell swoop. I reached my hands out in front of me and gave the signal.

"Shadow Magic, activate."

I'd been making a genuine effort to take Commander Saran's advice to heart and never use Shadow Magic when other people were around to see it. I wasn't too worried about my ability being seen—the average person would probably just write it off as an obscure deviation of Dark Magic—but on the off chance I lost control of it again, it would be better to make sure that there were never any innocent bystanders nearby. That was why I was always using Detect Presence.

The shadows manifested in puddles on the ground, deeper and blacker than the skies above, then swirled around my feet like dogs begging to play fetch.

"Go ahead, boys. Eat 'em up," I ordered. "Fair warning, though: they probably won't taste as good as the monsters you're used to."

Their first meal as my underlings had been a minotaur. Next was Fenrir, then the Chimera... Virtually every time I'd summoned them to swallow up a foe, it had been a rare and powerful enemy, so they'd probably developed a pretty discerning palate.

As my Shadow Magic began swallowing up the nearby monsters, leaving not even a single drop of monster blood in their wake, the other monsters started to flee, scrambling over one another in their haste. Because of the momentary hesitation, each row of monsters was quickly trampled and crushed beneath the bodies of their comrades in the row ahead of them, and on and on in a domino effect of death.

"Damn. It's pretty horrifying to watch, but I gotta admit, it's quite the sight."

The horde of invading monsters, which had struck fear into the hearts and minds of the beastfolk townspeople, were now on the receiving end of that fear, crammed into tight spaces and being crushed underfoot. When I thought about the innocent beastfolk who'd had their homes destroyed, or the humans who were only here to work and gather money to send home to their families, I couldn't help but crack a smile at the despair of these invaders.

Suddenly, I sensed another person via my Detect Presence skill, so I commanded my Shadow Magic to return to me at once. I thanked them for their service as they coalesced back into my shadow, then started cleaving through a group of straggler monsters with the dagger I'd borrowed, swinging in wide arcs so as to carve through multiple enemies at once.

"Sorry about that, Akira!" said Senna, rushing out from a nearby alleyway. I waved back at him. "Hey, is it just me, or are their numbers pretty thinned out?"

"Beats me. Haven't been paying much attention." I shrugged as he scanned the surrounding area before lowering my hand again and slicing an ox-like monster's throat. "Maybe they went elsewhere because this area was proving too hard to control?"

Most of them had been swallowed by my magic, but there were still a few hundred stragglers, although none that could pose a challenge to us. *Perhaps it would be a good idea to offer support elsewhere when we're done,* I thought, taking a moment to survey our surroundings. I was looking to one side when a fireball suddenly whizzed by in front of my face.

"Sheesh. If you're just gonna stand there, make yourself useful," griped Senna.

"Hey, man. I held the line all by myself. I think I'm entitled to a break."

I could tell from Senna's joking tone that he didn't actually need my help.

Out of the corner of my eye, I noticed a large, tiger-like monster from Crow's materials list. *Pretty sure I just needed its claws, right?* I closed the distance in an instant and slashed through its entire body before harvesting the claws off its corpse.

"Don't mind if I do," I said, tucking them in my inside breast pocket.

"Looks like we're about done here. Guess I'll use my leftover mana to finish the job," Senna said with a wry smirk. Then he started casting a spell. I could tell this particular incantation required a lot more focus than the others. Not wanting his efforts to go to waste, I took great care to ensure no monster made it anywhere near him before he was finished. "O purgatory flames, bring forth thy conflagration and reduce these heretics to ash! Inferno!"

He finished casting, and I waited. I scanned the periphery, yet nothing seemed to be happening. It was only when I cocked my head and started wondering if the spell had been a misfire that the ground began to quake.

"This way, Akira," Senna said with a peculiar smile as the tremors grew stronger and stronger. It seemed the earthquake was focused only on the spots where monsters were standing.

"Whoa, what the hell is this?" I asked, but Senna simply chuckled and pressed his pointer finger to his lips.

Then, with an ungodly sound, the ground began to crack beneath the monsters' feet. Although they clearly wished to escape, it seemed their legs wouldn't move. Something spewed forth from the cracks in the earth, consuming the monsters whole in a matter of seconds, leaving only their mana stones behind. Thanks to my superhuman eyes, I was able to perceive exactly what that something was.

"Was that...magma?"

The only other time I could remember seeing magma was during a class field trip to Mount Aso, in one of those museum videos they had playing on repeat on the observation deck. It was a thick, bright-red liquid that moved slower than molasses yet could consume an entire mountainside's worth of trees as it rolled downhill.

"Hey, good eye!" said Senna. "That's correct. It's a spell that draws magma forth from deep underground, then sends it right back down after the job is done."

Well, that's not terrifying at all. There was nothing but abject horror in the eyes of the few remaining monsters who'd just watched their friends get taken out by some unknown force. There were even a few idiots who were begging us for their lives. I wondered why they weren't running away, but then I noticed that the immense heat from Senna's spell had fused their feet with the ground. *That explains why they aren't moving, I guess. Now they're just stuck here forever, probably in immense pain, knowing full well they'll be next.*

"What a cruel spell," I muttered, knowing that if Night were here, he'd probably call me a hypocrite for my wanton use of Shadow Magic. The difference there was my spells swallowed their victims whole in an instant, and when I sneaked up behind a monster to assassinate it, it was over before they ever had a chance to feel terror. This large-scale spell of Senna's, however, was practically akin to torture or a war crime. The mere thought of it being used on other people instead of just monsters was enough to make my skin crawl.

I watched as the remaining monsters vanished one by one, leaving nothing but mana stones to indicate they'd ever been there. And at last, the area we'd been assigned was completely free of monsters. Finally able to relax, I let out a deep and exhausted sigh.

Then I got a telepathic transmission from Night, who sounded like he was at his wits' end.

"Master! We have a problem! Lady Amelia's been kidnapped!"

My mind went blank. All I could feel was an overwhelming, white-hot rage.

POV: AMELIA ROSEQUARTZ

"HUFF, HUFF... There's too many of them... I can't hold them off much longer..."

Thankfully, my MP was never at risk of running out, but it was still exhausting having to expend so much of it in quick succession. I could only hope Night would make it back soon, but even then, it would take a good amount of time to help all these elderly folks to safety.

"I'll just have to keep them at bay until then..."

I held up my arms, covered with cuts and scrapes, and reached out to the sides. I could heal little cuts in a matter of minutes, but it was a futile effort since new ones would immediately take their place. I was standing face-to-face with a battalion of what must have been hundreds of monsters—and those were just the ones in my immediate field of vision. If you included those currently pillaging the abandoned houses and the ones no doubt looming in my blind spots, they likely numbered well over two thousand. I was lucky enough to be able to cast Resurrection Magic on myself so that I'd be automatically brought back to life if I died, but the side effects of consuming such an enormous amount of mana meant that I'd be rendered completely vulnerable, unable to even move for quite some time.

"Gravity!"

Every monster directly in front of me within a twenty-meter radius or so was squashed to a pulp, organs and viscera of dozens of monsters splattering across the vicinity. It was a gruesome scene certainly not fit for children's eyes—like one of those "R-rated movies" Akira had told me about. Unfortunately, I wasn't really in a position to be careful about property damage at the moment, so the force of my spells had also destroyed quite a few nearby buildings. It would likely take quite some time for this part of the city to be fit for habitation again, even after the monsters were gone, but I didn't feel too bad about it—there were lives on the line here, and I couldn't afford to hold back.

"Night, what's taking you so long?"

I prayed nothing had happened to him as I continued to fend off the oncoming wave of monsters, who ran over the corpses of their comrades without any hesitation.

"Well, well, well. I recognize that Gravity Magic... You're the little elven princess, aren't you?" said someone who sounded like a young boy.

I didn't know where the voice was coming from, but it was awfully foreboding to hear such ominous words in a child's voice. I looked around frantically, searching for the owner of the voice, having been under the impression that I was the only non-monster left in this entire district. Was it a young boy who we'd failed to evacuate? No... There was something about this voice. Something I recognized.

"Up here, silly. Do you really not have Detect Presence or any skills like that?"

I looked up and saw a cute little boy with emerald-green hair and eyes to match perched atop the head of a long-necked monster (which Akira probably would have compared to a giraffe if he were around). There was a twinkle in the boy's eyes indicating he was enjoying the chaos.

Then it dawned on me.

"You're...the demon who attacked the Sacred Forest all those years ago, aren't you?"

It was the same incident I'd recounted to Akira back in the Great Labyrinth of Kantinen, the one in which Kilika had accidentally caused monsters to flood out from the Great Forest Labyrinth. But I remembered now—there had been a demon leading the horde, and I could distinctly recall the same glint in his bright-green eyes and the way he'd said "See ya later!" in that boyish voice of his as he rode off. I had been just a child at the time, so I hadn't known it then, but when I got older and learned what the demons were, I realized the boy leading the pack must have been one of them. I'd only seen him for a split second, so I had been sure whether I should tell my father what I had seen. If the demons were attacking, it meant the Demon Lord was going on the offensive, and that wasn't the sort of thing you wanted to spread false alarm about. It could result in a large-scale counteroffensive that forced us to cooperate with other races who our people didn't much care for, and all based on a purported sighting by a lone elven girl.

"Hey, you remembered!" the boy exclaimed. "Yep, that's me! Gosh, I've still gotta thank your sister for giving us an excuse to come out and have a field day like that. That was the most fun I'd had in a long, long time!"

Just as I realized he was indeed a demon and had assumed a more guarded posture, the boy's voice became much shriller and more jovial. His cheeks were flushed pink, as if he were enamored with a new toy. The monsters had stopped their invasion and were now moving in to surround me on all sides as though I were their primary target. I'd never seen so many monsters in such a tight space before—not even in one of the labyrinth's many monster lairs. Even with my Gravity Magic, which could take out vast swaths of enemies in a single blast, the odds were stacked against me.

"So listen, Princess," the boy went on, lowering his voice. "I've actually got a little job I'm gonna need you to do. So as much as I'd like to just kill you right here and now, I'm afraid that's not gonna fly."

His green eyes glimmered ominously, and suddenly the monsters who'd been frozen in place began to move again. Not in a wild rampage, but in a more organized manner, like they were following orders. I wanted to let out a grunt of frustration, but I stopped myself, thinking that wouldn't be very ladylike, and simply furrowed my brow instead.

"But I *do* know about that magic of yours," he continued, "so I'm afraid I'll still need to incapacitate you a little bit, m'kay?"

He flashed a devilish grin, but his eyes remained so pure and childlike that I might've had a hard time believing he wasn't just a playful little kid if it weren't for the enormous amount of mana radiating from his body.

"Oh, but that assassin friend of yours? The one brought here via the hero summoning ritual? Yeah, I'm probably gonna have to kill him, FYI. His Majesty said he'll only get in the way of our plans, and on top of that, I just can't stand his ugly mug. I hate it when human worms like him don't know their place. Need to kill him to make sure he doesn't achieve his goal, y'know?"

If my brow were capable of furrowing any deeper, it would have. We already knew the Demon Lord was aware of Akira from the message he'd had Night pass along, of course, but we'd only come to this continent to get Akira's sword repaired so he'd stand a fighting chance against the Demon Lord, who had *explicitly summoned us* to his castle. How exactly were we "getting in the way of his plans"?

"But you're probably gonna want to stay alive so you can bring him back in case I *do* kill him, right? So you'd better hurry up and use that Resurrection Magic of yours to make sure you survive this! Don't worry—I promise I won't kill him before you have a chance to recuperate. And I'm a man of my word!"

The boy raised a hand, and the monsters started closing in on me.

"Oh, right! And the name's Aurum. Aurum Tres. Now don't go forgetting it, m'kay?"

The boy lowered his hand, and the monsters rushed me all at once.

POV: NIGHT

"*A*URUM TRES," I muttered to myself as I examined the scene of the carnage. I was about 90 percent sure it was him—I'd recognize the mana signature anywhere.

"Night, are you listening to me? Did you see the guys who kidnapped her or not?"

Master's voice was even deeper than usual. He was making quite the effort to appear calm and conceal the immense rage he was feeling, but it was still abundantly clear he wanted to hunt down the perpetrators as fast as humanly possible.

"*Yes, I know who it was...but I'm afraid you're no match for him. I would recommend waiting until you're stronger to go after him.*"

"Even though my stats are already higher than those of the previous Demon Lord? Are you serious?"

"*I assure you, I am.*"

I was keeping my voice a little softer than usual—perhaps I was feeling a bit shaken up by this as well. But if *he* was here, then His Majesty was planning something. I never would have imagined that, before becoming Master's familiar, such a thought would ever make me sick to my stomach.

"Can you at least tell me the name of the guy who kidnapped her?" Master asked as I leapt up to a higher vantage point and looked down at the bloody scene. The stronger one's mana, the more they carried in their blood, to the point that it was possible to distinguish whom a given bloodstain belonged to even a little while after it dried. There was no question the blood I was looking at was Amelia's, as it contained traces of mana strong enough to kill an ordinary man.

"His name is Aurum Tres. He was given the surname Tres because he's the demons' third-in-command. And yes, the current Demon Lord's subordinates are indeed so powerful that they've surpassed even the previous Demon Lord—Aurum Tres among them."

Master knelt down and grasped a fistful of the blood-soaked sand at his feet.

"Well, let's clear out the remaining monsters before we do anything else. They'll get no mercy from me after this."

Sure enough, a group of monster stragglers soon began to congregate around us, drawn either by the scent of Lady Amelia's blood or by our presence.

"Very well," I replied.

But Master didn't even look up.

"Shadow Magic, activate."

I wasn't sure if it was a result of Master's rage, or if he was simply channeling more mana than usual, but the number of shadows he summoned forth from the nearby craters (which had likely been formed by Lady Amelia's Gravity Magic) was staggering. Previously, I'd only known him to be capable of making use of his own shadow and maybe the shadows of a few other nearby objects.

I took a deep breath, then used Shapeshifter to transform. I'd made the mistake of taking the form of a dragon before despite not being able to accurately emulate the hardness of its scales, but not this time. I was now taking the form of a monster I'd fought directly on many occasions. When the light from the transformation sequence abated, I was quite a bit taller than my previous feline incarnation, and I had three sets of eyes to work with.

"A Cerberus, seriously? How many monsters in this world are gonna ape Greek mythology?"

I heard Master muttering about something, but as the drool dribbled from my ferocious mouths, I sensed my thoughts growing more and more beastlike by the second. Even now, I could only comprehend about half of what he'd just said. In this form, I was far more powerful, nimble, and resistant to basic attacks, but there were certainly drawbacks as well. I was reduced to no more than a frothing beast that felt nothing aside from a deep instinctual desire to kill, kill, kill. The biggest hurdle to taking forms like this was always finding someone capable of stopping me before I went too far, but now that I'd teamed up with Master, I was sure that wouldn't be an issue.

"Mas...ter... I'm going to...destroy them now... When I'm done... you need to stop me..."

I leapt forth without waiting for Master to answer, immediately pouncing on the nearest monster and ripping out its throat. Then I moved right on to the next before the first could even choke out its final breath. I grew wetter and stickier as the entrails of my victims splattered against my fur, but I didn't care. All I cared about was trying to quench my insatiable thirst for blood.

"Ohhh, I get it. You can't control yourself when you're in that form, can you?"

Master's voice resounded through my brain, but I couldn't respond.

"Yeah, I can relate. I was just having some trouble trying to control my Shadow Magic at full blast, but you've bought me enough time to get a handle on it. Thanks, big guy."

The words seeped through my ears, but I had no idea what they meant. I made a mental note to try to think back on them after I'd reverted to my original form.

POV: ODA AKIRA

WHEN I SAW the puddle of Amelia's blood on the ground, which was large enough to have been from a lethal wound, something snapped in my brain. I didn't lose control of myself and start breaking things, but I had a bit of a mental breakdown from the overwhelming rage, powerlessness, and sadness I was feeling. Some other monsters appeared afterward, but I was in no state to pay them any mind. I felt like a lost child who'd been left behind in a dark and unfamiliar city.

"Shadow Magic, activate."

Needing some outlet to vent my frustrations, I unleashed my Shadow Magic, carrying with it the full weight of my fury. I couldn't control it.

"Mas...ter... I'm going to...destroy them now... When I'm done... you need to stop me..."

I was too focused on trying to get a better hold on my Shadow Magic to even notice that Night had transformed himself into a Cerberus. Seriously, why were there so many monsters from Greek mythology in this world?

Night said not another word before leaping into the crowd of monsters and ripping out the throat of his first victim, sending blood spraying across the ground. The corpses continued to pile up as he gnashed and ripped apart multiple monsters with his three distinct heads.

"All right. I think I've got it under control now."

I couldn't just stand back and let him do all the work now that, with great effort, I'd managed to subdue the Shadow Magic raging like a wildfire within me and harness its powers as my own once again. There was still much about the ability that I didn't know or understand—how far my range of control over it extended, and what its limits were. It was clearly a power far stronger than I had any right to control, yet weirdly enough, that didn't intimidate me whatsoever. Using Shadow Magic to clear an opening in the middle of the monster horde, I leapt over to Night's side. In his drooling Cerberus form, he seemed to have lost all sense of reason. He was acting purely on one instinct: to destroy.

I thanked him for keeping the monsters occupied thus far as I joined him in the fight, though it didn't seem like any of my words were getting through to him, so I decided it would be best to save this conversation for later. With my dagger cloaked in Shadow Magic, I stabbed deep into my first victim's vital organs. The other shadows at my feet stretched out across the ground, somewhat of their own volition, and began gobbling up monsters left and right, devouring them whole.

"Wha... Hey, Night!"

When I looked up, I saw that my partner was no longer by my side, but instead continuing his rampage elsewhere. He was still within my line of sight, but much too far for either of us to provide support to the other if things got dicey. Perhaps the monsters were intentionally trying to separate us—it *did* seem like they were acting on the orders of a more intelligent being rather than just their own impulses.

"Must be those damn demons."

They were the only race capable of controlling monsters. It was the same power that made them so reviled by the other races, to the point that they had been exiled to the most inhospitable of Morrigan's four continents, the hellscape known only as Volcano. If the demons were attacking, then it could only mean one thing: the Demon Lord was on the offensive. I couldn't speak to what the royal family back in the Kingdom of Retice was truly planning, but it seemed the timing of their ritual to summon an unprecedented twenty-eight heroes was a little too perfect.

"Aurum Tres," I muttered, letting the name linger on my lips as I clenched my fist and let my shadows writhe. "You're not gonna get away with this."

As a bit of an unrelated aside, I'd never known what love was like back in my world. I loved my mom and my sister, Yui, of course, but I'd never been *in* love. Every girl I knew had thought I was a freak or a creep due to my appearance or my attitude and stayed far, far away from me, and it wasn't like I'd had some conveniently gorgeous childhood friend I could develop a relationship with either. Hell, I didn't have *any* long-term friends, and since high school, I'd been too busy with work to even think about my pathetic love life.

That meant Amelia was the first girl I'd ever properly fallen in love with. The fact that she was a princess didn't deter me in the least, and I was pretty sure that if she died, I'd never love again. I wanted nothing more than to cherish and protect her. When I failed her, it felt far worse than merely failing myself. And right now, she was somewhere far beyond my grasp. I didn't even know where she'd been taken. She could have been in immense pain at that very moment. She could have been calling my name, crying for help. Yet I had no way of running to her side. No matter how many of these monsters I killed, it wouldn't bring me any closer to Amelia.

"GRAAAAAGH!"

The thought filled me with a blinding fury. A darkness even blacker than the skies above fell over the vicinity—my Shadow Magic had broken out of its confines and spread out far beyond my reach.

"Begone, filth! Shadow Hell!"

The monsters sank slowly into the black-dyed streets, and like quicksand, the shadows had them stuck fast. By the time they'd sunk all the way in, my MP was almost completely depleted, and when the shadows came rushing back to me, the skies overhead returned to their natural blue. As I looked up to confirm the nightmare was over, my body fell limp.

"Hm...? Master?!" said Night, somehow managing to catch me before I hit the ground. I was surprised to see that he'd returned

to his giant feline form. *"It seems your Shadow Magic... Or rather, the new type of Shadow Magic you just used has the power to cancel out other types of magic as well. It broke me out of my transformation the moment I came in contact with it. But more importantly, what in the world were you thinking?! How could you be so reckless?! Couldn't you have just picked them off one by one?!"*

Night's angry voice rang through my dizzy, exhausted mind like a siren, making my throbbing headache all the more painful.

"Sorry, Night, but can you save the lecture for later? I gotta take a nap."

Night protested, but I closed my eyes regardless. I'd reached my limit. He was right, though—I had gone way too far. For once, I'd let my emotions get the better of me. If my MP hadn't run out, my shadows probably would've gone on to raze this entire neighborhood. I should've known better than to let myself lose control like that, but ever since I met Amelia, it was like I'd become a different person. And yet, as someone who'd never cared one iota for anyone outside my immediate family back in my world, I considered this ability to feel emotions for other people an improvement.

"Don't worry, Amelia... I'll save you... I promise..."

These were the last words I whispered before finally passing out.

"MASTER'S INJURIES HAVE EXCEEDED ACCEPTABLE PARAMETERS. FATAL DAMAGE SUSTAINED; EMERGENCY ACTION REQUIRED. AUTO-ENGAGING

SHADOW MAGIC, RECOVERY MODE... MASTER'S MP SUPPLY DEEMED INSUFFICIENT. RECOVERY WILL REQUIRE THE USE OF EMERGENCY MANA STORES. INITIATING RECOVERY... RECOVERY COMPLETE. DISENGAGING SHADOW MAGIC."

As the mechanical voice came out of my mouth, my body was enveloped in a gentle light that healed my wounds and sent me drifting off to sleep. My pale face, drained of all its mana, was restored to its original color. It was a phenomenon that had only happened to me once before, well before I met Amelia or Night, when I'd nearly died from the injuries I sustained during the Chimera boss fight.

Night, recognizing his master was no longer in mortal danger, ceased his desperate flight in search of help and slowed his gait.

When I came to, I found myself in an unfamiliar room.

"Mm?" I mumbled groggily.

"Oh, good. You're finally awake, Master."

As I sat up in bed and surveyed my surroundings, a house cat–sized Night greeted me from the windowsill next to my bed. He seemed fairly exhausted himself.

"Night, where are we?" I asked.

"In my humble abode," said a voice that was decidedly not Night's. Yet it was one I recognized.

"Crow?" I said as the black-furred feline blacksmith approached me, carrying something in his hands. Aside from the bed, the small room had little in the way of furniture—not even a closet. It was clear that its owner didn't use it for any purpose other than sleeping.

"How are you feeling?" he asked.

"Awful. How long was I out? And did you find Amelia?"

My body felt as heavy and lethargic as one would expect after an especially long sleep, and my brain still wasn't working properly. I felt like I hadn't gotten a good night's sleep since arriving in this world, as death seemed to always be right around the corner, yet today I awoke feeling perhaps a little *too* well rested. I assumed I must have been out cold for a good while. As the cogs in my head finally started moving again, I held a hand up to my forehead and tried to regain my bearings.

"Oh, so that's it, eh? Amelia got kidnapped by the demons?" asked Crow.

"*Unfortunately so. We managed to stave off the monster invasion, but we still don't know where Lady Amelia's been taken. And to answer your question, Master, you've been unconscious for the past three days.*"

I was a bit taken aback by this. Had I really slept for three whole days? The longest I'd ever been unconscious before was that time I got hit by a truck when I jumped in front of it to save a child who was playing in the middle of the street, and even then, I was only out for two days. Thankfully, I'd managed to slip between the tires when I fell, so I hadn't been injured too badly, and from what it looked like, I hadn't sustained any major injuries this time either. So why had I needed three whole days to regain consciousness? I looked over at Night, who had a pensive look on his face.

"Night? What's wrong?"

I scooped him up to pet him, and he started purring like the little cat he was. Amelia and I would often compete to see who could get him purring faster.

"Master, I... No, never mind. It's not important."

It sure as hell sounded important, but I knew better than to try to force Night to tell me something when he clearly didn't want to.

Crow, having waited patiently for us to finish speaking, stepped forward and placed the objects he'd been carrying in my lap. "Here's the item you asked me to work on. I assume you'll need it if you're gonna go off and pick a fight with the demons. I went ahead and spotted you for the materials and labor costs, but I expect to be repaid in full at your earliest convenience. I also went ahead and sharpened up that dagger you were using while I was at it. Tell the owner I hope they continue to make good use of it."

I looked down at the dagger I'd borrowed from the fallen adventurer, which now gleamed in the light as though it were brand-new.

"Thanks, I appreciate it," I said, before looking at the other two daggers sitting in my lap. "You had to split it in half, huh? Guess I must've really done a number on the poor thing."

"That you did. But hey, you're an assassin, right? Dual blades should be a little more your style anyway."

The two daggers were all black from sheath to hilt, and upon pulling one out, I confirmed the blades themselves were still every bit as black as I remembered. There could be no mistaking it—my trusty katana, the Yato-no-Kami, had been split in two. There'd been a huge crack right in the middle of the blade when I left it with Crow. From the way he explained it, the katana hadn't been beyond repair, but he made an executive decision to adapt it after taking my class into consideration.

"Oh, and I want you to have this as well," he added, dropping a small box in my lap.

I picked it up and looked it over.

Night seemed to already recognize whatever it was, as his eyes shot wide open. *"Wait a minute. Is that...?"*

"Yes, it's exactly what you think it is. Go ahead. Open it up."

At Crow's insistence, I hesitantly lifted the lid of the tiny box. "Is this...a ring?" I asked.

It was a fairly primitive-looking piece of jewelry, clearly designed for men, with a blood-red gemstone embedded in the center. It had no name engraved on it, yet there was a message written in English in a tiny font on the inside edge: "LET ME BE YOUR GUIDE." I read it aloud, then translated it for Night and Crow. My English wasn't great, but I knew enough to understand what it meant. More than anything, I was just surprised to see yet another language from my world had made its way into this one. I assumed the ring must have been forged by an adventurer who'd been summoned from somewhere in the Anglosphere at some point in the past.

"You can read that, huh? Guess I shouldn't expect any less from the hero," said Crow.

"Yeah, it's not the language of my home country, but it's one of the ones from my world." *And I'm not* the *hero, technically, but whatever.*

Crow nodded in understanding.

He'd probably figured I wouldn't be able to read it since it was written in a different language than the one engraved on the Yato-no-Kami, and since my Understand Language skill didn't seem to work on languages from outside this world, he would have been right if I hadn't studied hard for all those English exams. I usually slept through most of the school day, but I tried to stay awake for my Japanese, English, and math classes at the very least. Not because I thought those subjects would serve me well in the future or anything like that, but because those were the classes with the scariest teachers. My English teacher, in particular, was bright and bubbly on the surface but had an eagle eye for snoozing students. And if you *did* get caught dozing off, you could expect to be woken up with a pop quiz about the lecture you'd just slept through.

"Well, that's a pretty fitting inscription. That ring will light the way to whatever it is its wearer seeks. Just slide it on, then think really hard about what you most desire. The light from the ring will lead you right to it."

My heart skipped a beat. It could lead me straight to what I most desired? Could I use it to find where they'd taken Amelia? I slipped the ring onto my pointer finger and tried to picture Amelia in my mind.

"Whoa!"

A red beam of light shot out from the ring and hit one of the house's walls at a slight downward angle. I quickly surmised it was pointing in the direction of the Great Labyrinth of Brute.

"Hold on a minute. That ring is a national treasure, is it not? How in the world did you come to possess it?" Night asked Crow, clearly suspicious. The ring was apparently supposed to be locked up tight in a castle vault somewhere.

Crow shrugged and shook his head. "Got it as a gift from someone I helped out way back when. Couldn't tell you who, since they didn't reveal their identity to me, but it seemed useful, so I graciously accepted."

He then made a quip about how he was glad to finally have a guinea pig to try it on and confirm it wasn't cursed, a joke which Night clearly did not find amusing. He shot Crow a death glare that said he should thank his lucky stars it wasn't cursed, or else his entrails would be splattered across this house.

"Well, the good news is we can use this to find Amelia," I said, changing the subject. "How 'bout it, Crow? You wanna come with us? Night told me you're gonna be mentoring Amelia. Wouldn't it be only proper to go save your apprentice?"

"Sorry, since when am I her mentor?" Crow snapped, giving Night a dirty look. "I don't recall ever agreeing to anything of the sort."

"Well, that you've put up with her this long means you must be at least considering it, right?"

This question gave Crow pause. I couldn't tell what he was thinking; he just stared off into space for a while before finally answering. "Perhaps. I suppose if she makes it back here alive, I wouldn't mind giving her some pointers."

"Are you serious?!" Night was so overjoyed that he pounced on Crow in a way that was cute in his house cat form, but would have been lethal were he at his full size.

"Don't make me repeat myself. And that's only *if* she makes it back alive."

Heh. Despite his tough-guy front, Crow was a bit of a softie on the inside. I was relieved to hear he would lend Amelia a hand, even if it sounded like he had no intention of helping us rescue her.

"Can I ask you for one other favor, Crow? I want you to do a little digging and see if you can find out who's conspiring with the demons."

At this, Crow stopped trying to peel Night off his head and gave me a sour look; his expression was always a little sour, though, so it wasn't a big change.

"Way ahead of you," he replied. "The general public still doesn't know the demons were behind the attack, but it's only a matter of time before the king puts out an official statement. That means we've gotta figure out how they sneaked in, and with whose help, before they have a chance to flee."

I nodded in agreement. Even if this *was* a port town, it wasn't so lightly guarded that demons could have just slipped in unnoticed. If anything, the town was even more security-conscious because it was a port—I'd needed official permission from the elven king to even enter the country. The proximity to the labyrinth meant the town was home to a major guild branch and an ever-increasing number of skilled adventurers who increased the city's security. While it was true that humans and demons didn't look all that different on a superficial level, demons exuded such an immense amount of mana that even the most ignorant fool with no eye for magic could recognize them from a mile away. Not that there were many such fools among the beastfolk, who prided themselves on their alertness and were notorious for trying to pick fights.

"Well, if I were you, I'd start with Guildmaster Lingga and his little brother, Senna," I said, and Night and Crow both looked at me like I was insane.

"Master, surely you don't mean..."

"When Lingga was addressing the Guild before the attack, he explicitly said not to let 'the *demons* defile our town,' but no one had even caught the faintest whiff of any demons at that point. So why was he so sure they were involved?"

Unless you were like Night, who had a direct link with the demons, there was no way to know where they were or what they were up to—so where had Lingga's intel originated from? I'd also noted that, when the majority of adventurers gasped at the mention of said demons, Senna hadn't seemed fazed in the slightest, which struck me as pretty suspicious. And was it really standard procedure to force the yellow and red ranks to team up with strangers to go fight on the front lines? There were plenty of silver-rank adventurers who could've helped with that. Why hadn't he sent them to hold off the monsters and had the lower-ranking adventurers help the civilians evacuate? The guildmaster's plan hadn't accounted for the civilians at all...which would have forced any capable fighters stuck in more densely populated areas to stay back and fight off the monsters while helping the elderly and disabled evacuate.

"Unless it was all a setup?" I finally said, opening my eyes after a long silence.

"Master?" Night responded incredulously.

"I think there's a good chance Lingga's our informant. He's the one who decided where and how to dispatch the adventurers, and he doesn't seem like the type to make a stupid oversight like, say, completely forgetting to send capable fighters to defend unarmed civilians. Especially with the monsters in every corner of the city."

Night frowned, grasping my implication. Crow, for his part, scowled like he'd swallowed a bug.

"So what's your theory?"

"I think it's possible Lingga predicted Amelia would stay behind to help with the evacuation, and he intentionally tried to overwhelm her and keep her in one place."

Of course, this was all pure conjecture. There were plenty of other people who could have been pulling the strings, or maybe someone had seen a demon and was able to relay the information to Lingga from afar via some unique skill.

"So you think he organized the adventurers the way he did specifically to get the elf princess trapped and alone," Crow said. "I'll see if I can find any evidence to support that theory, but for now, I think you should get a little more rest."

I nodded and promptly sank back down into the bed, already on the verge of passing out again. I knew Shadow Magic consumed an immense amount of mana, and I always tried to use it sparingly unless it was an emergency, so this was a first for me. I'd never experienced what it felt like to use up all your mana, but I never could have imagined it would feel *this* terrible. I would be careful to not let it happen again. As soon as I closed my eyes, my mind drifted into sleep. I could hear Night and Crow discussing something quietly, but it sounded like radio static in my current state, and it only grew fainter as my consciousness sank deeper into darkness.

POV: NIGHT

I PANICKED A BIT when Master seemed to faint again, but Crow assured me that he was merely sleeping, so I let out a sigh of relief. There was no shortage of mages who'd met their end due to mana exhaustion—it was no laughing matter. My demon superiors had theorized every breath used up a small bit of mana, and with Master having just narrowly escaped death, I couldn't help worrying that something so minuscule would be the final nail in his coffin.

"Gotta admit, I'm impressed he made it out of there alive," Crow muttered.

I considered telling Crow about the strange phenomenon that had saved Master's life, but neither I nor Master had any idea of what had actually happened.

Crow gave me an impatient look. "What? If you've got something you wanna say, then say it. Otherwise, I'm gonna head out," he said coldly, looking down at me where I lay on the bed.

I couldn't stand against that look. I caved and told him all about Master using up his mana by casting an extremely strong Shadow Magic spell, and about the words I'd heard coming out of his mouth as I dragged his battered body to Crow's home.

"Huh. That doesn't sound like any automatic recovery magic I'm familiar with. And where the hell did the 'emergency mana stores' come from?"

I let Crow stew over the information for a while as I checked on Master. He winced a bit at the cold touch of my paw on his forehead before falling back asleep.

"*Hrm. Well, he doesn't seem to have a fever, and that's one of the telltale symptoms of mana exhaustion,*" I said. Suddenly, my patient grabbed me and tucked me under his head like a pillow. "*M-Master...? Erm, Crow? A little help, please?*" I didn't want to force my way out of Master's grasp and risk waking him, so I turned to Crow for assistance, only to discover he'd already left. "*Blast... Ugh. Master, what am I ever going to do with you? You realize that by losing control like that, you put* my *life in danger too, don't you?*"

Before he and I made a pact, I'd found the boy's wanton fearlessness in the face of death rather amusing, but now that we were bound, I wished he would start taking things a bit more seriously. My heart couldn't take much more excitement, and I wasn't ready to die just yet. When His Majesty assigned me to my post as the final boss of the Kantinen labyrinth, I'd accepted knowing full well I would likely die down there someday, but that resolve hadn't lasted for long. I'd found myself constantly wishing I could escape from that commitment, and while I eventually did, it certainly hadn't been in the manner I would have expected. But it was still better than being stuck down there forever.

Regardless, I wasn't ready to die, which was exactly why I'd made the pact in the first place. Despite knowing it would mean my own death if Master should ever perish, I told myself everything would be fine so long as I made sure to protect him. I hadn't expected him to flirt with death at every opportunity he could get, even if this was the first time his life had ever truly been in danger since we'd teamed up. An ordinary human would have died from that first arrow ambush back in the Sacred Forest, but thanks to his extraordinary skills, Master was evading fatal attacks on what felt like a daily basis.

"Please don't die, Master. I'm begging you..."

I nuzzled his cheek. It felt a little bit patronizing for a once-proud monster like myself to be reduced to a mere pillow, but I paid it no mind. Master had been treating me like a stuffed animal since we first became allies down in the labyrinth, so I was used to it by now. True to his word, he'd made cuddle sessions a mandatory event each day before bed, just as he'd promised he would when we first made our pact. I moved closer to his body and prayed, whispering the same three words over and over.

"Please don't die."

What I perhaps hadn't realized was that my fear of Master dying had long since transcended a simple desire to not die myself. It wasn't long before I gave in to his comforting warmth, laid my weary head on his arm, and drifted off to sleep.

"Mas...ter..."

Not long after this, Akira wearily opened his eyes to discover a soft, furry mass had fallen asleep in his arms.

"Don't worry, buddy. I promise I won't let anything happen. I'm not gonna go dying anytime soon. Not before I make it back home, at least."

He wrapped his arms tight around his familiar, then fell once more into a deep, deep slumber.

POV: ODA AKIRA

THE SKIES OUT THE WINDOW were dark when I next awoke. I tried to jump out of bed, insisting we start looking for Amelia at once, but I was talked down by Crow and Night.

"It's already nighttime, and it's only going to get darker outside. I know that might be favorable for an assassin, but don't forget, the darkness is advantageous for monsters as well," Night warned.

"Besides, you haven't fully recovered yet," Crow added. "Go back to bed."

I wasn't sure how the two of them could possibly be so calm about this, and I was soon overcome with immense frustration at the thought of making Amelia wait even a moment longer.

"What the hell, guys? Do you not have any sense of urgency?!"

I slammed my fist into the wall in a fit of rage. I knew throwing a tantrum wouldn't help matters, and I wouldn't even have been in this situation if I hadn't used my Shadow Magic without considering the consequences. I also knew the two of them were probably beside themselves with worry for Amelia as well, but I couldn't stop myself from taking my frustration out on them.

"Trust me, Master. We want to rush to her aid just as badly as you do."

"Speak for yourself. Far as I'm concerned, you can take all the time you want, Mr. Silent Assassin," Crow snarked, and I would have blown up at him if it weren't for the last two words he'd said.

"'Silent Assassin'?"

Crow smirked at my dumbfounded expression. I was used to his sarcastic smiles by now, but this one sent shivers down my spine.

"It's your new nickname, Master," Night said matter-of-factly.

Noooo! Damn it, don't tell me that! If you're gonna be the bearer of bad news, at least ease me into it first! This was a problem my friend Kyousuke had always had too. He'd walk up to you, drop an information bomb sure to ruin your day, then walk off like he didn't even realize he'd done it. Maybe he and Night were secretly related somehow.

"Apparently, a good number of civilians witnessed you using your Shadow Magic to wipe out the monsters," Crow explained. "They watched from the nearby hill they'd been evacuated to. It's not often a yellow-rank adventurer becomes famous enough to get their own alias. The Guild's even officially approved it. Isn't that swell? Must be nice to have such a cool title, huh?" Crow slapped me on the shoulder with a grin before waltzing outside.

I was left there in bed, clutching my head in my hands. "No, no, no! I can't have a nickname! I'm an assassin! How can I be stealthy if everyone and their mother knows who I am?!" I cried.

"It's true, being famous generally doesn't help one sneak around unnoticed. For what it's worth, I still think you do a far better job of keeping a low profile than any other assassin I've met," Night said, trying to reassure me.

That's not the point, Night! I thought. *Ugh, why did I have to get the most edgelord-sounding nickname imaginable?! And since when does the Guild get to decide what nicknames get approved?! I sure as hell wouldn't have approved this!* "I swear to god, my class-mates better not find out about this... *Especially* not Kyousuke or the hero. They'll never let me live it down..."

Kyousuke would probably just say "Good for you" and mean it, which was honestly even more embarrassing than being made fun of. The hero would probably look at me in horror and say "Oof, that sucks," which would be insulting enough on its own, but then he'd no doubt go and tell his harem, who'd then spread it around until everyone in class knew my shame. I let out a deep and pained sigh.

"Damn it, Night. Can't we at least try to get them to change it to something a *little* less cringeworthy?"

"It's not outside the realm of possibility, but now that the entire town is abuzz with gossip about the elusive 'Silent Assassin,' I think

you'll have a hard time getting them to switch over to something else. Though I hear there was a contingent of townspeople insisting on the name 'Dark Assassin' instead," Night said, shaking his head. He clearly did not understand the true severity of the situation.

"*Dark* Assassin? That's even worse! I use Shadow Magic, not Dark Magic! Is every single person in this city a moron?!" I asked grumpily, and I could almost feel my shadow nodding emphatically in agreement.

"*Well, I don't know. Perhaps it looked to them like you were controlling a cloud of darkness. You must also remember that your Shadow Magic is a rare, undocumented school of magic. How could you expect the average person to tell the difference? You did cloak the streets in a veil of darkness, after all."*

Night gave me a wry look as though he knew I wouldn't have a good comeback. And damn it, he was right. I also couldn't deny that, regardless of how edgy my nickname was, the fact remained that an assassin who went around defeating monsters by harnessing the power of his shadow was about as edgelordy as you could get. Maybe it would be better to silence everyone in town to make sure there was no risk of my grandchildren ever finding out.

"Let's just get some sleep, all right? We've got an early morning tomorrow!" I said before slamming my head down into the mattress. Apparently my body was still in dire need of rest, as I immediately felt my eyes growing heavy. I was also no stranger to falling asleep after flinging myself onto my bed in anger. My sister, Yui, loved to tease me about it.

"*Yes, yes. Whatever you say, Master.*"

"Don't be snippy with me," I grumbled hazily before I drifted off completely.

"You can't recover from mana exhaustion in only a few days, Master. Especially not after it nearly killed you," Night murmured before leaving the house.

My Shadow Magic had automatically replenished my mana, yes, but it had only brought me back to the bare minimum of what I needed to stay alive. The only way to recover was to gradually drink mana potions and rest. I was now about 70 percent recovered, but it would be best to wait until I was back to 100 percent. I knew this, yet I was so fraught with worry for Amelia that I couldn't stay asleep for long, which meant my recovery was taking much longer than it should have.

"C'mon, c'mon, c'mon... Hurry up, damn it..."

POV: SATOU TSUKASA

"ASSUMING OUR ULTIMATE GOAL is still to slay the Demon Lord, where do we go from here?"

After some much-needed R&R in the eastern country of Yamato, I and the other members of the hero's party were finally ready to gear up and get moving again.

"Well, we're gonna want to be prepared, I can tell you that much. From what I've heard, the previous generation's hero lost all his party members except for a single beastfolk representative at the hands of the demons and monsters before they even made it to the Demon Lord's throne."

This had happened nearly one hundred years ago, and the disgraced hero had long since died of natural causes. It was theorized that the current Demon Lord might be the same one from back then, since no one had been able to slay him, but no one was sure how long the average demon lived.

"Guess that means we should be careful not to underestimate the Demon Lord's cronies, huh?" Hosoyama said.

I nodded. "Well, we don't know exactly how strong the last hero's party was, but we can certainly assume it was composed of the finest living warriors from across three continents at the time."

"In other words, there's no doubt they were far, far stronger than we are now," Asahina muttered to himself.

For the past several days, we'd been taking on requests posted at the local Adventurer's Guild. There weren't a ton to choose from, given that there was no labyrinth in the area, but since Yamato wasn't a popular stop for adventurers, there were plenty of requests to defeat low-level monsters that were trivial for us but intimidating for the average civilian. We split up and took care of each and every one, and we were finally reconvening to take a breather. There didn't seem to be any powerful monsters in this part of the continent—certainly nothing as strong as the minotaur we had fought down in the labyrinth, at least. Even the training Sir Saran and Sir Gilles had put us through had been more taxing than fighting the nearby monsters, none of which were stronger than those found in the first few levels of the Great Labyrinth of Kantinen.

"We'd best be careful we don't get too big for our britches, then," Ueno grumbled, her arms crossed as she mulled over our options. It seemed everyone in the group was at a loss regarding what our next step should be aside from myself and Asahina.

"Well, we just reached yellow rank, which is great, but there's not much more we can do to get stronger in a city that only has weak fodder monsters and no labyrinth... So if you ask me, there's only one thing we *can* do."

As Ueno said, it was imperative we took things slow to make sure we didn't get ahead of ourselves, but there wasn't much more to be gained from staying here, and plenty we could learn from venturing elsewhere.

"Man, I really don't wanna have to say goodbye to Japanese food again..."

"Don't worry about that. I'm sure Tsuda will do his best."

"Why does it always have to be me?" grumbled our party's primary chef, Tsuda Tomoya. He was a knight class, but his cooking was so good that he'd become something of a maternal figure for the group. Our two female party members also had the Cooking skill, but he had done the cooking for his entire family, so his skill level was by far the highest.

For reference, the last remaining member of the party was Waki Daisuke—the guy who was always saying "praise the lord" in reaction to any remotely auspicious happenstance. His animal trainer class wasn't always the most useful; its biggest applications had been taming some little monkeys in the nearby forests and befriending stray cats around town. He was a pretty lackadaisical guy in every respect, and he was prone to going off on tangents in every conversation. He was the oldest child in his family, but in our group he was definitely the annoying baby brother.

His skills would be invaluable if they could be used to tame monsters, but unfortunately that wasn't how it worked. Apparently there *were* so-called "monsterlords" who could domesticate monsters like the demons did, but they only came around once every several hundred years or so. I didn't understand why anyone would want to keep something so hostile as a pet, but to each their own.

"Guys, I'm not a miracle worker. I can't cook every dish on the planet, and it's not like there's a ton of good ingredients to go around either," Chef Tsuda grumbled. Nanase patted him reassuringly on the back.

Nanase Rintarou was a master in the art of communication and understanding, as evidenced by his ability to hold a conversation with even the most curmudgeonly students in our class (read: Akira). I'd even heard he'd once managed to get Asahina, a man of few words, to open up to him and gush about his favorite anime, though these rumors were unconfirmed. Still, Nanase was probably the middle child of the group, which I suppose made me the oldest.

"Don't take it personally, Tomoya," said Nanase. "He's only saying that 'cause everyone here loves your cooking. And I get that it's hard to get the right ingredients for traditional Japanese cuisine here in this world, but you could probably at least season things in a pseudo-Japanese way, couldn't you?"

"I guess I could probably come up with something, yeah," Tsuda agreed.

"Whoa! For real?! Dude, work on that ASAP! I need this in my life!" Waki begged.

"Same! I can be yer taste tester if ya want!" added our disenchanter, Ueno Yuki. She was a ray of sunlight for our group. I had a feeling that if she or Waki ever stopped smiling, it would be the first sign of the apocalypse. I'd probably place her as the second-oldest daughter of the family.

"I'll eat anything as long as it sets my mouth on fire," Hosoyama Shiori said with a delicate, feminine expression at odds with what she was saying. A well-known lover of spicy foods, she couldn't eat anything here without burying it under a heap of foul-smelling blue seasoning of dubious origin. I wasn't sure if she had been the same back in our world and just done a better job of hiding it, or if this was a new development. Regardless, I'd probably place her as the eldest daughter.

Which left Asahina, who I suppose would be the father of the group.

"Okay, enough about food, people! We still haven't decided what our next move should be!" I shouted in a desperate attempt to steer the conversation back on track. Everyone fell silent as I scanned their faces to see if anyone had any decent ideas.

"We need weapons," said Asahina, leaning up against a wall. He could always be relied upon to offer helpful input regardless of the subject.

"You make a good point. I've got my holy sword, so I'm all set, but Tsuda's sword is so beat up that it'll probably break soon."

"We've got plenty of money; maybe it's about time we got everyone some new equipment."

"Oh, in that case, maybe it'd be a good idea to get me and Yuki some weapons to defend ourselves with too! Things got pretty dicey for a minute there yesterday."

Our current formation was as follows: me, Asahina, and Tsuda in the front, with casters Nanase, Ueno, and Hosoyama pulling up the rear and Waki as a floater. This still left us vulnerable to attacks from behind, and while we all had the Detect Presence skill, none of us had reached a particularly high level in it. We still needed to keep a watchful eye out to make sure we didn't get ambushed.

"Why don't we head over to the beastfolk continent? I've heard they've got the best blacksmiths in the world over there," Nanase suggested, and suddenly all eyes were on him. "I mean, I guess it was just a rumor, but I even heard that the beastfolk survivor from the previous hero's party has his own workshop over in the port town of Ur."

"I believe the Great Labyrinth of Brute is in Ur as well," said Asahina.

Welp, I guess that settles it, then! "All right, folks! Tomorrow morning, we leave on the first ship to Ur in order to buy ourselves some shiny new weapons! Would be nice if we could enlist the services of that world-famous blacksmith, but let's not get our hopes up. As long as we can find some weapons that work for us, that's all that matters."

Everyone raised their fists and cheered in agreement, and I let out a sigh of relief. Finally, it was beginning to feel like we were getting ahead of Akira in the race to slay the Demon Lord.

My Status *as an*
Assassin Obviously
Exceeds *the* Hero's

CHAPTER 4

The Great Labyrinth of Brute

POV: ODA AKIRA

"*A*RE YOU SURE *this is where the ring was pointing, Master?*" Night asked, looking up at me as we stood before the entrance to the Great Labyrinth of Brute.

The towering doors had already been repaired after the recent monster invasion, and they were shut tight. The Adventurer's Guild certainly worked fast.

There was no one else around, so we could get inside quite easily—it was the getting out part I was worried about. There was no guarantee we'd find a convenient teleportation circle at the bottom like in the Great Labyrinth of Kantinen, so going in was a bit of a gamble.

I looked down at the ring on my right hand. The light pointed directly at the doors. "Yup, this is the place, no doubt about it," I confirmed, opening the doors. Night sighed before enlarging himself, and I hopped up on his back. "Now remember: we're just gonna bomb right through as fast we can, okay?"

"Leave it to me."

We'd agreed beforehand that since our goal was to find Amelia as quickly as possible, we would do our best to avoid as many fights as we could. There was no telling how deep into the labyrinth Aurum Tres had taken her, so the plan was to just have Night run through every standard floor between boss arenas. I was sure I was well enough to run alongside him now, but he stubbornly refused, insisting I ride on his back out of an abundance of caution. Sometimes it felt like Night was the master and I was the familiar.

"Actually, hold up a minute," I said, stopping Night just before he was about to run inside. I had felt something—a presence. I pulled out a throwing knife and threw it into a shadowy corner.

"Eek?!" cried a voice, and the beastfolk girl who'd been spying on us stepped into the light. Her face was covered by a hood, and she was fairly tall for a girl—maybe just slightly shorter than I was. But something struck me as strange; her voice was almost familiar. I scrunched my brows together as I struggled to remember.

"Who goes there?!" Night roared, causing the very air around us to tremble.

Naturally, the girl froze at Night's voice and was now shaking in her boots.

"Dial the Intimidate down a notch, would ya?" I reprimanded him. "We're not gonna be able to get much information out of her if you scare her literally speechless."

"Very well," Night responded before lowering the intensity of his Intimidate skill enough to let her speak, but not enough to let her escape.

"Um..." said the girl, her voice clear as crystal.

Then it hit me. "Wait a minute... Aren't you that girl I spoke to outside the Great Labyrinth of Kantinen? The one who was being all angsty about the hero summoning ritual? Something about it requiring a lot of sacrifices or whatever?"

"Hang on. Then you're... No, now's not the time. Sorry to spring this on you out of nowhere, but would you mind if I tagged along?!" the hooded girl asked, shaking her head bashfully.

"We don't know if you can be trusted, and we're already in a hurry as it is. We don't have time to babysit you," said Night, giving voice to my thoughts. Our feline friend was very kind to me and Amelia, but he had no patience for strangers. A relic of his time as a monster, perhaps.

"So you want me to introduce myself, is that it?" the girl asked. She lowered her hood to reveal her husky-like ears and brilliant cobalt-blue eyes, which felt as though they could pierce straight through me. "I'm Lia. Lia Lagoon, princess of the great nation of Uruk."

Her steadfast gaze reminded me a little bit of Amelia's.

"Well, well. And what in the world is a princess of Uruk doing in a place like this?"

The girl's voice shook in the face of Night's Intimidate skill, and I could tell from her frightened expression that she hadn't

seen much actual combat. Night was only using the skill at a level equivalent to that of low-level monsters on the upper levels of the Great Labyrinth of Kantinen. This told me that, even if we were to let Lia tag along with us, she certainly wouldn't be taking part in any battles.

"I need to speak with Amelia, Princess of the Elves," the girl said.

"What business have you with Lady Amelia?!" Night snarled.

Upon hearing this, I was unable to maintain my composure. I hopped down from Night's back and grabbed Lia by the collar.

"Gghk?!"

"Amelia only got captured because she stayed behind and fought off hundreds of monsters to buy *your* people enough time to get their slow asses to safety," I spat, pulling out a throwing knife and holding it up against her throat. "Now tell me: how in the world did *you* know this is where they're keeping her prisoner?"

I tightened my grip on the knife, accidentally piercing her skin, and a tiny droplet of blood ran down the girl's quivering neck.

I whispered in her ear. "I hate to break it to you, but I've had some pretty negative run-ins with princesses in the past, Amelia excluded, so you'll have to forgive me if your title doesn't command much respect from me. If I don't like your answer, I'll have no problem killing you right here and now. Now talk."

I let up on my own Intimidate skill to give her a chance to explain herself. *Man, I really lose my cool when it comes to Amelia, don't I?*

She coughed to clear her throat. "You're right, I don't have any fighting capabilities, but I do know how to protect. And I'm not here on behalf of my people, but to give her a warning as a fellow princess."

Her eyes spoke true. I had plenty of questions I wanted to ask her, but I decided it was probably safe to release my grip on her collar. I didn't put down my knife, however.

"You didn't answer my question. How did you know this was the place? I didn't sense you following us here, so you must have been planning to come here all along," I said, giving her my most intimidating glare.

"I used my Scent Tracker skill. I followed her scent trail, and it led me right to the entrance of the labyrinth."

Scent Tracker? I cocked my head and looked up at Night.

"It just means she has a heightened sense of smell, essentially. There are skills for heightened versions of all of the five senses, all of which are more likely to manifest in beastfolk than any other race," he explained, and I nodded in understanding. I figured it would be a good idea to give the old World Eyes a spin to see if Lia was telling us the truth.

LIA LAGOON	
RACE: Beastfolk	**CLASS:** Guardian (Lv. 52)
HP: 2500/2500	**MP:** 2000/2000
ATTACK: 150	**DEFENSE:** 5000
SKILLS:	
Scent Tracker (Lv. 7)	Royal Grace (Lv. 2)
Short Swords (Lv. 2)	

EXTRA SKILLS:

Spirit Barrier

Well, she didn't seem to be lying about her Scent Tracker ability, and its skill level was fairly high to boot. Maybe she really had tracked down Amelia using scent alone—though that didn't explain how she'd recognized Amelia's scent in the first place. Her claims about not having any combat prowess seemed to be true as well. Her stats looked to be on par with some of the casters in my class when they had been at Level 1. I knew beastfolk were supposedly naturally gifted with certain skills regardless of whether they used them or not, but hers seemed to be much too low for that—other than her Defense stat, which was enormous in comparison. Though even more than that, there was something else that caught my eye.

"You're not a trueborn royal, are you?" I asked.

"Wh-who told you that?!" she gasped.

But I wasn't in the mood to get into it, so I simply hopped back up on Night's back. "Climb aboard," I said, reaching a hand down to help her up.

She just stood there, looking dumbfounded.

"Are you sure about this, Master?" Night asked, looking at me over his shoulder. *"Even if she wasn't lying about her abilities, she could still be lying about her motives. We shouldn't blindly believe every word that comes out of her mouth."*

"Who said I did? I just wanna get a move on, that's all. We're wasting daylight here, and I'm sure our little princess knows what she's getting herself into. Now, are you coming or not?" I asked without even looking down at her.

With trembling hands, Lia grabbed hold of Night's fur. "I'm coming. I have to convey this message to Princess Amelia no matter what it takes," she said confidently.

"Fair enough... Step on it, Night," I ordered, ignoring the look of protest on his face.

I could feel his fur rustling beneath me for a moment, then his body became bathed in light. It was his trademark Shapeshifter ability. When the light receded, my kitty companion had transformed himself into a giant, black-furred cheetah in the interest of speed.

"Hold on tight. If one of you falls off, I won't turn around to come back for you unless your name is Master," Night said, looking back at Lia as his muscles bunched beneath us in preparation for takeoff.

One leap, and we were out of the sunlight and into the darkness of the labyrinth. Another, and we landed right in front of a group of monsters. A third, and we had long since passed them by. Lia clung to me for dear life and shrieked directly in my ear. The only girl whose breasts I wanted pressing up against my back was Amelia, so this was more annoying than titillating, but I did my best to put up with it anyway. Hers were a bit bigger than Amelia's, but I wasn't even a boobs guy, so it made no difference to me. *Though I won't say what kind of guy I am either.*

"All right, you can tell me your story now," I yelled, turning carefully around to face Lia while clutching Night's fur. "Just be careful not to accidentally bite your tongue."

No longer able to cling to me, Lia scrambled to get a good grip on Night's fur coat. "W-well, y-you're right that I wasn't born into the royal family," she admitted.

This was something I had surmised based on the order of skills on her stat page. Skills were listed in the order in which you obtained them, as far as I could tell. Amelia's Royal Grace skill was the very first one listed on her stat page, whereas Lia's was listed second. This led me to believe that if one were truly of royal blood, the skill would be there from the moment you were born and thus appear in the first slot. The only explanation I could think of to explain the discrepancy was that Lia had gained the skill sometime *after* birth, and she therefore must have been adopted into the royal family. Judging by her reaction, my theory was correct. I wondered if perhaps they had adopted her for her unique class or her Extra Skill.

"I was the daughter of a fairly ordinary, if slightly upper-class, household," she began after adjusting to the high velocity we were traveling at. "My family were once very powerful nobles, but they fell from grace several generations ago, leaving them no more respected than the average family by my father's time."

Now this I had not predicted. Night made a sharp turn into a different corridor, and Lia hunkered down, holding tight to his fur so as not to fall off.

"A-anyway, I was only adopted into the royal family about five years ago, and before that, I lived in a little village out in the countryside. One day, our village was attacked by a monster, and everyone aside from me was killed, including my mom and dad... or so I thought." She paused and bit her lip.

I had to admit, I was intrigued.

"What kind of monster was it, if you don't mind telling me?" I asked.

"A slime," she replied, intense hatred burning in her eyes. "A stupid, pathetic monster I should've been able to take out in a single blow. But this was no ordinary slime. It was a disgusting, pitch-black slime the likes of which I'd never seen before or since, and it swallowed every single villager in its goop."

I gulped. That sounded an awful lot like the slime I'd found Amelia trapped inside of—the type made by scumbag slavers to kidnap beautiful elven women. I found it hard to believe such a slime could have kidnapped Amelia all the way over on the human continent, but I had never really considered it. If Lia was saying the same slimes were taking victims here in Brute, that was a different story entirely. This revelation certainly poked some holes in my theory that the traffickers we encountered back in the elven domain had been knights working on direct orders from Uruk. At least, I *hoped* beastfolk wouldn't attack one of their own villages.

"I'm convinced that slime was made artificially in some way, to serve some sort of purpose," Lia said, apparently having arrived at the same conclusion as Amelia and I had.

"You mentioned that you only *thought* the other villagers were dead a minute ago. What was that about?" I asked.

Her expression darkened. "Remember what I told you when we first met? That it takes unfathomable sacrifices to conduct the hero summoning ritual?"

"Hang on a minute. You're not about to tell me those beast-folk were being kidnapped to be used as sacrifices, are you?"

It was something I'd considered back when she'd spoken to me outside the Great Labyrinth of Kantinen, but I'd quickly pushed it into a corner of my mind and forgotten about it. At the time, I couldn't imagine why such sacrifices would be necessary, and I didn't want to think of so many dying to bring me and my classmates to Morrigan.

Unfortunately, my fears were about to be confirmed as the truth.

"That's exactly what I'm telling you," Lia said. "See, when I first found out I was a guardian, I cast a protective barrier on every one of my fellow villagers, just in case.

Guardians are different from barrier mages in that they can cast barriers on specific people that stay with them, rather than just casting a big stationary forcefield around a predetermined location."

Interesting. So it works almost like an elemental buff, then. I was eager to find out where this conversation was going.

"If a person dies while the barrier is still in effect—like, say, from being poisoned or something—then the barrier will automatically be dispelled the moment they die. I can feel my spell breaking when that happens...but guess what? I didn't notice it at first, probably because I was too shaken up from the attack, but not a single one of my barriers disappeared after the slime swallowed the villagers, which told me they had to still be alive. I searched everywhere to find out where they'd been taken, until one day, all of a sudden, I felt all the barriers vanish almost at once. I'd already been adopted into the royal family by that point, so I used every power at my disposal to launch a full-scale investigation into what happened to them."

I lowered my gaze. I could guess what had happened next.

"My investigators didn't turn up anything here in Brute, but they finally found a lead on the human continent. A cursed ritual had taken place at almost the exact same time as the barriers disappeared. The ritual required an enormous amount of mana to create a very special type of summoning circle. It was then that I set out for Kantinen to see what these supposed 'heroes' looked like with my own two eyes."

And that's when she met me, huh.

Come to think of it, Lia probably didn't realize I was one of those "heroes" who'd been summoned via that ritual, did she? I hadn't been marching with the other heroes when I sneaked up behind her outside the labyrinth. Even assuming she'd done a background check on me before she came here to meet Amelia (since I was one of Amelia's companions), she was more likely to come across rumors about me being a "monsterlord" or my "Silent Assassin" nickname than she was to find out I'd been brought here from another world. I was pretty sure Lingga was the only person on this continent who knew that, and I didn't find it likely he'd gone out of his way to inform a royal princess of that fact. But perhaps what made me surer of this than anything was that she became immediately hostile any time the subject of heroes came up, yet that hatred was never directed at me.

Maybe it would be a good idea to tell her the truth sooner rather than later.

My main reasoning for letting her tag along was that I wasn't sure just how powerful the demons would be, and I thought it would be nice to have someone with some defensive abilities on our side. It had always been my intention to do the fighting solo, so Lia backing out now wouldn't be the worst thing in the world. Besides, even if I did tell her I was one of those summoned heroes, she was in no position to do anything about it.

"My father was a simple accessories maker, and the royal family was quite fond of his work, so when the village was lost, they were more than happy to adopt me into their care. Though I think the fact that I was a guardian had plenty to do with it too," Lia finished. Then, upon seeing my perplexed face, she got flustered and went on. "Er, sorry! I kinda got a little carried away and scrambled up the order of events, didn't I? Anyway, there's my life story. I know it's pretty boring, so feel free to forget everything I just said."

Are you kidding me?! Like hell it's boring! I wanted to scream, but I held it in. Instead, I decided to ask her the biggest question still weighing on my mind. I'd decide whether to tell her about my hero status depending on her answer.

"Okay, so what is it you need to tell Amelia so badly? I realize I don't know the whole story here, but it doesn't seem to me like you two would have that much to talk about."

Given that Lia had merely been adopted into the royal family, and thus wasn't in the line of succession, it seemed highly unlikely that the two of them were already acquainted with each other, especially given that relations between the elves and the beastfolk were at an all-time low.

Lia hesitated for a minute before answering. "I came to warn her that we've received intel stating the Demon Lord has launched an offensive...for the express purpose of capturing her. He's after her Resurrection Magic."

I furrowed my brow. This was all getting so complicated that I wished Lia could write out a bullet-point list; not that it would be very easy to write at the moment, with Night moving at top speed, even if I'd had a pen and paper on hand.

"There it is, Master. The tenth-floor boss arena," Night said, interrupting for the first time since we'd entered the labyrinth.

I turned to look over my shoulder and saw the massive doors up ahead. "Damn, that was fast. Feels like we've only been in here a couple minutes..."

"Just who do you think you're talking to, Master?" Night huffed, then added, *"So, what's the plan?"*

"We're bustin' in," I said, turning to face forward. I closed my eyes and braced for impact.

"Copy that!"

Night burst through the doors without hesitation. Lia shrieked and clung to me once more.

"Shadow Magic... Remote Activation!"

The moment the door broke down, my eyes shot wide open. The already dimly lit arena was bathed in even deeper darkness. A moment later, it disappeared entirely. I smirked at the distinct feeling of power.

"Eek!" Lia squealed, catching sight of the desecrated carcass of what had once been the boss as Night dashed to the staircase leading to the next floor.

Until now, I'd only been able to activate my Shadow Magic using my own shadow and the shadows that overlapped it, but with the remote mana control I'd learned back in the Great Labyrinth of Kantinen, as well as my recent experience learning just how far my Shadow Magic could go, I was now able to make use of shadows completely distinct from my own, as long as they were in my field of view.

"You scared?" I asked over my shoulder. Night had already found the stairs leading down to the twelfth floor. His brisk pace was triggering all sorts of traps, but it didn't matter, since we were long gone by the time they went off.

"I'd be lying if I said I wasn't," Lia replied. "But I was the one who asked you to let me tag along, so I've got no room to complain."

I felt her fists tighten around my clothes. I could tell she was trying to act brave, but deep down she probably wished she were anywhere else; that was just the way people were designed—there was nothing we could do to escape that primal fear.

"Just who are you, anyway?" she asked.

I considered her question for a moment before answering. "Well, I guess you could say I'm Amelia's boyfriend, but more than that, I'm just a simple assassin who got summoned here against his will... That's right. I'm one of those heroes you so resent."

"Huh?!" Lia gasped.

As I gave her a minute to let this sink in, I mulled over what she'd just told me. So it was *Amelia* the Demon Lord was after, eh? I could have sworn it was me he wanted, but maybe he'd only sent Night to summon me to his castle in order to get Amelia there as well. But why was he after her Resurrection Magic? Was he on his deathbed and hoping it would save him? I had a hard time seeing why anyone would want to live in this messed-up world longer than their already ridiculous lifespan allowed, but maybe that was just me.

"So you were brought here via the hero summoning ritual?" Lia asked.

"Yep, that's right, and no doubt at the cost of your friends' and family's lives. How does that make you feel? Do you despise me now? Would killing me make you feel better?"

I knew it wasn't fair for her to hold something like that against me when I had no choice in the matter, but I also thought it would be good to at least try and show her some empathy. I certainly wasn't going to let her kill me, of course, but if she wanted to slap me or something, I was prepared to let her do it.

Yet it seemed I had underestimated the girl.

"No, there's no blood on your hands. I recognize the hero summoning ritual is unfair for both its victims as well as the people it summons. It's those villains over in Retice whom I'll never forgive."

It felt like I'd been emotionally suplexed. I could feel Night chuckling beneath me.

"Looks like you could learn a thing or two about maturity from her, Master."

"Oh, shut up, you," I grumbled, before turning back to face Lia again. This time, she adjusted to holding Night's fur without issue. "Let me ask you a different question, then: do you want to kill the *hero*?"

With how much spite I'd felt exuding from her the day we first met, I couldn't imagine she had zero desire for vengeance. She claimed to bear no ill will toward me, yes, but perhaps my classmate Satou Tsukasa, the hero at the center of it all, was a different story.

And just as I'd suspected, Lia nodded. "I do get that the hero didn't *choose* to be summoned either, but..." She faltered, hanging her head. I guess it wasn't that easy for her to simply let go of those feelings. Personally, I didn't care much one way or the other whether that stupid hero got himself killed, so I certainly wasn't offended.

"Well, let's get back on topic, shall we? You came to warn Amelia, and her scent led you here, where you bumped into us, and now we're going to save her together," I summarized, rubbing my chin as I tried to get a handle on the sequence of events thus far.

"Yes, that's correct... Um, actually, could I ask you a question?" Lia asked hesitantly, and I gave her a little nod without looking up. "Do you know who kidnapped her?"

"We do. It was a demon by the name of Aurum Tres."

Lia's eyes grew wide as I bit my lip in anger. The fact that she'd been kidnapped by a demon meant it the Demon Lord himself had likely given the order. And since Aurum Tres was the demons' third-in-command, that meant it really only *could* have been the Demon Lord—or his second-in-command—who'd sent him here. I still didn't know what exactly the Demon Lord wanted Amelia for, but I knew I wouldn't like it. We had to do whatever it took to rescue Amelia before they had a chance to whisk her off to his castle.

POV: AMELIA ROSEQUARTZ

M UCH TO MY DISMAY, the first thing I saw upon waking was not the piercing jet-black eyes of my beloved, but a big pair of vibrant emerald eyes instead.

"Oh, hey! You're awake!"

The sight of a creepy little boy smiling down at me woke me right up. I tried to get away, but try as I might, my body wasn't moving the way I wanted it to.

"Whoops, sorry! You actually can't move a muscle right now; I made sure of that. But it's for your own good! You just came back to life via your Resurrection Magic, so your body's really weak right now, y'know?"

I strained my neck to at least get a decent look at my surroundings. I wasn't being restrained by chains or ropes—my body had simply been rendered incapable of moving, perhaps by some sort of magic. I recognized the feeling of the sandy dirt against my cheek. It was a different place, to be sure, but the atmosphere was nearly identical.

"A labyrinth?"

THE GREAT LABYRINTH OF BRUTE

"Got it in one! You're very observant, Princess." The boy nodded happily.

I glared at him. I felt like he'd told me his name before he killed me, but I hadn't exactly been in the mood to memorize it at the time, and I had promptly forgotten. The boy continued grinning like an idiot—my death glare hadn't fazed him at all.

"Well, jeez, you don't have to look so ticked off about it. Kind of a waste of such a pretty face, don'tcha think?"

I gritted my teeth at the boy's obnoxious demeanor. My body still wouldn't move an inch. All I could feel was the cold, hard ground against my cheek and the aching pain in my back from laying on my side on such a rugged surface.

The little boy trotted closer to me. "What did I just say? You can't move right now. His Majesty said not to put a scratch on you, so I had to do *something* to keep you in pristine condition," he said, waltzing around a bit before shoving his face directly in front of mine. "Y'know, I always wondered what would happen if I used my monster-controlling abilities on an elf, a human, or a beastfolk. And thanks to you, now I finally know!"

He was within arm's reach of me now, and I couldn't do a thing about it. It was entirely possible that he was too strong for me to fight on my own anyway. I couldn't even run and hide. A weakling like me didn't deserve to be Akira's partner.

"They didn't allow me to actually control you, per se, but the fact that I was able to stop you from moving entirely is quite interesting. You elves generally have quite a bit of mana, after all. Second only to us demons, of course." He smirked before stepping away.

I cared less about his stupid research and more about what Akira might say when he saw me incapacitated like this. If he decided I wasn't fit to accompany him, I didn't know how I would go on living... No, now wasn't the time to get trapped in a negative spiral. I needed to try to squeeze as much intel out of this little boy as possible.

"Why are we in the labyrinth?" I asked, and the boy's eyes twinkled with delight.

Apparently he'd been hoping I'd strike up a conversation with him. The demon really was just a little boy at heart, even if he was hundreds of years older than me.

"Yeah, so get this! My, um...superior, I guess you could say? He's the demons' second-in-command. Anyway, he knows how to use magic circles like nobody's business, and he made a teleportation circle so we could warp straight into this here labyrinth and sneak into the country. In order to warp back home, we've gotta go aaaaall the way back to the bottom of the labyrinth and use that same teleportation circle. Honestly, I dunno why he had to put it all the way down there, y'know? I mean, I guess he's just being overly cautious, but still."

Amazingly, the boy didn't hesitate before divulging a mountain of what probably should have been confidential information, and my jaw dropped—well, not literally, since I couldn't move, but in spirit. So the second-in-command was a master of magic circles, was he? And he could make them strong enough to teleport all the way from Volcano to Brute. Not quite as unbelievable as the one that had warped us from Kantinen to the Sacred Forest, but still pretty impressive. If he could create them on the spot to warp even short distances, then he could probably teleport right into your blind spot and get you from behind.

As long as the circle was drawn quickly and enough mana was channeled into it, the method could be much faster than casting by incantation. On the flip side, circles used up much more mana, so they weren't an option for humans or beastfolk. Even elves barely had the mana to pull off the most basic of magic circles, and ones designed for teleportation were most certainly off the table. The demons had invented magic circles; it might have been accurate to say they were the only ones who could have invented them. The other races had long since given up their research efforts due to the enormous mana costs. Though I had heard of one human researcher who supposedly found a way to mitigate the costs several years back, but he had been kidnapped by the demons before he could release his findings. No one knew where he was now, but most assumed he was dead.

"I know! What a pain in the butt, right? I totally agree," the boy continued. "The final boss monster was kind enough to give me a lift to the surface on my way up, but the moment my Monster Control wore off, he hightailed it outta there! So now we've gotta walk all the way back down. We're just taking a breather right now, though."

It seemed he'd interpreted my wide-eyed expression as a reaction to our circumstances and not his lack of restraint when it came to confidentiality. That suited me well enough.

"How many floors until the bottom?" I asked weakly.

"Mmm... I don't remember, honestly, but I wanna say about twenty? Oh, and I've been carrying you with the help of a little levitation magic, in case you were worried about that!"

We were probably on the eightieth floor, then. If he rode Night the whole way, Akira might be able to make it in time... assuming they were coming for me at all, of course. If I had to die, I wanted it to be with Akira by my side. While I had no intention of dying just yet, I had to admit things were looking pretty bleak. All I could was try to keep this boy in a good mood and get more information out of him.

God. Some spirit medium I am. If I'm supposed to be able to make the world bend to my will, then how the heck did I get into this mess? I'd never really understood how my divine class was supposed to work, nor why it had chosen me, of all people. Other classes had it easy... Assassins assassinated, and wind mages used wind magic, but no one could even tell me what a spirit medium was supposed to do. There were hardly any records of past spirit mediums anywhere.

All my life, I'd had everything handed to me on a silver platter as the heir apparent, while my sister was laser-focused on pursuing the art of the sword. I was jealous of her, to be honest. What did I have that I could say I was truly good at? It felt like everything I tried, I was only "pretty good" at. I'd never developed an intense passion for anything—maybe that sounded like a privileged, upper-class problem to the common people who were only trying to make ends meet. I couldn't help but yearn for something more—some greater purpose I could devote my life to. I envied Akira in that regard.

The demon boy, growing annoyed with my silence, began to pout.

"Hey, c'mon! Say something! Tell me about yourself or whatever. Feels like I'm doing all the talking here." The boy's face appeared in front of mine again, catching me off guard. His big, round, green eyes looked sullen and downcast. "Let's see here... You've got a little sister, right? The one that set the stage for me to throw that big ol' monster party all across the elven domain, right? I've got a little sister too, y'know! That's something we have in common. Why don't you tell me about yours?"

For a moment, I was taken aback by this revelation, but when I calmed down and thought about it, it made sense that demons would have siblings, parents, and loved ones like any other race. The other three races taught their children from birth that the demons were an evil race to be feared. In stories and plays, the demons were always the villains, and they were never painted in a sympathetic light. Of course, plenty of innocent people had died at their hands over the course of history, but the stories were still propaganda designed to brainwash us into thinking of them as villainous beings incapable of love, which probably didn't seem all that fair from the demons' point of view. That just went to show how afraid of the demons the other races were. Even I had to admit my mental image of them was of heartless and unapologetic killers, so my brain was having a hard time reconciling that lifelong perception with the knowledge that this little demon boy had a little sister he loved very much.

"My sister's a very strong woman," I began. "Though recently I learned she's actually quite fragile deep down."

I now knew just how jealous of me she truly was—she resented me to the point of trying to have me killed. But I'd always been just as envious of her. If she hadn't gone off the deep end, I probably would have done it myself sooner or later.

"When she realized she had a natural affinity for swordsmanship, which is a rarity among us elves, who generally only use long-range weapons, she practiced tirelessly day and night so that she could protect our bow-wielding countrymen."

Every day, I'd watch her head off to the labyrinth in the morning, and every night, she'd practice her technique against a dummy tree. I never understood what compelled her to work so hard at it. She probably wanted people to treat her as well as they treated me, to recognize her as equally valid. We were sisters born only minutes apart, but to her it must've felt like she was a totally different species just because she came out of the womb second.

"She's a gold-rank adventurer too. In terms of pure combat prowess, not even you demons would have an easy time against her."

"So how come you just said she's fragile?" the boy asked.

I sighed, embarrassed with myself. All this time, I'd been harboring the exact same feelings of inadequacy that Kilika had been dealing with. How had I not realized it sooner? "She was jealous of me. Though she did an excellent job of hiding her envy from me and my father," I said.

Everyone always said our personalities were nothing alike, but I disagreed. Perhaps they would have changed their tune if they'd seen my heart was plagued by feelings of jealousy too.

"But then one day, she lost it, and I realized for the first time that she wasn't the infallible, self-confident girl I thought I knew. She threw a tantrum like a crying child begging to be acknowledged, deceived our father, and brainwashed our countrymen. All because she was jealous of the attention I'd always gotten."

Even that, I was a little jealous of. The version of Amelia the elven people wanted to see would never be permitted to do such a thing. All my life, I'd denied myself the right to act or even think in a way the common people might find unbecoming of their princess.

"That's when I realized just how fragile Kilika truly was."

What did that say about me? Was Kilika weak simply because she'd lost control of the emotions she'd bottled up for years? If that was the case, then I was even weaker than she was, because I simply held on to those feelings of envy and never mustered up the strength to act on them.

"Gotcha... See, I only remember bumping into *you* all those years ago in the Sacred Forest, so I was wondering what your little sister might be like. Okay, my turn! Let me tell you about *my* little sister now."

The boy's eager inflection cast a bright light on the darkness that had fallen over my thoughts. I had to admit, I was pretty interested to know what other people's sibling relationships were like.

"My little sis is really talented! When it comes to controlling monsters, she's even better than I am! Maybe even the best of all demonkind!" the boy boasted, his eyes glimmering with pride. His emerald eyes lit up the dark and desolate labyrinth like the rays of the sun. "Man, I really love my little sis... Er, not in a weird way or anything! Just as a family member, obviously. But sometimes, it kinda feels like she hates my guts. She's always ignoring me and stuff."

The sun went dark; the peaks and valleys of this boy's emotions came and went like a raging storm. This was a bit much for me, since neither Akira nor I were particularly expressive, and Night was even less so. I'd recently learned how to tell more or less what they were thinking by the look in their eyes.

"And, well, you know me. I figured maybe she found me too obnoxious or something, so a little while ago I decided I'd try to give her some more personal space and see how that went."

There'd been a period when Kilika and I kept our distance from each other as well—though that might have been more a result of our lives being extremely busy and our schedules never lining up. When we finally saw each other for the first time in almost a year, we both broke down and cried. Those were the days... That was back before Father wiped all memory of Kilika from the minds of the people.

"But get this: then my sister started following me around *everywhere* all of a sudden!" The boy snickered. He looked nothing like the demon who had relished in murdering me; even I, as an outsider, could tell he loved his sister an awful lot. "And so I was like 'What gives? I thought you hated me!' And she was like 'Huh? When did I ever say that?!' The look on her face was so priceless! God, Luné's so cute. Though lately she's started ignoring me again for whatever reason."

Oh, so she was just like Crow, then—she put on a tough, prickly facade, but was really a big softie deep down. Akira once said something about this being a popular "character archetype" (whatever that meant) back in his home country, and ever since, I'd been noticing I knew a lot of people who fit that mold.

I was amazed at just how carefree this boy was being, laughing it up with me after ordering his monsters to kill me. He seemed pretty personable and easy to talk to (certainly more so than Akira); I'd always had the impression that demons were emotionless drones, yet this boy was anything but.

"Does every demon laugh as much as you do?" I asked.

The boy laughed yet again. "Oh, Luné doesn't laugh too much, and His Majesty's a bit of a stick in the mud too. Cyrus, our fourth-in-command, is always pissed off about something or other. I guess there's Mahiro. He's the second-in-command, and he laughs from time to time."

Why was he smiling and laughing as he divulged all of this valuable information to me? I started to feel a little uneasy. He was supposed to be their third-in-command, right? Surely he wouldn't reveal so much intel to me unless he was confident I would never have the chance to share it.

"Now then, I think we'd better get a move on. I'm sure your friends will be hot on our tails. I've been taking it pretty slow, so it took me several days just to make it down this far... I think. Don't you just hate how there's no sunlight down in these places to tell you how much time has passed?" he said before standing up and placing a faintly glowing hand to my forehead. "Sorry, but I can't have you struggling, so I'm gonna have to put you to sleep for a bit, m'kay?"

As my consciousness began to fade, all I could see were his emerald eyes shining, as ever, like beacons in the darkness.

POV: ODA AKIRA

"W-WAIT, so, um...are you sure this Aurum Tres guy is a demon?"

I almost couldn't hear Lia's voice over the sound of the wind rushing past my ears, now that Night had kicked it into high gear. I had almost forgotten she was still sitting behind me, and it gave me a bit of a fright; I had a bad habit of getting lost in thought, though, so that was on me.

"Yeah, there's no doubt about it. Night told me so, and I felt the residual mana on the scene too. Nothing short of a demon would have been capable of leaving so much."

The place where Amelia's blood had been spilled had been overflowing with traces of a mana the likes of which I'd never felt before. If it were just in the blood, that would have been one thing, but I had tasted the mana lingering in the air itself. Such a thing was usually impossible even for me, who had far more mana than even the average elf. It had to have been a demon.

"I see... The Demon Lord really is up to something, then. I dunno if the crown has changed hands, but I know the last time the demons attacked, they sent monsters flooding out from the labyrinths on every continent... It's very possible the attack was as much an attempt to kidnap Princess Amelia as it was a declaration of war."

I nodded, then asked Lia what might have sounded like a rhetorical question: "Why does the Demon Lord feel the need to attack the other races?"

Everyone here seemed to accept that the Demon Lord was the evil overlord of the world, and that the demons and monsters went around doing his bidding...but I'd never really sat down to think about why he felt compelled to invade and ravage the other continents. Was it a desire to conquer the world, or did he want to enslave the other races?

"I can't speak to what actually goes through His Majesty's head," Night began, *"but I can tell you the first Demon Lord originally only attacked the other races to exact revenge for his people, who had been forcibly exiled to the desolate land of Volcano."*

Right. I did remember Commander Saran mentioning that to me at one point. Something about how the other races didn't trust the demons due to their ability to control monsters, and so they drove them away to the nigh-uninhabitable continent of Volcano. I didn't have very fond memories of that particular part of my life in Morrigan, so my memories from then were a little hazy. I hadn't even lived in this world for a year, yet my friendship with the commander felt as if it had happened an entire lifetime ago.

Back then, I never would have dreamed I'd end up riding on the back of a giant monster with a beastfolk princess clinging to my back on our way to rescue an elven princess. What an eclectic cast of characters we'd amassed in such a short time. If you included Aurum Tres, then there was even a representative from each of the four races participating in the current predicament.

"I guess that makes sense. But what about the other Demon Lords throughout history? What were their justifications?" I asked.

Night nodded as he trampled a few monsters on his way to the next staircase. *"After the fall of the first Demon Lord, the other races of the world started to hail the first hero as the savior of the world, and they continued to portray the Demon Lord as the root of all evil in the stories and folklore passed down through the generations. Over time, a few misguided nincompoops even saw fit to make a pilgrimage to the Demon Lord's castle in the hopes they might follow in the first hero's footsteps. Some of them, either through special presence-concealing skills like yours or sheer brute force, even made it all the way to the royal bedchambers before being caught."*

My eyes widened. Who the hell did the Demon Lord hire to be in charge of his security detail?! What was it with this world and leaving their castles wide open to invaders?! The castle of Retice had been the exact same way!

"And I don't mean just a handful of times either. While I'm ashamed to admit it, it's not uncommon for demons to get cocky and grow careless because they feel like the other races could never pose a threat to them."

Night clarified these events had all occurred long before his lifetime, so he was only relaying what was in the castle records. We slaughtered the twentieth-floor boss while we were having this conversation, and this time, Lia didn't even bat an eye after all the carnage she'd witnessed thus far. We'd increased our pace significantly after the tenth floor. With any luck, we'd be able to make it to the bottom floor in a matter of hours. *Atta boy, Night.*

"But then, during the reign of one Demon Lord several generations back, one of these boorish invaders was foolish enough to murder the Demon Lord's wife," Night continued, his voice ringing loud and clear over the wind rushing past and the bloodcurdling screams of the monsters trampled underfoot. *"This king detested fighting in all its forms, mind you, and had never laid a finger on any human, elf, or beastman. So much did he despise meaningless wars that he even lowered himself in order to propose a peace treaty with the other races. He was a good, kindhearted king who loved his wife, his children, his countrymen, and his monsters. Yet just because he bore the mere title of 'Demon Lord,' his wife was assassinated."*

I understood exactly what Night was getting at, and I agreed it was unfair. I'd heard the relatives of murderers back home were often treated with a similar level of hatred by the rest of the world, subconsciously or otherwise, simply on account of being related to the killer.

"So what you're telling me is some dumbass wanted to play hero and tried to do it in the stupidest way imaginable." I sighed.

Society at large was generally quite predictable in this regard. People who did good things were heroes, and people who did bad things were villains. No one cared what their respective backgrounds were—all that mattered was whether you were good or evil. Once you'd been branded as one or the other, you'd be either lauded or hated for the rest of your days. But even if there were probably some people who were so diabolically evil that they were beyond redemption, something told me the vast majority of people labeled as villains only did the things they did because they truly felt they had no other choice.

"Correct... And after that, the Demon Lord retracted his peace treaty proposal, declared war against the entire beastfolk race, of which his wife's murderer was a member, and laid waste to two entire cities on the continent of Brute."

He'd responded with the fury of a thousand suns, essentially. According to Night, the murderer's family members were brought out and slowly tortured to death right before the man's eyes.

"Man, that's grim. The guy who killed the king's wife probably thought he was totally in the right to kill her too. Probably thought he'd come home and be hailed as a hero, when he was really sentencing his own family to a cruel and painful death."

I couldn't imagine having to watch my mom and Yui get tortured over a mistake I'd made. I'd much sooner be tortured instead.

"The other races of the world have feared the demons ever since, and chances are they'll never come close to a peace treaty again. So remember, Master: the demons are only 'evil' from the non-demons' perspective. It's important you understand that."

I couldn't see Night's face from my position, yet there was a sincerity in his voice I'd never heard before. I mulled this over a bit before responding. "Yeah, I dunno about all that. Guess I'll just have to see for myself." I shrugged.

I felt Night buck below me, apparently unsatisfied with my noncommittal response. I decided to clarify before he had the chance to get uppity about it.

"Hey, I never said I wouldn't listen to the Demon Lord's side of the story. I'm sure the old Demon Lord in your story really was a good, stand-up guy, but to be honest with you, I've kinda got a bad first impression of the current one due to the whole 'sent his cronies on a rampage killing countless beastfolk civilians to kidnap my girlfriend' thing. Just sayin'." I wasn't about to go destroying two entire cities over it, but I did feel like I had every right to pay him back for what he'd done. "If I find out he ordered this invasion, then I don't care what you say, I'm sorry—I'm not letting him off the hook for that. Are we clear?" I asked.

"*Yes, Master,*" Night responded.

I had a hunch that Night hadn't really written off the demons as much as he claimed, but that was understandable, given that the Demon Lord was the closest thing to a parent he had. Now that the guy had kidnapped Amelia, though, there would be no mercy for him. The sob story about the old Demon Lord's wife was sad and all, but this was a different matter. I might reconsider it if Amelia forgave him herself, though.

An awkward silence fell between Night and I before it was broken by Lia. "Wow, I didn't know that story at all. I wonder if the beastfolk royalty at the time tried to suppress it or something. There are certainly records of the Demon Lord you spoke of, but that peace treaty you mentioned is presented as having been a ruse to get us to lower our guard so they could attack..."

Yeah, no duh they censored that story. Are you kidding me? I could see why they would want to keep that information from getting out, but the thought of them just twiddling their thumbs and hiding the truth from their people to deepen their existing prejudices pissed me off to no end. God, why did it feel like no matter what world you were in, people couldn't just learn to live in harmony and stop being jerks to one another?

"Look, I don't really care that much who was in the wrong and who was in the right in that specific instance, all right? Not like the truth really matters all that much in a world where memory-wiping magic exists... If you really want me to believe something, I'm gonna need more than just words. You've gotta let me see it with my own eyes."

Take me, for example. I was going around telling everyone I was an assassin, yet I had yet to kill a single human, elf, or beast-folk. I didn't have the will or desire to do so either. I was strong enough, sure, and I had plenty of powerful magic at my disposal, but I just didn't have it in me. I didn't want to kill or be killed. I knew that likely wouldn't fly forever. Sooner or later, I was gonna have to make up my mind and pick a side.

I wondered what Kyousuke would do if he were in my shoes.

We didn't talk much for the next few hours as we made our way all the way down past the seventieth floor. Night seemed to realize I was running a little low on mana after casting Shadow Magic so many times since we'd entered the labyrinth, so he'd been mercilessly crushing boss after boss to pick up my slack. I couldn't help but feel kind of sorry for the poor little things. At long last, someone had made it to their respective boss arenas and they would get their time to shine...only to be squashed in a matter of seconds. And by a fellow boss monster, no less. If that wasn't the epitome of cruel irony, I didn't know what was.

But after we passed the seventieth floor, things got a lot more intense, and I had more important things to worry about than sympathizing with monsters. All of a sudden, the mana in the air started to feel a lot thicker—and a lot more demonic. The mana density was such that the average human likely would have struggled to even breathe down here. How could anyone, even a demon, leave *this* much residual mana in the air just by passing through? I figured it would be wiser to just focus on recovering Amelia and give up on the idea of exacting my revenge against the demons.

"I'm gonna use Shadow Magic this time, Night," I said as we approached the next boss arena.

"Very well, Master. I'll leave it to you," Night replied reluctantly.

The defense and HP of the boss on the seventieth floor had been higher than we expected, so a single trouncing from Night wasn't enough to kill it off. This forced him to change course and swivel back around at high speed to deal the finishing blow, which sent Lia flying from his back with the change of momentum. It took quite the sturdy opponent to withstand a full-speed body blow with all of Night's weight behind it, and if the seventieth-floor boss was strong enough to handle it, I could only assume the eightieth-floor boss would be as well. As soon as we burst through the doors, I began to cast Shadow Magic using the shadows in the arena to prepare an immediate attack.

"Shadow Magic, activate!"

"What in the world?! Master, wait! Don't do it!" Night yelled, but it was too late. My shadows were well on their way to the boss monster in the center of the arena (which looked like a shark that had grown limbs and a pair of wings for good measure).

"Wha?!"

Just as the shadows were about to pierce the monster's chest, they vaporized.

"Oh, come on! Don't tell me this thing's immune to magic!" I whined.

"Unfortunately, it is." Night sighed. *"Its name is Poseidon, and it is a master of both land and sea. As you suspected, it's immune to all forms of magic."*

Yikes. You mean to tell me they gave Night a crappy name like "Black Cat," but this guy gets to be freakin' Poseidon?! And again, what's with all the Greek mythology names?! I'm pretty sure the Poseidon from legend wasn't a weird anthropomorphic shark monster. And if he's supposed to be a ruler of the seas, what the hell's he doing so far underground?!

"Man, I can't stand sharks. They just remind me of that one amusement park ride I got traumatized by as a child."

It wouldn't have been nearly as bad if we hadn't gone at night. At least during the day, you could sort of predict where the shark was gonna come from, but nope, it just sneaked up in the dim light... My mom insisted we go on the ride and offered to buy a stuffed animal Yui was begging for in exchange for us riding it with her. I still remember my dad and Yui playing around with those shark masks they sold at the souvenir shop. That had been our one and only family vacation.

I'd been afraid of both sharks and the ocean ever since. Shallow water I could deal with, but being in any large body of water where I couldn't see the bottom made me sick to my stomach. I'd been pretty shaken for the whole ship ride from the elven domain to the beastfolk continent, though I'd tried not to let it show. I'd wanted to be brave in front of Amelia, but I had been unable to stop sweating, and I'm sure she noticed my hands shaking.

Without the ability to use Shadow Magic, I'd have to get up close and personal with my trauma and take the monster out with close-quarters combat.

"I'm sorry to hear that, Master. But if we can't defeat it, we'll never catch up to Lady Amelia in time. Aurum Tres could reach the bottom any minute now."

"I know," I said, chills running down my spine. *This is all for Amelia's sake. I can handle a shark or two for her, no sweat.* I drew the two daggers Crow had forged for me from the Yato-no-Kami.

"GRRREEEEEAAAAAAGH!"

Mr. Sharkface let out a disgusting wail before lunging at us. When it opened its gaping mouth, I saw rows upon rows of razor-sharp teeth lining its maw—I certainly didn't want to get caught between those jaws. I gripped my daggers tightly.

"Humph!"

The giant beast reached out with a massive hand to try to grab me. I dodged and ran up its arm. It fired a few blades of water magic at me to try to stop my ascent, but I easily evaded those as well. Then I drove my twin daggers deep into the monster's hide.

POV: LIA LAGOON

IT WASN'T AS IF I had *no* combat experience, but this boy was on a different level. Before becoming a member of the royal family, I'd made a living by going on hunts with the other villagers. While I didn't have any special skills or adventurer ranks to show for it, I did feel I'd garnered a fair amount of experience. Hence why I'd come to the labyrinth with no backup.

"What in the world..." I muttered in amazement as I beheld the scene playing out before my very eyes.

The boss lay in a heap on the ground with its wings plucked, and one of its legs had been carved off and sent flying off into the wall, where it crumpled into a formless lump of meat. Perhaps most notably of all, the beast's fearsome shark-like head had been removed from its body, leaving nothing but a bloody stump. I shifted my gaze and found the head rolling around on the ground nearby, wearing a baffled expression.

I couldn't blame the beast either, as it had happened so fast even I wasn't sure what I'd just seen. The last thing I was sure of seeing was Akira brandishing his two black daggers, then the beast's head was severed, and its wings and one of its legs were gone as well. I prided myself on having pretty good vision, but even I hadn't been able to follow the action.

"Was that really your doing, Akira?" I asked in wonder.

"Uh, yeah? Who else could it have been?" he asked, blood splattered all over his body.

He was right, of course. Rationally, he was the only person who *could* have done it, since it hadn't been me or Night. "Right, uh... I guess I'm just having trouble believing those little daggers could slice through a neck as thick as a giant tree trunk in the blink of an eye, that's all." It felt a bit like my understanding of what was and wasn't possible had just shifted, and that was terrifying.

"Master, you need to understand your movements are far too fast for the average person to follow. Why, it even took me a while to grow accustomed," Night explained on my behalf.

I'd grown a lot less afraid of the feline monster over the past few hours, despite his reputation as the Nightmare of Adorea. I could only assume the rumors about him had been blown out of proportion. He did seem to be every bit as powerful as they claimed, but as far as I could tell, he was less of a city-destroying monster and more Akira's loyal kitty cat.

"Huh, really?" Akira asked, genuinely surprised by this as he clambered back onto Night's back. "Well, you're right to think these little daggers couldn't take off that big lug's neck all by themselves, but here's a little hint for you: just because something's immune to magic doesn't mean it's immune to *mana*. You with me now?"

Unfortunately, I was still pretty lost. I mean, I'd never heard of anyone using mana by itself before. My understanding was that mana was the fuel that made magic work, just like a fire needed kindling. And similar to how kindling couldn't burn without a spark, I always assumed mana wasn't capable of inflicting harm without a spell to ignite it.

"I guess since magic channels mana, I sort of figured anything immune to magic would be immune to mana by default," I replied.

"Not a bad theory, but magic and mana aren't one and the same. Magic is a specific phenomenon that's *brought to life* by mana, but there's no mana in the magic itself. So being immune to magic doesn't say anything about your resistance to mana... At least, that's how I understand it."

In other words, I needed to stop thinking of magic as a channeled form of mana—and start thinking of mana as a form of energy expended in order to *create* magic. In that case, my fire and kindling analogy was still pretty apt.

"Okay, it's starting to make sense to me now. But where in the world did you learn how to control raw mana?" I asked. Perhaps he was self-taught. I'd heard that the Hero of Legend was supposedly capable of a similar feat, but no one else who ever tried had been able to figure out how he did it.

"I didn't 'learn' it anywhere. I was forced to figure it out for myself."

"O-oh? You don't say," I replied casually after picking my jaw up off the floor.

For the first time in my life, it felt like I was speaking to a bona fide prodigy. He proceeded to go on a rant about how "Amelia forced me to try to take out a white bat without using my Shadow Magic," but I was hardly listening by then. If he'd just randomly figured out something only the Hero of Legend had ever been known to be capable of, then did that mean he possessed the same level of potential as the strongest person who had ever lived in this world?

"Akira, are you *sure* you're really just an assassin?"

I'd heard rumors claiming the current summoned hero was proving to be quite the layabout and hadn't even left the humans' castle yet. That was another reason I felt like I could forgive Akira but not the hero—he seemed to feel no remorse nor sense of duty. Even though I recognized it hadn't been his choice to get summoned here, he was still supposed to be the hero. But apparently my family members had been sacrificed for a lazy oaf who just sat around the castle doing nothing. *Akira* should have been the hero, if you asked me.

"I'm definitely an assassin. I can assure you of that much... even if I haven't technically killed anyone yet. And even if I don't really fight like one," he replied, his shrewd and discerning eyes peering deep into mine; it felt like he could see straight through me. "Now c'mon, let's get moving."

Even after killing the eightieth-floor boss so quickly, his fire was still burning bright. Something told me that nothing in this world was capable of stopping this boy except maybe the demons, and he still seemed to be seeking out ways to attain more power.

"What...what are you really after, Akira? What is it that you seek?"

"A way home."

CHAPTER 5

Demons

POV: ODA AKIRA

HAVING SLAIN the eightieth-floor boss without much issue, the three of us quickly made our way down to the ninetieth floor. The boss there was a big, golem-like creature, also immune to magic. Since my twin daggers wouldn't be of much use against a walking rock wall, I had to resort to using mana once again to take him out. But then I got careless, and the golem used its final breath to hit me with a mighty body slam. Thankfully, Lia cast a barrier on me at the last second, so I made it out unharmed—if that attack had hit me with its full force, it likely would have shattered every bone in my body. The lower-floor bosses were not to be messed with.

"Just three more floors, and we'll be at one hundred, eh?" I asked as Night dashed into the ninety-eighth floor. I had to assume he was approaching the limits of his stamina too.

"Master... I think I can make it the rest of the way, but I doubt I'll be able to assist you in the battle. You'll have to save Lady Amelia yourself."

I patted him on the neck to reassure him that he'd already done more than enough.

"Hey, Lia?" I asked. "Could you cast barriers on Night and me, just to be safe? And on Amelia too, once we get there? Don't forget to cast one on yourself, as well."

Considering I was about to go toe-to-toe with demons, I figured there was a good chance of them getting caught in the crossfire. Perhaps I was worrying too much, but I figured a little insurance couldn't hurt.

"You got it!" she replied.

I could feel the demonic presence getting closer and closer; I was sure we'd run into them any second now. The mana in the air was so thick that it was making me nauseated, but the effect was relieved a bit after Lia cast her barriers.

"Aha! There they are!" yelled Night.

At last, we had managed to chase down the demon by the name of Aurum Tres. He was a short-statured boy with green hair and matching eyes wearing a devilish little smile. Even through the barrier, I could feel the overwhelming might of his mana; Night had told me what to expect, and he hadn't sold Aurum short.

And right there, by the demon's side, levitating just slightly off the ground, was Amelia's limp and unconscious body.

"Well, hey there!" the boy cried excitedly. "Didn't think you'd actually catch up to us in time! I mean, you were out cold from mana exhaustion for at least three days straight, weren't you?"

I didn't answer. It seemed the boy's personality was about as mature as his appearance.

"Although I guess I shouldn't have expected any less from *you*, Black Cat," the boy went on. "Pretty smart of you to take Speedah's form to tap into his trademark speed, but you must be way too tuckered out from all that running to fight now, huh? Surely you don't think a mere human and a beastgirl will be enough to take on a demon, right?"

Whoa, whoa, whoa. Back it up. I've got plenty of choice words for you, young man, but before we get to that: are you telling me the Demon Lord had a pet cheetah, and he named it Speedah*?! What is with this dude and his penchant for awful names?! Poseidon was the only one thus far that was even remotely decent, even if I had plenty of other problems with his design! But anyway!*

"You sure love to hear yourself talk, don't you, kid?" I shot back. "Yes, I'm a human, and she's a beastgirl, and we're here to take you on. You got a problem with that, punk?"

"Uh, excuse me? A human and a beastgirl combined still isn't much of a threat, y'know. Didn't history teach you that your kind can't win against us demons? Maybe if you were the hero, it'd be a different story, but you just look like a plain old assassin. And that beastgirl hiding behind you can't even fight!" Aurum's cackle turned into a hearty belly laugh. I gripped my twin daggers in both hands. "Heh heh heh! Y'know, I was planning to just kill you and get it over with, but I think I've changed my mind! I'll torture you to death in front of your beloved Princess Elfie. That way, she can suffer right along with you. It'll be like killing two birds with one stone!"

His smile disappeared and the room became deathly quiet. Lia, trembling, hid behind Night's legs.

"Go ahead and try, kid. I've never even seen a demon before. Try to at least make this interesting for me, will ya?"

Aurum was standing in front of the stairway leading down to the ninety-ninth floor. I needed to ensure he didn't escape. I told Night telepathically to try to block the exit when he got a chance, then gripped my daggers tightly and used World Eyes to take a look at Aurum's stats.

AURUM TRES	
RACE: Demon	**CLASS:** Spearmaster (Lv. 70)
HP: 35000/35000	**MP:** 20000/28000
ATTACK: 42000	**DEFENSE:** 21000
SKILLS:	
Weaponcraft (Lv. 7)	Polearms (Lv. 9)
Swordsmanship (Lv. 8)	Buff Up (Lv. 9)
Detect Danger (Lv. 9)	Detect Presence (Lv. 9)
Intimidate (Lv. 9)	
EXTRA SKILLS:	
Monster Control	

I almost gasped, but I managed to hold it in. It seemed I'd underestimated just how powerful a demon could be. We were about the same level, yet his basic stats were significantly higher than mine, and he seemed to be skilled with swords as well, despite being a spearmaster. The only saving grace was that he didn't appear to have any sort of magic at his disposal.

My palms were sweating. I was talking a big game, but this

was the first time since arriving in this world that I'd felt genuinely threatened by an imposing foe. I wasn't shaking in my boots or anything, but I was definitely mentally preparing myself for the chance that I might die. *Should I use Conceal Presence just to be safe? No, that wouldn't sit right with me. I need to face this prick head-on!*

"I'm gonna shut that annoying mouth of yours for good, kid," I announced.

"Not before I rearrange your ugly mug," he shot back.

After a moment's pause, we both kicked off the ground and charged at each other.

CLANG!

The sound of metal striking metal reverberated through the corridor. The wind howled violently around the spot where we'd clashed. Aurum was now wielding a long, thin spear he'd produced seemingly out of nowhere. Behind our crossed weapons, I saw his eyes widen. Then he grinned, pleasantly surprised.

"Well, well. Looks like you can talk the talk *and* walk the walk. You're the first human who's ever managed to block one of my attacks. This might turn out to be kinda fun!"

He pushed out of the weapon lock, sending me flying—I managed to twist my body around in midair and land on both feet. I couldn't believe the amount of power this boy wielded in his shrimpy arms; he might have been the strongest person I'd met in this world—maybe even stronger than Commander Saran.

"No time to stop and think! C'mon, let's keep it up!" the boy said, his childish voice growing madder by the minute. His pupils were dilated and burning brightly. This little boy was a berserker at heart.

"Ngh!"

As the boy leapt at me with another downward thrust, I crossed my daggers to block his spear, but the earth beneath me shattered with the resulting impact, and my feet sank a little way into the ground.

"Ha ha! Gosh, there aren't even many *demons* who can last this long against me!"

"Aw, thanks... I'm so *flattered*!"

I mustered all of my strength and deflected his spear to the side. *Okay, playing it defensively and going for counters clearly isn't working. It's about time I went on the attack.*

POV: AMELIA ROSEQUARTZ

A S I LAY THERE, floating within a sea of unending darkness, I thought I heard Akira's voice, followed by what felt like two clashing egos, both out for blood. These things combined to wake my weary consciousness from its torpor.

"Aki...ra... Akira...?"

I sensed him nearby. I could feel earth-shattering shockwaves causing the walls around me to crumble, but I remained unharmed.

"Ha ha! Looks like Sleeping Beauty's finally awake!"

A child's voice rang in my ears. I recognized it as the voice of the green-eyed boy who'd taken me captive.

"Would you pick a nickname and stick to it?! What happened to 'Princess Elfie'?!"

"Gosh, you're dumb. Do you not pay attention to context, or what? Sleeping Beauty is the *perfect* nickname for a princess who's just woken up!"

I could hear their weapons clashing as the wall behind me trembled and quaked.

"This is no time to be referencing fairy tales, you stupid-ass kid! There's only gonna be a happily ever after for one of us, and it sure as hell ain't gonna be you!"

I blinked a few times, and finally the scenery surrounding me came into view. My body regained feeling; I could move my fingers again, and though my arms were still numb, I used them to prop myself up against the wall of the labyrinth.

"Akira!" I cried.

"Just stay right there, Amelia. Don't worry… I won't let him take you away from me again," Akira yelled back.

Without even turning to face me, he unclasped his cloak and sent it flying in my direction. As I wrapped it around myself, I was completely enveloped in Akira's scent, which calmed me down immediately. I moved slowly along the wall, and just as I felt like I was about to collapse again, something soft and fluffy propped me up. "Night?" I asked.

"Don't overexert yourself, Lady Amelia. Believe in Master and let him settle this."

Night gazed down at me with his warm, golden eyes. Even though he wasn't in his usual cat form, I could still tell it was him.

Using his tail, he enveloped my cold, weak body to help heat me up again. This, combined with Akira's reassuring scent, did wonders to relax my mind.

"I do. I believe in both you and Akira," I replied.

Akira, already bleeding from several wounds, was meeting the long spear of the little boy with his daggers, who was yet unharmed. Akira was clearly losing the battle, yet the fact that he was able to go toe-to-toe with a demon and only take a few cuts and scrapes was incredible.

"Akira looks like he's having fun," I observed.

"Master's abilities are far beyond those of any other man or beast in this world. He can kill just about any opponent in a single blow. Not that he would ever go around seeking opponents just for the sport of it, mind you," Night said, looking in their direction. Even though Akira was bleeding all over and probably in a lot of pain, he was grinning with delight. I'd never seen him actually *enjoying* a fight this much before. *"I can understand why he might relish the chance to test his abilities against someone who can actually put up a good fight. So much so that he can't help but crack a smile. If he really wanted to, he could probably use Conceal Presence and take the boy out like any other foe, but he's intentionally chosen to fight him fair and square. Master tries very hard to tell himself he gets no thrill out of fighting, yet it's plain to see that he most certainly does."*

I couldn't deny it. He clearly *was* enjoying it. It almost reminded me of Kilika, training tirelessly day and night to hone her swordsmanship.

"I'm a little jealous," I admitted quietly, letting my true feelings slip out. I hoped Night hadn't heard.

"What's the matter, buddy? You still haven't landed a single hit!" the boy teased. "Sure, it's cool that you've lasted this long against a demon and all, but what's the point if you're just prolonging the inevitable?!"

He had a point. While Akira hadn't suffered any grievous wounds just yet, he was still losing a lot of blood, and his face was starting to turn pale. His blood was coalescing in little puddles all across the ground in a pattern that looked almost intentional.

"That's where you're wrong," Akira replied. "I was just getting warmed up. Now my preparations are complete."

"Oh, please," the boy laughed, holding his hands out to his sides in a shrugging gesture. "What could you *possibly* still have up your sleeve?"

"Shadow Magic, activate!"

All of the shadows in the dimly lit corridor converged into one—not just Akira's and the boy's, but mine and Night's as well.

"Go!" he commanded, and the shadows dispersed and spread out across the ground.

I'd never seen this technique before. I'd only known Akira to be capable of using his own shadow. When had he learned how to control the shadows of the people around him as well? The shadows, meanwhile, seemed to be spreading out in a particular manner, as if they were being guided.

"*The blood...*" Night murmured. I looked around and noticed the shadows were indeed reconverging at the sites of the largest blood puddles scattered across the ground.

"They're reacting to the residual mana in Akira's blood and gathering in those locations…? Wait, no—are they recombining?"

Akira held out his hand, then clenched it into a fist. "Shadowbeast!"

The shadows atop the various blood puddles wriggled and squirmed out of the ground, taking on the shapes of four-legged, bloodthirsty beasts. The wolf-like specters charged the boy, deftly avoiding the wide sweeps of his spear, and started gnashing away at his legs, arms, and torso.

"Ngh!"

The boy spun around to shake off the beasts, tearing bits of his flesh away in the process. This time, it was the boy's blood splattering across the floor, and in far greater amounts than Akira's had.

All of a sudden, the tides had turned.

"Wow, kid. Your blood must be pretty tasty for them to be so ravenous. My Shadow Magic sends its compliments to the chef," said Akira as the wolves circled around him like loyal dogs awaiting their next command.

The boy simply stood there speechless for a while, gazing down at his own bloodstains on the floor. Then he suddenly began to laugh. "Heh heh heh! AH HA HA HA HA HA HA HA HA!"

Akira seemed taken aback by this, as he recoiled a bit. After a moment, the shadow beasts disappeared, seeping back into the ground before returning back to the feet of their respective owners.

"So this is what pain feels like... *This* is what my blood looks like..." the boy muttered, clutching at the geyser of blood shooting out from his belly.

As Akira and I winced at the sight of his descent into madness, Night simply looked down at the boy with an unaffected stare.

"While it's a well-known fact that demons have extremely high mana and attack power, it's not as commonly known that their defense is also much, much higher than any other race. Normal weapons won't even so much as scrape their skin, and even magic rarely proves effective... I knew several demons in my time at the castle who hadn't shed a single drop of blood for as long as they'd been alive."

If that was true, then I had to assume this boy's defense stat was very high, judging from his reaction. It looked to me like he was *delighted* by the sight of his own blood, like he was *enjoying* feeling pain, like there was some thrill for him in the knowledge that he was indeed mortal like any of the other races.

"Aha ha ha ha ha ha! Wow, this is incredible. The other demons are gonna flip when they find out there's a human like you to play with." The boy laughed, so lost in the throes of rapture that his spear fell from his grasp and clattered to the ground. With his other hand, he produced a small flute. "Okay, you got to do your special move. Now it's my turn."

One look at that flute, and the moment just before my death flashed back into my mind.

"No! Akira, get out of there!"

"Too late," the boy giggled as he raised the flute to his lips.

POV: LIA LAGOON

THE DEMON BOY named Aurum Tres blew into the flute, but it produced no sound. For some reason, Princess Amelia seemed insistent that it was very dangerous and that Akira needed to get the heck out of there. Heeding her warning, I turned to run away, but I discovered my legs wouldn't move. Perhaps my body was suffering from the effects of prolonged exposure to demon-tier mana, despite the barrier I had cast on myself. *Welp, I'm dead meat. This must be what frogs feel like when they realize they're about to become a snake's dinner.*

"You forgot that we demons can control monsters and order them to do our bidding," the boy said. "I can manipulate and use monsters as if they were extensions of my own body, even if they aren't directly under my employ."

Then, each and every wall around us opened up to unleash a horde of monsters. There weren't just a couple dozen, or even a hundred—this was a veritable army that probably numbered well over a thousand. This was my first time delving deep into the labyrinth, but I'd heard plenty of stories about all the lethal traps littered about its halls, and how if you weren't careful, you could get overwhelmed by a horde of beasts like this in an instant. Recalling these stories snapped me out of my stupor.

"Strengthen Spirit Barrier!"

All I could do at the moment was reinforce the barriers I'd already cast on my allies. I had been watching the previous battle from a safe distance, which unfortunately meant that I was now separated from the rest of the group by countless monsters. I grimaced as their disgusting faces closed in on me.

"No! Stay away from me!"

I pulled out a dagger in an attempt to fight them off, but these were high-level monsters from the deepest depths of the labyrinth, and my pathetic Short Swords skill (which the castle knights had forced me to learn) wasn't going to put a dent in them. I was sure Akira would do fine on his own, and Princess Amelia had Night with her, so they would probably be okay. Thankfully, it didn't seem like Aurum's powers were capable of superseding Night's pact with Akira and taking control of him.

That made me the weakest link in the chain. A small subset of the monsters was keeping Akira and Night occupied while the rest came after me. Monsters generally rushed at whoever was closest, but they seemed capable of complex thought and planning when a demon was around to give them orders.

"Sorry, gonna have to take you out first. Mahiro told me that if you let a guardian live, they'll only make things more annoying in the long run," said Aurum Tres.

He'd somehow made his way over to me without anyone noticing, and he was now grinning sweetly down at me from atop a large monster. The feeling of his overwhelming mana so close to me was enough to make my body quake, and I could no longer move my arms and legs. My dagger fell from my hand, clattering to the ground. I dropped to my knees and fell forward onto the cold, hard labyrinth floor. I could still move my eyes, with great effort, though all I could see was my impending death.

My life was on the line here, and I knew it. This was my punishment for insisting on warning Princess Amelia, for coming all the way down to this dark and desolate place despite my lack of strength. My life flashed before my eyes, and memories I thought I'd forgotten shot through my mind one after another, as if begging not to be left behind.

Right. I can't let their memories die with me. I can't let it all have been for nothing.

"I can't afford to die down here... I'm gonna live, no matter what it takes!"

As soon as the words left my mouth, I felt strength coursing through my body once again—I'd finally adjusted to Aurum's mana. With trembling arms, I lifted my upper body up off the ground. I scanned my surroundings and saw my trusty staff lying on the ground nearby—the staff that I'd never let slip from my grasp, not even for an instant, not when I fell off of Night, not when Akira grabbed me by the collar and tried to choke me...not even when my family died. It was forever my partner. I reached out and picked it up, then used it to support myself as I got shakily to my feet.

"Wow, you're still kicking, huh? Your death would've been a lot less painful if you'd just stayed conked out on the ground, y'know," the boy tutted.

Perhaps he was right. Maybe death would have given me some amount of relief—it would have at least freed me from this burdensome life I'd become obliged to bear.

"I can't die yet... Not until I see him again... Not until I can express how I feel..."

Seeing how deeply Akira obviously cared for Princess Amelia made me feel a mixture of both envy and regret. It made me wonder if I should have told *him* how I felt back when we went our separate ways; if there was anything more I could have done for him; if I would have ever gone as far for him as Akira had for Princess Amelia. Thinking back on it now, I'd virtually always been on the receiving end of things, and I had almost never acted based on my own convictions or emotions. If I had, it was only after I'd been brought into the royal family.

But after meeting and observing Akira, my self-perception had changed. I didn't want to be the one watching and envying others from the sidelines. I had to actually act on my emotions. Seeing Akira and Amelia's relationship only drove home just how pathetic and foolish I'd been for trying to snuff out my feelings. I'd been using *him* as an excuse to run away from myself.

"I won't run away anymore. I won't just go along with what others decide for me. I... I won't go back on my word ever again!"

The mana stone embedded in my staff began to glow with blue light. He had made me this staff from the mana stone of a monster he'd slain. With this staff in hand, I knew I had nothing to fear.

"I'm gonna see him again, no matter what it takes!"

I wanted to soothe his weary soul the way he'd soothed mine back when I was trapped and could think of nothing but revenge; the mana stone grew brighter in tandem with my convictions.

"Inverted Spirit Barrier!"

The mana stone grew brighter still, and my body began to glow as well. Judging by their surprised gasps, I could only assume that Akira, Night, and Princess Amelia were also experiencing the same phenomenon. This was a brand-new spell of my own design—a barrier I'd come up with after consuming volumes upon volumes of books in the castle library. I'd known all along that it was theoretically possible, yet whenever I'd tried it, a critical piece of the puzzle had always been missing. Now I knew what that missing piece was—it was my own conviction.

And now that I'd found it at last, the spell was complete.

"Huh, that's not a spell I've heard of any past guardians having. Interesting. Is this what Mahiro was afraid of? Doesn't look all that different from your usual barriers to me... Whatever. I'll just have to attack you and find out what it does!" Aurum said. He then barked an order to all of the monsters in my vicinity: "Kill her!"

All at once, I was besieged by a flurry of fangs, claws, and magic. But I didn't even flinch. I kept my eyes wide open, refusing to run and hide. I wasn't frozen in fear or succumbing to despair; I no longer had anything *to* fear. I took it all head-on.

"What the?!" Aurum gasped.

It was all over in the blink of an eye. When the light receded, all that remained in my field of view was Akira, Night (whom Amelia was probably hiding behind), and Aurum Tres's deliciously flabbergasted face.

POV: ODA AKIRA

WHEN AURUM BLEW into his flute, I felt inaudible sound waves reverberating through the corridor. He was still only one guy, even if he had the might of thousands combined. But there was strength in numbers too, and the monsters he summoned from within the labyrinth walls quickly surrounded and separated us. To make matters worse, Aurum rode one of the monsters in Lia's direction. I knew she had a small dagger for self-defense, but that wouldn't help her much against a demon and a horde of the labyrinth's most powerful monsters. Maybe Night, Amelia, or I could have held them off for a little while, but Lia just didn't have the stats.

I could have just used my Shadow Magic to clear the rabble out all at once, but as long as Aurum was still alive, it was too risky to consume such a huge chunk of my mana. If only I had a less costly spell, like Amelia's Gravity Magic...

"Gravity!"

Speak of the devil. Right on cue, her voice resounded through the corridor and squashed the monsters currently surrounding us like bugs. The area was cleared in an instant. I looked around and saw Amelia garbed in my cloak, leaning up against Night for support. *Right, I tossed that over to her in the midst of the battle, didn't I?*

"Amelia! Night!"

I leapt over the fallen monsters and dashed over to the two of them.

"I thought I heard you asking for my help," Amelia said, her face pained.

Wow, it's almost like she read my mind. I hadn't realized the spell would take so much from her, but she didn't seem to be in that much pain, so at least things had turned out all right.

"Yeah, you did great," I replied, running my fingers through her hair for the first time in a good while. At this, she nuzzled up to me like a purring cat. She must have been awfully scared and lonely without me.

"Look, Master. Our barriers are still in effect. Which must mean..."

Leave it to Night to get us back on track. I supposed Amelia and I might have gotten a little carried away with our reunion, but he was right—now was not the time. "Right, that means Lia must still be alive. If anything, it feels like our barriers just got stronger," I replied.

I tried to prick my arm with my dagger to test it out, but the weapon bounced right off, followed by a pale flash of light. Maybe now I could withstand more of Aurum's attacks. I was impressed; when we'd first entered the labyrinth, I'd thought Lia's abilities were pretty lackluster, but it seemed she'd just been saving up for the main event. The fact that she was still alive meant she was stronger than I'd thought, and according to Lia, she could feel when any of her barriers disappeared, so she had to know that we were still alive as well.

Nice. Then we're all still accounted for.

"Wait. Who's Lia? You're not cheating on me, are you?" asked Amelia, her ears having pricked up at the sound of another woman's name. She looked up at me with teary eyes.

How cute... Er, I mean... "C'mon, Amelia. You know I'd never cheat on you," I reassured her. "Lia's a guardian and a beastfolk princess. She came here to warn you that the demons were out to kidnap you... Obviously she didn't make it in time, but still."

"Oh, really? I've never met a guardian before."

Evidently, guardian was a pretty rare class. Maybe not as rare as spirit medium, but certainly not common. It often felt like I was surrounded by nothing *but* rare classes. Almost made the word lose all meaning to me.

"Well, guardian or not, she won't last very long against a demon," Night warned, and I nodded.

He was right again. We didn't have time to be standing around talking like this, but something told me that Lia would be just fine. Maybe it was the fact that my Detect Danger skill, which had become like something of a sixth sense for me, wasn't going off at all.

That being said, we didn't have any reason *not* to go help Lia out, and Amelia had already taken out all the monsters on our end of the corridor, so we headed over to flank the monsters surrounding Lia from behind. Luckily, Aurum hadn't realized we'd already cleared out so many of his goons, so we could sneak up on them without being noticed. Just as we were about to launch our attack, a powerful voice rang out from the center of the monster congregation.

"Inverted Spirit Barrier!"

A glowing light shot out from the middle of the horde of monsters, and our bodies began to glow as well.

"Wh-what's this?!"

"Calm down. It's not anything bad."

"Another barrier?"

As the three of us shared in our mutual confusion, Aurum ordered the monsters to descend upon Lia with all their might.

But after a moment of silence, the monsters assailing Lia all fell lifeless to the ground. The ones with sharp claws had scratch marks all over their bodies, the ones with giant fangs were covered in bite marks, and the casters seemed to have been singed by their very own magic. It seemed the monster's attacks had been reflected back at them.

"Well, well. Never seen a barrier used like *that* before," I marveled.

"Likely because it's never happened before. No guardian throughout history—that I know of—has ever been capable of anything like that," Night said, his eyes wide with awe.

"Dang. You think it's an original of hers, then?" I asked.

"You mean, she just created a new spell out of thin air? Even though she doesn't have Spellcraft like me?" Amelia asked, equally astonished.

I grabbed one of the few stragglers by the scalp and hurled it against the wall. It exploded in a gory mess. Amelia, meanwhile, picked off a few monsters trying to sneak up on Night from behind with a tiny bit of focused Gravity Magic. I looked over at Lia, and we made eye contact.

"Sure seems that way," I replied. "And she looks a lot more confident now than she did earlier."

As our gazes met, I sensed a newfound resolve in those cobalt-blue eyes of hers. Perhaps she'd found a new purpose in life in the face of certain death. The monsters that had been surrounding her were now utterly wiped out. All that remained was Aurum and the monster he was riding on.

"Would you all like to know a fun fact?" asked Aurum.

He was unfazed by the tables turning significantly in our favor. If anything, he seemed even *more* overconfident. My Detect Danger skill hadn't gone off earlier, but now it was ringing like crazy.

"We can control monsters even without that little flute, y'know. Maybe your traitorous kitty cat friend didn't know this, but the flute actually serves two distinct purposes. The first is that it allows us to give the monsters more precise orders," Aurum explained, then paused and looked over our heads with an ominous smirk.

"And secondly, it allows us to let our fellow demons know when we're in need of help, no matter how far away they might be," came an unfamiliar voice from behind us.

The moment we turned to see who it was, there was the sound of glass shattering, and the light enveloping our bodies suddenly began to fade. Our spirit barriers had all been broken simultaneously—no doubt the work of this newcomer.

"It's not like you to call for help," said the new voice. "How'd you get those wounds?"

Standing at the other end of the corridor was a young man with long black hair and eyes to match, whose youthful face was adorned by a pair of refined glasses. With his pale hands, he smoothed out his frizzled hair (though a single stray strand stuck defiantly up) and pushed his glasses up the bridge of his nose. He was grinning, yet his eyes indicated that he was anything but amused. His mana was incredibly overwhelming, and it sent a chill running down my spine. Lia had already passed out from its sheer magnitude.

"Sheesh, Mahiro! Took you long enough! And yeah, I know! I wouldn't have called you out here if I didn't actually need the help, silly!" said Aurum. His grievous wounds had done nothing to affect his childish personality, it seemed. His injuries would have certainly been enough to kill anything less than a demon, yet he looked right as rain. That had to be thanks to his substantial HP.

"I was wondering what was taking you so long. Didn't think you'd get tripped up by a bunch of kids. Come on, let's go," said the young man, who suddenly appeared directly behind us.

"What the?!" I gasped.

I'd been watching his every move extremely closely, so I had no idea how he could have slipped behind us without me noticing. There wasn't even any indication he'd used some sort of teleportation magic. It was obvious this guy was much more powerful than Aurum.

"Mahiro... He's their second-in-command. The little boy told me so," Amelia said.

So he *did* outrank Aurum, if only by a single promotion.

The young man by the name of Mahiro took a quick look at Aurum's wounds before shaking his head in disappointment and turning to look at me. "I guess he was no match for *you*, was he, Oda Akira?"

I tensed up. It had been a long time since I'd been called by my full name in proper Japanese order. This, combined with the young man's facial features, made me realize something. "Wait... You're Japanese too, aren't you?" I asked.

In this world, everyone went by their given name first, surname second, and since the language was different too, you could always tell when someone wasn't a native speaker from their accent. This guy had a very Japanese intonation, not to mention a very Japanese name.

"Yes, I suppose you could say that," he replied. "I'm a bit different from you and your group, but I am indeed Japanese. The name's Abe Mahiro. I'd say it's nice to meet you, but I'd be lying through my teeth."

A bit different from us? What did he mean by that? And if he was originally from our world, then how could he be a demon?

"Oh, dear, look at the time," Mahiro continued. "I'd love to stay and chat, but I'm afraid we'll need you to hand over the princess so we can be on our way now."

I stepped forward to put myself between him and Amelia. Night crouched into a combat-ready stance as well. I felt bad for leaving Lia in her unconscious state, but right now, I needed to focus on protecting Amelia.

"Good grief. You'd think the third-in-command would be able to handle kidnapping a single elven princess on his own, but apparently not. Just goes to show that if you want something done right, you have to do it yourself." Mahiro sighed, then clapped his hands together.

A piercing sound shot through the corridor, and when he pulled his hands apart again, strange runes came flying out of his palms by the dozens. They spun around him, then arranged themselves neatly in a circular pattern, forming a magic circle.

The symbols glimmered beautifully in the darkness, and I stood there mystified for a moment. It wasn't long before Mahiro sent his finished magic circle into action.

"Marionette!" he cried, channeling his mana into the magic circle. The circle glowed red before shooting through the air in our direction.

"Amelia, look out!" I screamed.

"Eek!"

I'd been prepared for him to target me, but the circle flew toward Amelia instead. I tried to warn her, but it was too late. The magic circle hit its mark, sending Amelia careening into a nearby wall. She crumpled to the ground, motionless.

"Damn it! Amelia!"

I dashed over to her and scooped up her limp body. Blood was pouring from a cut on her scalp, but it appeared she was still alive and was merely unconscious; any human would have surely died from the impact.

"You rat bastard!" I yelled at Mahiro.

"Dear me, has anyone ever told you that you've got the eyes of a common lowlife? Why, one look at your ugly mug and you've got me clutching my coin purse in fear!" the man said, trying to taunt me.

It worked—my blood was boiling.

"Don't let him get under your skin, Master," Night warned, having gone over to assist Lia.

I clenched my fists. I wanted to sock him right in the kisser, yet I knew deep down that I probably didn't stand a chance against him. I needed to get the hell out of here, and fast. Hell, the whole plan had been to rescue Amelia and run for our lives from the beginning, though Aurum had thrown a wrench in that idea.

"I take it you've officially marked yourself as a turncoat now, Black Cat?" Mahiro asked. "I don't want to get reprimanded later if you're on some undercover operation I wasn't briefed on."

Night changed back into his usual black cat form, then glared down at Mahiro with his beady golden eyes. *"Never again will I return to His Majesty's throne room, for I am Black Cat no longer. You may call me Night,"* he said proudly.

"Very well. Then I suppose I won't get in trouble if I skin you alive and make a nice fur coat out of you, will I?" Mahiro smirked, and Night gritted his teeth.

"I'd like to see you try."

POV: NIGHT

MAHIRO ABE.

A crafter of magic circles, an art form thought lost by the other races, and a man who surely numbered among the top two or three strongest I'd ever known. He had more mana than any other demon, and he was the only man who could rein His Majesty in whenever he lost control. And now I was baring my fangs at him. To be blunt, there was no way in hell I could defeat him, especially not after expending so much of my stamina running down here and suffering several injuries in the previous battle. I only had about enough mana left for one more use of

Shapeshifter. Even if I somehow eked out a victory against him, there would still be Aurum Tres to worry about, so I wasn't optimistic about my chances of making it out of here alive.

I turned around and looked down at Lady Amelia, who'd suffered a traumatic head injury, and Master, who was trying desperately to stop the flow of blood. These were the two who had saved me from my fate of dying a worthless death at the bottom of a labyrinth. Only Akira Oda was my master, yet Lady Amelia was just as important to me. I would never forgive anyone who injured her so gravely.

"Tell me, were you always this feisty?" asked Mahiro. "I seem to remember you being a good, obedient little kitty."

"You have harmed my master and the one he loves dearly. I have nothing more to say to you," I responded matter-of-factly.

"If you insist."

Mahiro brought his hands together again. When he pulled them apart, he gave birth to a magic circle of unfathomable, mind-boggling complexity. The fact that he could handle such a complicated conjuration all by himself, and with such blinding speed, was what made him the demons' second-in-command.

"If you had just died a lonely death like a good little servant down in that labyrinth, it would have never had to come to this... Such a shame," he lamented.

As the blinding light from his conjuration pierced my eyes, I tried to picture someone in my mind—an image of the strongest man I'd ever done battle with. The only man I thought might conceivably stand a chance against Mahiro.

"Night, is that...?" Master began, dumbfounded. I was impressed that he recognized the person I was shapeshifting into while I was still mid-transformation, and from behind, no less. But I supposed I shouldn't have expected any different. The man *had* met his end right before Master's eyes, after all.

"Well, well... If it isn't the late sage, Sir Saran Mithray," said Mahiro.

Standing now on two feet instead of four, with shining white armor on my back and long golden locks flowing in the air behind me, I glared over at Mahiro with cold, unfeeling eyes. I was now the very image of Master's savior and mentor, Saran Mithray.

"It takes an awful lot of mana to shapeshift into a person, you know. I'll need to recuperate for quite a while after this, so let's make this quick, shall we?"

As an animal myself, trying to take the form of a human required a Herculean amount of effort. I would have preferred not to take this particular form in front of Master, but the dire state of our current affairs hadn't given me much of a choice. I raised my left hand skyward and began to recite an incantation.

"O heavenly gavel, let thy judgment rain down upon those who would do my master harm! Hammer of Light!"

The dead man's light magic was unbelievably powerful, even for a sage, and it was honestly a bit hard for me to bear as a creature of the dark myself. But that went for Mahiro as well. The light collected in the air above my raised hand, and when I brought my elbow down, it condensed into the form of a mighty mallet; it was easy to imagine what an earth-shattering event it might be were I to bring that hammer crashing down.

"Bwa ha ha ha ha! Yes, that's the ticket! Oh, it's been ages since I last saw *that* one!" Mahiro cackled, clapping his hands together once more. This time, the magic circle he created was so massive, it would have likely taken well over a dozen mages to craft under normal circumstances. Yet there he was, a single demon, conjuring it in a matter of seconds.

"Storm Ruler! Golden Ray!"

He channeled mana into this new magic circle as well, as the one he'd conjured previously, to cast two distinct spells at once. My eyes widened upon hearing the names of these spells; they were both types of magic I'd witnessed before.

Storm Ruler was, as the name suggested, a spell capable of bringing thunder and lightning crashing down upon a wide area with such force that a single cast could bring an entire country to its knees. Golden Ray was a type of light magic whose strength was either on par with or exceeded that of Hammer of Light. And while demons had, with few exceptions, no propensity for light magic, a runic mage like Mahiro could imbue his magic circles with spells of any element he pleased. It was a skill of his that I had been quite thankful for back when we were allies, but I was deathly afraid of it now that we were fighting on opposite sides.

Just as I was about to bring down my Hammer of Light, intending to stop Mahiro from channeling mana into his magic circles, I heard a soft whisper echo through the corridor.

"Shadow Magic, activate."

"Master?!"

I spun around to see Master drape his cloak over Amelia and lean her against the labyrinth wall before ruffling her hair and turning back toward the center of the action. "I can't let you do this alone, Night," he said. "And besides, all this extra light is perfect for my purposes."

It was true—the light from my Hammer of Light and Mahiro's magic circle had the auxiliary effect of casting enormous shadows all across the formerly dim corridor. It seemed Master had realized my Hammer of Light and Mahiro's Golden Ray were comparable in strength and would only cancel each other out. This meant I'd be leaving us wide open for his Storm Ruler area-of-effect spell to kill us all, and we couldn't have that I would sacrifice myself to protect them from the spell if it came down to it.

"If you die, I die too, remember?" Master said. "I'm afraid I'm not ready to give up the ghost just yet. You just focus on your own spell. I'll try to do something about his."

I had been prepared to give my life for Master all along. We would simply need to terminate our pact, and he could survive. Maintaining a master-familiar bond required both parties mutually agreeing on the pact, after all. If I wished to annul it, then it would lose its efficacy, and as long as Master didn't stubbornly insist on maintaining the pact, then either of us could die without affecting the other.

However, he seemed insistent on keeping me alive.

"If you think I'm gonna let you die here without telling me

how you knew the commander, you're wrong... Besides, we fight better as a team anyway," said Master.

It was true. He and I generally split up to take out separate groups of enemies, as combining our powers was overkill for the vast majority of foes, so we didn't often fight side by side. It felt surprisingly good to fight alongside a partner who had your back. The most recent time we'd fought together had been the day Lady Amelia was kidnapped, I supposed, though I didn't remember much of that considering the ravenous beast I'd transformed into at the time. Which reminded me—Master had tried to tell me something back then, hadn't he? *Well, drat. Now I really need to make it out of this alive, or else I might never find out what it was.*

"Very well, Master. I leave it to you."

I left Lady Amelia's protection in his hands and focused all my mental strength on pouring as much mana as I could into my Hammer of Light. At last, it was done.

"Now die," uttered Mahiro.

Our spells clashed—his Golden Ray firing upward as my Hammer of Light came crashing down, knocking it out of midair with an earth-shattering impact. The two spells had effectively canceled each other out. This had given Mahiro more than enough time to activate his Storm Ruler spell...but it also gave Master's Shadow Magic ample time to stretch through the air and swallow up that spell, magic circle and all.

"Wha?!" Mahiro gasped in bewilderment as the light of the spell he'd been counting on was extinguished by the shadows. This must have been quite the eye-opening experience for him—I couldn't imagine he'd ever had one of his magic circles *eaten* before.

POV: ODA AKIRA

AFTER MY SHADOW MAGIC swallowed up Mahiro's magic circle, I fell to my knees.

"Master?!"

Shadow Magic really did expend an exorbitant amount of mana. If it was just firing shadows like bullets through my enemies, I could do it countless times, but little attacks like that wouldn't work on a demon, and over time the fatigue would build up regardless. I was trying to save my mana so I didn't end up incapacitated, but when Night tried to sacrifice himself, I didn't really have much of a choice. And now my mana was almost all gone.

"His Majesty told me about you, but I didn't expect you to have grown this much in such a short time. Certainly wouldn't have expected you to be able to gobble up one of my magic circles. But I assume that used up the last of your mana reserves, so let's finish this, shall we?"

Mahiro snapped his fingers, and I watched him carefully, bracing myself for whatever was about to happen.

But nothing did.

"Master!"

Night, his mouth agape, seemed to be gawking at something behind me. I spun around to try to see whatever it was, but I was stopped dead in my tracks before I could even get that far.

"Nghk?! Wha?"

"*Master!*"

A deep red liquid began to trickle out of my mouth, dribbling down to form an expanding puddle on the ground. The smell of blood pervaded the area. Presumably, my Detect Danger skill hadn't triggered because I was all out of mana, or perhaps it would have never anticipated any sort of danger coming from this particular source.

"Isn't it beautiful, being killed by the one you love? Hate to be the bearer of bad news, but I'm afraid His Majesty has deemed you an obstacle in his path toward revenge against this world. Now be a good little boy and exit stage right," said Mahiro.

I looked down to discover a thin, delicate arm jutting out of my stomach—someone had impaled me with their bare hands from behind.

"No... NOOOO!" I heard a voice cry behind me.

I twisted my neck to see Amelia staring down in horror at the hand she'd just plunged through my abdomen.

"I didn't do that! Why did my body just move on its own?!" she screamed. Her body was emitting a pale red light.

It was then that I realized she was being controlled, no doubt the purpose of the magic circle Mahiro had initially thrown at her.

A twisted sneer spread across the demon's face. "My Marionette spell draws out 100 percent of its victim's latent physical and mental abilities, then adds my own stats on top of that," he said. "So even a weak little princess like her could impale your already battered body."

"Ame...lia... Ghgk!"

I was losing more blood by the second. Soon, all the strength drained from my body, and when Amelia pulled her arm out, I collapsed to the ground as if she'd just ripped out the very essence of my life, root and stem.

"NOOOOOO!" she screamed, her sorrowful cries echoing through my rapidly fading consciousness.

"My, oh, my. Killing the man you love most... Are you a closet psychopath?" Mahiro teased as though this weren't all his doing.

I felt my blood boiling even as my mind continued to fade.

"M-Master?"

Fighting through the pain and numbness of my blood-drained body, I slowly lifted myself off the ground once more. I raised my head to look Mahiro directly in the eye. When he noticed me, his one stray hair shot straight up like a soldier at attention.

"Are you *sure* you're only human? Why, you're almost as resilient as a demon."

But I ignored this question and turned to face Amelia instead.

"A-Amelia... I'll be okay. Don't worry about me."

"Akira..."

I wiped the tears from her drenched cheeks, accidentally smearing a bit of my blood on her face in the process. Then my knees gave out, and I fell against her. She stumbled, but she held my weight just fine.

I was so cold, but my blood flowed seemingly without end. Perhaps straining to sit up hadn't been a good idea after all, but

I had to do *something* to try to feign that I was okay. Otherwise Amelia would never forgive herself.

"You're like an annoying little cockroach in the kitchen that refuses to die, you know that? Why, you even kind of look like one in that black armor of yours," Mahiro said, facepalming. Then he snapped his fingers once more, and Amelia's face twisted in fear.

"N-no! Stop it!" she cried.

"Marionette's an awfully tricky spell," he continued. "Even an old hand like me needs to be very careful with it. But it's perfect for catching someone off guard with a little betrayal from a trusted ally, wouldn't you agree? That's the sort of death idiotic normies like you deserve, if you ask me."

Amelia's hand impaled me once more. My body quivered, though I couldn't tell which one of us was shaking.

"Grghk!"

I was so unbelievably cold. I remembered thinking to myself a while back that if I had to die at someone else's hands, I wanted it to be Amelia's. But now that it was actually happening, and I was forced to watch the tears run down her face, I wanted to slap my past self in the face for ever thinking that. Had I truly forgotten what it felt like when Commander Saran died? How it felt when my father abandoned us that day, leaving us lost and alone? Had I already forgotten the lesson I learned from that trauma?

A person's death is far more painful for the people they leave behind.

I didn't want Amelia to ever have to go through that. And I still hadn't achieved any of the things I'd sworn to myself that I'd accomplish.

I'm cold.

I couldn't die yet.

So cold.

I had to defeat Mahiro.

So cold.

I couldn't let them take Amelia.

So cold.

I still had to avenge Commander Saran.

So cold.

So very, very cold.

All the strength had drained from my body. Amelia was screaming uncontrollably. Night simply looked on in an open-mouthed daze, while Mahiro's lips twisted into an evil grin.

No. I can't die yet.

"MASTER'S INJURIES HAVE EXCEEDED ACCEPT-ABLE PARAMETERS. AUTO-ENGAGING SHADOW MAGIC, RECOVERY MODE."

My lips moved, but not of my own volition. What *was* this phenomenon? I tried to writhe about on the ground to resist it but to no avail. I could only watch as my shadow wriggled beneath me before enveloping my entire body.

"MASTER'S MP SUPPLY DEEMED INSUFFICIENT.

RECOVERY WILL REQUIRE THE USE OF EMERGENCY MANA STORES."

My body began to grow lighter. The bitter cold was gone. The pain too. I had no idea what was happening to me, but it seemed like my Shadow Magic had somehow activated itself on its own.

"RECOVERY COMPLETE. PROCEEDING TO ELIMI-NATE REMAINING HOSTILES."

The two gaping holes in my abdomen had been completely healed. That done, the shadows around my torso dispersed and wrapped around my arms and legs instead.

"HOSTILE DETECTED. DEMON. NAME: MAHIRO ABE. CLASS: RUNIC MAGE."

My body was moving on its own—or rather, the shadows wrapped around my limbs were compelling me to move. I now knew all too well what Amelia must have felt like only a moment ago. Losing control of your own body was not a pleasant feeling whatsoever.

POV: NIGHT

IT WAS THE SAME PHENOMENON that had occurred the day Lady Amelia was kidnapped. Master had used up all his mana again and suffered lethal wounds, to boot, but his Shadow Magic had once more kicked in automatically, replenished his MP, and healed his wounds. I wasn't sure if it was a skill set to activate whenever he was on the verge of death or a subconscious command he wasn't even aware of, but any sort of magic that could save someone from the brink of death was a very powerful tool in the hands of a man like Master—even if it wasn't quite as powerful as Lady Amelia's Resurrection Magic.

"NOW ENGAGING COMBAT MODE. ELIMINATING ENEMY: MAHIRO ABE."

Master's Shadow Magic was speaking through his mouth, the same as before. The voice was still his own, yet the odd phrasing and bizarre intonation belonged to someone else. This time, I noticed the shadows had wrapped themselves around his arms and legs and were manipulating his body.

"I'm not sure what this bizarre charade is about, but do you really think you still stand a chance?" Mahiro asked. "You humans are simply lesser beings. That's all there is to it. Now go back to wriggling around on the ground like the lowly worm you are."

With that, Mahiro snapped his fingers, and a new dazzling magic circle was born. Lady Amelia (who was still standing behind Master) assumed a battle stance.

"H-he's controlling me again! Akira, watch out!" she cried.

Against her will, she raised her arms up in the air and brought them back down, casting her signature Gravity Magic. Suddenly, Master's entire body was forced down by the pressure of unfathomable g-forces, and the ground cracked beneath his feet. But he was not brought to his knees—he remained standing, defiant and undeterred. This left him a sitting duck for the spell Mahiro was about to cast with his newest magic circle.

"Whirlwind Scythes!"

An unending barrage of whirling blades was unleashed upon the corridor. Somehow, none of them hit me or Lady Amelia— they were all homing in on Master specifically. This was peculiar, as Whirlwind Scythes, like Storm Ruler, was an area-of-effect spell designed to kill all enemies in the vicinity. It must have taken quite a bit of mana to focus such a spell on a single target.

"To think he was capable of such a thing..." I muttered to myself.

The Mahiro I knew was a fairly lax individual—his lone stray hair always dangling to and fro as if it were a representation of his fickle personality. I had never once seen him let his emotions show on his face beyond a simple smile. He was ever the enigma. No one seemed to know who he was, where he'd come from, or how long he'd been here, but somehow he was the only one who had the power to rein in His Majesty as the demons' second-in-command. This was a fact I had always internalized, yet I apparently had never grasped the true scope of his might. To have such complete control over one's magic was astounding indeed.

The only attacks I had ever suffered from Saran Mithray, and thus the only ones I was capable of emulating in his form, were Hammer of Light and one other, but there were special requirements for using the second attack that had not yet been met.

The whirlwind of blades ceased, but the dust had yet to settle, so I still couldn't quite make out Master's figure. I knew he had to be alive, though.

And so it had been Master who protected me in the end once again. I wondered if there would ever come another day when we would truly fight alongside each other as equals, like we had earlier.

"I poured an awful lot of mana into that last spell, you know," Mahiro murmured. "Every last blade hit its mark. So tell me: how exactly are you still alive?"

Finally, the dust settled, and I saw Master standing there, right where he had been all along, his posture unchanged. The combination of Lady Amelia's Gravity Magic and Mahiro's Whirlwind Scythes hadn't even been enough to make him flinch.

"RETURN TO ME, YATO-NO-KAMI," said the specter controlling Master's body.

I looked around and saw the two daggers that had once been Yato-no-Kami lying on the ground a short distance away. At Master's command, they vanished into thin air before reappearing in his hands.

Where in the world did he learn to do that?

"Those blades..." uttered Mahiro as he gawked at the two daggers. He could likely sense a certain power from them.

I'd never seen Master recall them like that before. Even when he threw them at enemies, he always ran off to collect them right afterward, even when the situation didn't really permit. This implied that the Shadow Magic controlling Master's body was more familiar with how to use the blades than even Master was.

"Wha?!" Mahiro flinched as Master closed the gap between them in an instant, slicing off a few strands of Mahiro's hair with a slash, which snapped him right out of his reverie.

Master's movements were almost impossibly fast now. It seemed the Shadow Magic controlling his limbs was pushing them well beyond what they were capable of doing under human power. I had to wonder if such a thing was safe, even if the shadows *did* have the ability to heal any injuries they might sustain.

"Ngh! How are your slashes so strong?!" Mahiro asked through gritted teeth as he crafted magic circle after magic circle to use as makeshift shields against Master's successive swipes. But the speed and ferocity of Master's strikes cut straight through each and every one.

"SHADOW MAGIC—SHADOWBIND."

The shadows splayed out between Master and Mahiro shot out of the ground and restrained Mahiro like a prisoner in chains. Master had likely surmised through observation that Mahiro needed to clap his hands or snap his fingers every time he wanted to create or activate a magic circle. He was therefore attempting to bind Mahiro in a way that rendered him incapable of doing so.

"YOU WILL RELEASE AMELIA ROSEQUARTZ FROM YOUR SPELL," said the Shadow Magic, pressing a dagger up against Mahiro's throat.

Even this did not break the demon's smile. "Hate to break it to you, but I don't need my *hands* specifically to craft magic circles," Mahiro laughed. "We runic mages are far too clever to let ourselves be bested by an Achilles' heel like that. Speaking of which..."

It was a fatal oversight. The shadows were primarily focused on binding his hands, but his legs were still free to move however they wished. With one last smirk, Mahiro clicked his heels together, and the same aura of light produced every time he snapped his fingers began to emanate from his feet.

POV: ODA AKIRA

WHEN A BLINDING LIGHT suddenly flashed before my eyes, I (or more accurately, the Shadow Magic controlling me) closed my eyelids to shield them. Closing one's eyes in the midst of combat was a mistake that could have lethal consequences. The spell Mahiro cast with his feet shot through my torso like a harpoon. *Just how many times am I going to be impaled today, anyway?*

"DAMAGE SUSTAINED. INJURIES EXCEED ACCEPTABLE PARAMETERS."

Ha! What *parameters? You're just taking my body for a joyride!* I wanted to laugh, but the noise refused to leave my throat. I didn't have the power to break out of this phenomenon, and there didn't seem to be any sort of kill switch to turn off my Shadow Magic once this had begun. It *had* saved my life, however, so I decided I'd shut up and defer to its judgment for now.

"SWITCHING TO RECOVERY MODE."

The gaping hole in my body created by Mahiro's magic closed up in an instant. What a bizarre feeling it was to be saved by the volition of one's own magic.

"What's gotten into you, anyway?" Mahiro asked suspiciously. "Those magic daggers, those shadows swirling around your body, that bizarre way you're speaking... If I didn't know any better, I'd say you were possessed by something. Am I right?"

Right on the money. If I could move my hands right now, I probably would have applauded him for being so observant.

"I NEED NOT ANSWER THAT QUERY," said the Shadow Magic, much to my surprise.

I felt my body tense up, through no will of my own. Mahiro, having broken free of his restraints, brought his hands together once again. *How does he still have mana left over after cooking up all those magic circles?* Nevertheless, the air was yet humid with his oppressively thick mana.

"Fine, then. I guess I'll just have to take you in and *torture* the answer out of you. And here I was only planning to bring the princess back to His Majesty, but you just changed my mind. In fact, I'm more interested in you now than her."

I appreciate your interest in me, but I'm straight, thanks.

"Hand of the Divine!" chanted Mahiro.

From the demon's back, a giant hand made of glimmering light was born, which shot over in my direction to try to apprehend me. My Shadow Magic didn't even flinch.

"A GREATER LIGHT ONLY BRINGS WITH IT DEEPER AND DARKER SHADOWS. I WILL CARRY OUT MY MASTER'S WISHES," hissed the Shadow Magic, seemingly addressing me directly. It was then that I learned beyond a shadow of a doubt that the magic did indeed have sentience of its own. It raised my hands high above my head, then addressed Mahiro once more: *"IF YOU DIE, YOUR SPELL ON AMELIA ROSEQUARTZ WILL BE BROKEN. NOW, PREPARE TO BE EVISCERATED."*

The shadow said only this, then the fearsome and threatening Hand of the Divine vanished without a trace. Or rather, it was *swallowed* without a trace. At this, even Mahiro seemed at a loss for words.

"KNOW YOUR PLACE, DEMON. YOU DO NOT STAND A CHANCE AGAINST ME."

Mahiro's jaw dropped. He tried to collect himself and flash a confident smile, albeit one that was twitching with rage. "Well now..." he began.

Out of the corner of my eye, I noticed Night and the others taking a step back and bracing themselves for the demon's next attack. Hell, I probably would have too, if I'd had any control over my body. It seemed awfully ballsy to mess with the demons' second-in-command.

"You've got quite the mouth on you for a lowly human," Mahiro snarled. For the first time, his smile was nowhere to be seen. It wasn't as if his constant smiling was a result of joviality or an indicator of his mood or anything—it was clearly the default expression he wore for show, probably as an intimidation tactic. Still, it was harrowing to watch it vanish without a trace. "Your kind can never hope to defeat us demons. That's just an inevitable fact of life, I'm afraid. Accept your fate and submit."

More than anything in the world, I hated being talked down to or treated like I was lesser, but I had to admit there was a kernel of truth in what Mahiro was saying: humans were generally too weak to take on demons. The only reason I stood a chance against him at all was because my stats were basically glitched. I was pretty sure this one demon could handily take out the hero and my other classmates combined without even breaking a sweat.

We'd been fighting for a good while now, and his mana showed no signs of depleting. Moreover, the only reason I'd been able to put a dent in Aurum was because he'd been careless.

Apparently, my Shadow Magic felt differently about all this.

"IF IT IS MY MASTER YOU REFER TO, THEN I SUGGEST YOU THINK AGAIN. YES, HARD WORK WILL NOT ALWAYS ALLOW ONE TO TRANSCEND THE MEANS OF THEIR BIRTH. NOT ALL PEOPLE ARE CREATED EQUALLY IN THIS WORLD, AND SOME OBSTACLES ARE TOO GREAT TO OVERCOME. BUT THAT DOES NOT MEAN ONE SHOULD SIMPLY GIVE IN WITHOUT EVEN TRYING."

A vein bulged on Mahiro's forehead. Apparently he was beginning to lose his temper. "What do they teach you humans in schools, anyway? Just take a look at any history book. Humans have never won against the demons. *Never*," he reiterated. "Well, not including heroes, of course."

He didn't think summoned heroes could be lumped in with the regular humans of this world. Interesting.

Mahiro clapped his hands together, and the red aura surrounding Amelia's body grew thicker and more vibrant. She let out an agonized scream as her body contorted in response to whatever new spell Mahiro was putting into effect.

"You can gobble up magic with those shadows of yours, right? Well, go on then! Eat your fill!" Mahiro cackled.

Every time I watched my Shadow Magic swallow another spell or a group of monsters, I found myself wondering, *Are there any limits to how much it can eat?* From my experiences thus far, I had no evidence to say one way or the other. According to Commander Saran, there was no such thing as Shadow Magic in all of recorded history, so what *was* this power I had, anyway? It had almost razed an entire forest in the past—what if swallowing too much of Mahiro's magic made me lose control of it again? *Oh, wait... I already have lost control of it, duh. It's taken over my whole body this time.*

"Aqua Needle!" Mahiro shouted.

All at once, dozens of magic circles appeared throughout the corridor, summoning forth a flurry of high-velocity needles made of water, all of which shot through the air in Amelia's direction. Still under Mahiro's control, she was helpless to dodge the assault. I tried to reach out my hand in her direction, knowing full well that my body would not listen. But I just couldn't bear to see Amelia get hurt anymore.

"HNNNGH!"

To my surprise, it seemed my emotions won out over the control of my Shadow Magic, and I was able to dash over and wrap Amelia in my arms to protect her from the storm of needles. The needles were merely liquid, yet at such high speeds, I had no doubt they would feel like icicles piercing through me like pins into a pincushion. I wasn't ready to die today, but more importantly, I wasn't ready to watch Amelia suffer any more than she already had.

"Master!" I heard Night say in a harsh whisper as I braced myself for the imminent bombardment.

I had to wonder just how many times I was going to be impaled today.

In the end, though, I would not be killed by this attack. Both Amelia and I would make it out just fine...because we were saved just in the nick of time by a dark figure with a long black tail.

"You two all right?" asked our savior.

"Crow... What are you doing here?" Night asked.

Crow didn't answer the question; he simply snorted and shot Lia a knowing glance before turning to face our mutual enemy.

"Great. First a human, now a beastman. And the infamous Crow, no less," said Mahiro, his smiling face betraying just the slightest hint of unease.

"Infamous, you say?" Crow grinned deviously. "Oh, I'd love to hear what kind of stories they tell about me back in Volcano, demon boy."

As sparks began to fly between the two of them, Night herded the rest of us back to a safe distance near the corridor wall. It seemed that somehow the spell on Amelia had been broken, and the Shadow Magic controlling me had also disappeared.

"Do Crow and Mahiro know each other, Night?" I asked, leaning my battered body up against the wall for support.

Night, still in the form of Commander Saran, quickly did the same beside me. Amelia stood a short distance away, probably still rattled after being forced to try to kill me. Thankfully, I'd come away without any major injuries and just a bit of blood loss.

"Crow was a member of the previous hero's party who fled after failing to slay His Majesty. Yet the beastfolk king and the citizenry

did not hold Crow's failure against him, as by the time they reached His Majesty's castle, there were only two of them left alive to take him on. The odds were more than stacked against them, and they did better than any reasonable person could expect. They nearly succeeded."

My eyes widened, but I noticed Amelia's didn't seem that surprised. Perhaps she already knew all of this. It definitely did strike me as strange that a failed hero would be reaccepted by society, even if he was by no means living the high life in his little blacksmith's atelier. Crow's was the sort of immense failure that often drove people to suicide, yet I supposed if they really had nearly taken the castle all by themselves, maybe people had been more understanding.

"I was by His Majesty's side at the time, so I didn't witness any of this firsthand. I simply thought the hero's party was beaten handily early on and fled with their tails between their legs. It wasn't until a while after the fact that I heard from one of my subordinates that two of them actually did make it almost all the way to the throne room."

I had to wonder what any of this had to do with Crow being able to break the spells Mahiro cast on Amelia and me. I shot Night an impatient look, and he rolled his eyes as if to say "Hold your horses, I'm getting to it."

"Apparently, it was Mahiro who delivered the final blow that convinced Crow and the hero to retreat. But Crow was already not at his best by the time he reached Mahiro, so the two have never fought on level ground before. According to Mahiro's report, Crow was still able to counter each and every one of his spells."

Night and I both turned to look at the two men in question. Mahiro's overconfident facade was nowhere to be found; he seemed extremely annoyed, almost as if he knew deep down that he didn't stand a chance against Crow.

"Long time no see, Mahiro Abe," said Crow.

"You beastfolk are only supposed to live, what, about a hundred years longer than humans? How in the hell are you still kicking, you geriatric old coot?" asked Mahiro.

He had a point. If Crow had been involved in the Nightmare of Adorea debacle a hundred years ago, and his stint as a member of the hero's party had happened even before that—and if you considered that he must've needed an awful lot of time to get as strong as he was before *that*... He had to be approaching the end of his life expectancy by now, right? It was pretty hard to tell a beastman's age just by looking at him, though.

"Don't talk down to me, you little runt," Crow growled. "I may be past my prime, but I'm still more than capable enough to handle a brat like you."

"So it would seem," Mahiro said, shooting a quick glance in our direction. "As evidenced by the fact that you effortlessly broke them out of my spells."

"Yeah, well, your Marionette spell was practically undone before I even got here. Did you just lose your focus and let it slip? Or did you take a hit that *made* you lose your focus?"

"Don't act like you don't already know, you crotchety old fart."

It was plain from his tone that Mahiro was getting more frustrated by the second. With his usual pompous and overconfident smile, you'd think he'd be one of those characters who never broke out of formal speech, but apparently not. Crow was clearly a bit tickled by Mahiro's obvious agitation too.

"I guess the last hero summoning ritual wasn't a waste of time after all. Looks like we got at least one decent fighter out of it, anyway," Crow said, presumably referring to me. His impression of me had apparently changed quite a bit since we first met. The two men glared at each other for a while, until at last Mahiro caved and pulled back.

"I'll let you live this time, Crow. But next time, you won't be so lucky."

"Funny, that's exactly what I was about to say to you."

Crow had officially won the stare-down. Mahiro clicked his tongue in frustration, and he scooped Aurum into his arms from where he lay unconscious atop his mount. I hadn't noticed him faint; I'd been wondering why he'd been so quiet during my battle with Mahiro. I stood up and glared at Mahiro just as he was about to leave. Noticing my gaze, Mahiro walked over to me with Aurum still in his arms.

"We're falling back this time, but don't think I'll go easy on you just because we're both Japanese, you pitiful human," he said.

"Don't make me laugh. You hurt Amelia, and I'm going to make you pay for it. You can count on it, bub," I retorted. We locked eyes for a moment, but then Night pulled me back.

"Master, we need to leave."

I turned around to see that Crow was already on his way out of the corridor with Lia in his arms. I turned to Amelia, who was still looking anxiously down at the ground, and grabbed her by the hand. Startled, she looked up at me.

"C'mon. Let's get out of here," I said.

"Nngh..."

When I awoke, I didn't know how many days had passed. All I knew was that it was dark outside, and that I was in a familiar room. *Right*. This was where they'd taken me after I collapsed due to mana exhaustion. Which meant this was Crow's house. I could hear Amelia, Night, and Crow talking over in the next room. I couldn't tell what they were saying, but Night seemed a little offended by something, and hearing Amelia safe and sound put my mind at ease.

After we made it out of the labyrinth, we'd all headed straight for Crow's house as fast as our exhausted bodies could take us. We hadn't even stuck around to confirm that Mahiro and Aurum had teleported out of the labyrinth, though that seemed like a pretty safe bet.

"All right, now eat some food and get some sleep. We can talk things over later."

Once we arrived at the house, Crow brought out some fruit and bread for us to snack on. I didn't know just how long we'd been fighting with the demons down there, but I was starving, so I gratefully accepted the vittles. I remembered nothing after the food. I didn't even remember climbing into bed, so I assumed someone must have carried me there. I was so exhausted that I'd probably conked out halfway through my little meal. *Tends to happen whenever I use Shadow Magic.*

"Looks like your feisty companion's woken up," I heard Crow say from the next room.

Then I heard the sound of Amelia and Night getting out of their seats and dashing over. When they opened the door, I had to shield my eyes from the light coming in from the next room.

"Akira!"

"Master!"

Before my eyes could even adjust to the light, they had pounced on me, and I fell promptly back into the bed. It seemed like I still hadn't fully recovered my strength.

"Akira, I was so worried, I...I..." Amelia sputtered as she pressed her face into my chest.

I ran my fingers through her hair, unable to find the right words. I knew she probably still felt horrible for having almost killed me, even if it had been no fault of her own. If my Shadow Magic hadn't kicked in to save my life, I probably would have been six feet under by now. Something told me Amelia was going to hold it against herself no matter what I said, so I decided that perhaps it was best to just not bring it up and hope time healed those wounds.

"How long was I out, Night?" I asked as my feline companion hopped up to his usual perch on my shoulders.

He let out a sigh and shook his head as though I were a child who'd just gotten himself into trouble again—a gesture which mildly annoyed me, but I let it slide. *"Only a day this time. You didn't deplete all of your mana again, thankfully, so it was probably just plain old exhaustion. Though I must say I expected better of you. Why, Lady Amelia and I recovered within a matter of hours, you know,"* he teased. *"Oh, and Crow has already escorted Lady Lia back to the palace, just so you're aware."*

I knew Night was only teasing me to try to lighten the mood to lift Amelia's spirits, but it was still a little irksome. Okay, maybe more than just a little. But I held my annoyance back and lowered my clenched fists.

"So what's new? Anything?" I asked. I couldn't imagine that nothing of import had happened the entire day I was out cold. However, I didn't expect this question to make both Amelia and Night immediately stiffen.

"Yeah, we can talk about that after you come out here. You've got guests."

I turned in the direction of Crow's voice and saw someone else standing in the doorway—someone I never would have expected to see. My jaw hanging wide open, I threw the covers back and sat up in bed. Night was sent flying off my shoulders from the momentum, and while I normally would have scooped him back up and apologized, I had more pressing matters to attend to right now.

"Vice Commander Gilles?!" I gasped.

"In the flesh. Been a while, hasn't it?"

I ran over to the man, who greeted me not with his usual worrywart expression but with a wry smile. He wasn't dressed in his usual knight's garb, instead wearing a set of light armor designed for traveling, but there was no doubt about it. This was the same Sir Gilles I'd come to know back in the Kingdom of Retice. I glanced over my shoulder at Amelia and Night. He was still grumbling on the floor after being flung aside, so she was trying to console him.

Seeing this comedic display, Vice Commander Gilles laughed heartily. "Looks like you've found yourself a fine set of companions," he said.

"Y-yeah, I guess you could say that," I replied, scratching my cheek bashfully. I couldn't hide anything from Vice Commander Gilles. He was almost as much of a mind-reader as Commander Saran had been before him.

He laughed at my hesitant reply.

Night, having leapt back up onto my shoulders, was peering teasingly into my eyes. *"You 'guess,' Master? Go on, tell him we're the finest companions a boy like you could ever hope for. No need to be shy."*

Don't push your luck, bub. I grabbed him by the scruff of his neck and flung him back onto the bed. I didn't have time for any of his mewling right now. I held out my hand to Amelia, who took it tentatively.

"Let's go, Amelia."

"O-okay."

She still seemed a little bit tense, but her hand in mine was every bit as warm and reassuring as usual. As we walked together through the doorway, I was met with yet another surprise. While I maybe should have expected as much given that Crow said I had "guests"—plural and not singular—I was still completely thrown for a loop when I saw the people sitting patiently in the next room.

"Hey, Akira."

"K-Kyousuke...?"

There in the sitting area were seven of the classmates I'd left behind when I fled Retice Castle. There was my friend Kyousuke, the hero Satou, and...well, I couldn't remember the others' names. I'd seen all of their stat pages back when we were first summoned, but so much had happened since then that I'd completely forgotten. My classmates, for their part, seemed less interested in me than the lovely lady whose hand I was holding.

"What are you guys all doing here?" I asked as I took the seat across from Kyousuke. Unfortunately for them, I wasn't going to address their curiosity regarding Amelia unless they came right out and asked me who she was.

"My Intuition skill told me we'd find you here," said Kyousuke. "And we were on our way to Ur anyway to seek out a skilled blacksmith when we bumped into Sir Gilles on the ship over."

Apparently Vice Commander Gilles and Crow were acquaintances, and he had just so happened to be on his way to the same exact place. So, he'd joined up with Kyousuke and my other classmates to come here and introduce them to Crow, who was about as skilled a blacksmith as they could hope to find, if you were able to look past his personality.

"Wow. I'm surprised the castle's allowing you to be away for so long, Vice Commander," I said.

To my surprise, though, Sir Gilles shuddered uncomfortably at this simple offhand remark. "Er, yes. About that..." he began. "Please stop calling me Vice Commander, would you? I've resigned from my post as a member of the Knights of Retice."

I blinked a few times. Now *there* was a surprise. I had found it odd how casual his tone seemed to be, compared to when we'd last spoken, but I never would have expected him to have quit entirely.

"Well, perhaps it's more accurate to say I was *forced* to resign," he added. "I guess the king felt that my fellow knights and I were becoming too much of an obstacle to his master plan."

Now that I could understand. With Commander Saran gone, I was a little worried about what might be going on back at the castle if Sir Gilles wasn't there to keep an eye on things, but apparently I'd underestimated just how conniving the king could be.

"So tell me, Crow: what exactly are all these people doing here?" I asked, thinking it far too convenient to be a mere coincidence.

"Don't ask me," he said, furrowing his brow. "Little Gilles here is the only one *I* asked to come. Those kids just decided to tag along with him."

"Little" Gilles, huh. It felt weird for him to be talking about a grown man as though he were a little kid, but maybe that was just a result of Crow looking awfully young for his age.

"Well, I can't speak for the other six," said Kyousuke, "but *I* came because I wanted to join up with you, Akira. Would you mind if I tagged along?"

Night quickly leapt up onto my shoulders.

"I already told you, that's not going to happen! Master only has room for one partner, and that's me! You think I'd just hand him over to a no-name ruffian of dubious origin like yourself?!"

This must have been what I heard Night complaining about from the other room when I first woke up. Though Kyousuke was decidedly not just some "no-name ruffian" of dubious origin—if anything, Night was the one who was of dubious origin here.

"I'm talking to Akira right now, Night. Please try to keep it down," said Kyousuke.

"Who gave you permission to call me by that name?!" Night hissed.

Was this what the fearsome Nightmare of Adorea had been reduced too? An easily offended pussycat? And since when was Kyousuke so talkative? Why, he was talking so much that my other classmates were looking at him like he was a completely different person. In any event, I couldn't stand to have Night hissing in my ear, so I grabbed him once again by the scruff of his neck and set him down on a nearby table.

"Hey, if you guys wanna duke it out, take it outside. I just woke up and you're already giving me a headache," I said, and the two of them both stopped dead in their tracks. Amelia looked over at me, impressed with the amount of authority I was displaying.

"How are you feeling, Akira? Doing okay?" asked the hero, who I'd been making a distinct effort to ignore up until this point.

"Yeah, more or less," I replied, and he let out a sigh of relief.

This puzzled me, I had to admit. It was no secret that he and I hated each other's guts, though I'd always been under the impression that it was *he* who wanted nothing to do with me, and I was simply keeping my distance. Where this sudden change of heart was coming from, I couldn't say.

Before I could pursue this train of thought any further, Crow stepped forward as if he had something to say. He looked around at the people who'd intruded on his humble abode with a look that was cold and inhospitable even by his standards. Gilles, meanwhile, simply sat and sipped his tea.

"Listen," said Crow, staring directly at me. "I get that your little friends here are just worried about you and want to make sure you make a full recovery, so as much as I hate unwanted guests, I'm gonna make an exception just this once. But if they can't behave themselves, just know that I reserve the right to kick them all to the curb."

Always so testy, this one, I thought with a sigh. I appreciated that he was trying to be considerate of me, but he didn't have to be so prickly about it.

There weren't a lot of chairs, so all of my classmates aside from the hero and Kyousuke were forced to stand. Gilles stood opposite Crow, who stood next to me, and Amelia stood on my other side. I could tell that the hero, who was sitting across from Amelia, was feeling a little flustered by her beauty, but Amelia wouldn't even so much as look at him. Kyousuke, who was sitting across from me, was still having a stare-down with the kitty cat. Sparks were flying all around.

"Well, for starters, Crow... Were you able to dig up any information on Lingga?" I asked, referring to the matter I'd asked him to look into back when I passed out due to mana exhaustion. I figured he probably wanted to get down to business, but I wasn't really interested in being the facilitator, so I decided to steer the conversation in that direction. Suddenly, all eyes were on him, and he frowned and took another sip of his tea before responding.

"Yeah. He's totally innocent," Crow replied at last.

This was not an answer I'd been prepared for. I was all but certain it had been Lingga who'd paved the way for the demons to invade the city. He was by far the most likely culprit given the circumstances. Sure, the common belief was that the Demon Lord created the labyrinths, but did that really make it possible for his lackeys to teleport between them with such pinpoint accuracy? I remembered Commander Saran telling me once that magic was a very inexact science. So while there did exist magic that could teleport you to wherever you wanted to go in an instant, it was apparently nigh-impossible to teleport somewhere you hadn't been before. There would have needed to be some sort of symbol or landmark near the destination Mahiro had been aiming for, at the very least. And since Lingga just so happened to be the guildmaster of a city with a labyrinth, and just so happened to have that Inconspicuous skill that would make it easy for him to sneak down to the bottom floor and place said symbol, I was fairly certain he was guilty.

"But I do know of someone *else* who I think might be our guy," Crow said, clenching his fists. He was digging his claws so deep into his palms that blood began to trickle out, but he didn't seem to notice. "He's the guildmaster of the Uruk branch, and I can tell you from experience that he's as rotten as they come."

"What's his name?" I asked.

I could see Night's fur bristling. Amelia, too, stiffened up. Then, with clear-cut malice burning in his eyes, Crow finally uttered the villain's name:

"Name's Gram. He's the current king's nephew, and he used to be prime minister. Also happens to be the guy I've been waiting a hundred years to get revenge against."

My ears immediately perked up at the name Gram, though I couldn't quite remember why. I looked over at Night to see if he could help refresh my memory.

"No, you're not imagining things, Master. That was the name of the supposed ringleader of those ruffians who attempted to kidnap Lady Amelia back in the elven domain. The ones we suspected might have been official knights of Uruk."

Come to think of it, Night mentioned the name ringing a bell back then, didn't he? He'd said there was once a prime minister by the name of Gram, so this had to be our guy. To think he'd become guildmaster for the Uruk branch since then...and that Crow had beef with him.

"This is the first I'm hearing of any revenge, Crow. Did you guys already know about this?" I asked Amelia and Night. It sounded like there'd been some sort of communication breakdown. Not that we'd had much time to share intel lately, what with me being unconscious and Amelia getting kidnapped and all.

"Yeah, Night told me about it back on the day Aurum attacked the city," said Amelia.

"You can tell him about it later. I don't wanna hear it," said Crow, looking away.

Must be a touchy subject for him. I'll just have to have Amelia fill me in later. "So what makes you think this Gram guy could have been behind the invasion?" I asked, shifting gears.

"Well, for starters, he's got a history of stuff like this. One need only do a little digging to find plenty of evidence of corruption and backdoor deals he's been a part of. The man is basically evil incarnate," Crow replied, looking back at me.

Evil incarnate, eh? Seemed fitting for the man who tried to kidnap Amelia.

"Embezzlement, larceny, kidnapping and imprisonment, slavery and trafficking..." Crow went on. "You name it, he's done it. Only thing you might actually have a hard time pinning on him is murder, because he makes his cronies do the actual dirty work. But the man's definitely killed a lot of people, make no mistake."

I assumed the trafficking was referring to the elf trafficking, specifically. But I had to wonder: if this guy's rap sheet was so long, why wasn't he in prison right now? I was about to ask this question when I realized the answer was probably pretty simple.

"Let me guess: he gets away with it because he's a member of the royal family," I said.

Crow nodded, and Amelia bit her lip. It must have been hard for her, as a member of another royal family, to see someone else abuse their power so blatantly.

"He's been using his status as the king's nephew to his advantage and getting involved in all sorts of dirty business ever since he was named prime minister. He got caught red-handed once, so he was forced to step down from that post, but that didn't stop him. He's pulling the exact same crap today as guildmaster."

I glanced down at the amber liquid in my teacup. I couldn't believe such a villain was roaming free in this world. He might have even been more wicked than the royal family back in Retice.

"You can't pin anything on a member of the royal family. Rumor has it there have been plenty of assassination attempts too, but the skilled mercenaries under his employ always put a stop to those, then retaliate with a vengeance... The man's a waste of flesh that doesn't deserve to live, plain and simple."

It was hard to disagree with that appraisal after what I'd just heard. That being said, I still wanted to do some investigating of my own into this Gram fellow. I didn't want to assume guilt right off the bat like that stupid hero wannabe who had killed the good Demon Lord's wife.

"So what evidence do you have that suggests he had a hand in letting the demons into the Great Labyrinth of Brute?" I asked.

"Apparently, he's made some sort of back-alley deal with the demons."

At this, I looked up from my teacup. I'd been under the impression that demons would never bother conducting business with the "lesser races" whatsoever, shady or not, but evidently I was wrong—though I'd only met two demons myself, and they could have been outliers.

"And from what my acquaintances in the Ur branch were able to tell me, I learned an interesting little tidbit: Gram was permitted entry into that very labyrinth only a few short days ago."

Okay, *now* this was starting to get pretty damning. I was all but convinced at this point. There was no reason for a man who had an entire army of trained mercenaries at his back to go into the labyrinth. Why would *he* ever need to fight enemies or get stronger? From what I'd heard so far, I was picturing him as the quintessential lazy villain who just sat on his ass bossing his little minions around. That was how it always was with his ilk... though, come to think of it, the king of Retice had been pretty slim. Borderline gaunt, almost. Villains with his body type were usually saved for the final boss.

"And wouldn't you know, the Guild employees *also* told me Gram was wearing a very large cloak that day to conceal his identity, coincidentally enough. They said they wouldn't have even known it was him if he hadn't been forced to show them his dog tags to be granted entry," Crow went on, and I sighed in disbelief as our suspect dug himself an ever deeper grave.

"It may have been a monster-repelling cloak," suggested Night, and suddenly all eyes were on him.

"What's that?" asked Crow, and Night quickly obliged.

"It's a vestment that allows demons to travel while making their presence and mana signatures undetectable to all but the most powerful of monsters. Obviously, no demon would have any trouble with such weak monsters, but the whole reason Mahiro designed it was because he couldn't be bothered to deal with them all the time. There

are magic circles woven into its interior that allow one to safely pass by any monsters as weak as those on the lowest floor of the labyrinth."

Well, if Mahiro had designed it, I could see why it would be so effective, but had he really just called the lower-level monsters "weak"? In that case, I didn't even want to know how powerful the monsters were over in the demons' domain.

"Sounds like an open-and-shut case, then. Gram's our guy," said Crow, standing up from his chair as if to say the conversation was over. He seemed antsy, like he wanted to go do something about it without further delay, and he stepped out of the building. After the door slammed behind him, I turned back toward the hero.

"So where do you guys plan on going from here?" I asked.

The hero seemed startled by my direct address (which was probably warranted, to be fair). One of the other boys who always tried to talk to me in class answered for him.

"We're still focused on moving toward our ultimate goal: slaying the Demon Lord."

"You *lot are going to try to slay His Majesty? Don't make me laugh!*" Night snorted, and one of the other boys (who seemed to be an animal tamer of some sort, judging from the little monkey perched on his head and the kitten on his shoulder) didn't take kindly to this.

"Uh, 'scuse you? What's your problem, pussycat? Whose side are you on, anyway?" the boy said.

"Yeah, no kiddin'!" a girl with a Kansai accent chimed in. "He was bein' awful rude to Asahina a li'l while ago too! What gives?!"

Apparently the other students had only been so docile out of fear of Crow's wrath, and now that he was gone, they were prepared to be as unruly as they pleased.

"I'm on the side of Master and Lady Amelia, for your information! And if Master couldn't even defeat the demons' second-in-command, you meddlesome kids don't stand a chance of defeating His Majesty himself!"

"You don't know that!" cried one student.

"Yeah! We've gotten really strong too!" said another.

I wasn't sure just how much stronger they'd gotten, but I was willing to bet Night was probably right, judging by the way the knight-looking boy seemed to be on the verge of tears. His teary-eyed face and delicate figure sure did make him seem effeminate.

"Do you people want to sleep outside tonight, or what?" Kyousuke said matter-of-factly, and the argumentative students shut their mouths. "If we're going to defeat the Demon Lord, we'll need to greatly increase our collective strength first. We know full well we're no match for him as we are now, hence why we've come to this town known for having both a highly skilled blacksmith *and* a labyrinth in which we can hone our abilities."

That was all well and good, though I had a feeling it would be a while before the labyrinth was open to the public again, and Crow didn't seem like he was really in the mood to take on any new requests at the moment. Their trip here might have been a rather pointless one.

"Given that the labyrinth is unusable at the moment, and that our finances are in a pretty good state right now," said the hero, choosing his words carefully, "I was thinking the rest of us should join your team along with Asahina."

"Absolutely not," I said almost reflexively. The hero must have been expecting this answer, as his expression didn't change whatsoever. "That goes for you too, Kyousuke. Sorry, but I can't take on any new companions that can't hold their own when fighting alongside me. You guys would be nothing more than a liability, and we don't need any more healers or support classes either."

It was harsh but true; we were never going to beat the Demon Lord if I had to worry about protecting our weaker party members at the same time. I shot a quick glance over at Kyousuke, who was biting his lip and looking down at the ground, then stood up from my seat.

"I need to speak with Crow real quick. In the meantime, I'll let you guys have some space to think things through. Just don't try to come up with a way to change my mind, because you'll be wasting your breath," I said. I placed my hand on Amelia's head, and she twitched in surprise. "Amelia here is the only one I fight for. If you can somehow convince her that you won't be a liability, maybe I'll reconsider. Just don't get your hopes up."

I whispered to Amelia that I was counting on her, then promptly left the building. The hero and Kyousuke watched me closely as I stepped out the door, but I didn't once look back.

I wasn't lying just to remove myself from the situation—there really was something I wanted to ask Crow about, so it was time to figure out where he'd gone off to. Thankfully, I didn't have to look far, as I found him right next door in his workshop, looking pensively over his various smithing tools.

"Crow," I said, and he slowly raised his head.

"Oh. Hey," he replied, only looking briefly over at me out of the corner of his eye.

I leaned my back against the door frame and looked the man over, his catlike features illuminated by the pale moonlight leaking in through the opened door. I wasn't sure what he'd come in here to think about without even turning the lights on, but I decided to get straight to the point. "There's something I wanted to ask you."

He scrunched up his face. "Sorry, can it wait? I'm a little busy right n—"

"What is it that you're most afraid of?" I interrupted.

With this, I finally managed to grab his attention. He turned to face me with a bewildered look in his eyes. "Where the hell is this coming from?"

"Just my own curiosity, really. What scares you more than anything else in the world?" It really was just plain old curiosity, but I had a feeling that Crow and I might have similar feelings about stuff like this, so I figured I should just ask and see what he said. Something told me that if anyone could relate to the feelings of helplessness and anxiety I'd had when Amelia had first been kidnapped, it was him.

"The thing that terrifies me more than anything else in the world..."

Crow turned his gaze to the moon shining through the door behind me. There was no hint of his usual shrewd and calculating persona in those eyes—only the look of a vulnerable and broken man who'd lost more than anyone could ever know.

"...is when I try to reach out for something, and my fingers touch nothing."

AFTERWORD

THANK YOU SO MUCH for taking such an interest in Akira's tale that you chose to pick up this book and see where his travels took him after Volume 1. Once again, my name is Matsuri Akai, and I am the author of the *Assassin* series.

As I was reviewing the content of Volume 2 prior to publication, the thing that struck me most was how little interaction there is between Akira and Amelia in these chapters. I mean, they only have a few one-on-one scenes together throughout the entire book! I suppose that's to be expected, given the fact that she gets kidnapped, and the spotlight is more on Night's and Crow's respective backstories this time around anyway, but I still feel bad for anyone who was looking forward to more flirty fun between our two main characters.

So the demons have finally joined the fray, and the stakes are starting to ramp up for our little band of heroes. Some of you are probably starting to wonder by now what the point of giving the main character all these cool assassin abilities was if he wasn't even going to assassinate anybody with them, and, well...all I can say to those people is that I hope you'll look forward to Volume 3. It might just change things up a bit. No promises, though.

Lastly, I'd just like to take this opportunity to once again thank everyone who had a hand in this book's publication and turning it from a simple story in my head to the tangible volume you now hold in your hands.